THE DARKER

Tales
of a City
Different

THE
DARKER

Tales
of a City
Different

by Angelo Jaramillo

Ruth (Ms. Holmes)

If it wasn't for you, this publication would not exist and neither would my life as I know it. You are the angel that first rescued me from the darkness and the inspiration behind this eternal love for letters. Thank You Always.

Love,

SUNSTONE PRESS
SANTA FE

Book and cover design by Vicki Ahl

Sunstone books may be purchased for educational, business, or sales promotional use. For information please write: Special Markets Department, Sunstone Press, P.O. Box 2321, Santa Fe, New Mexico 87504-2321.

Library of Congress Cataloging-in-Publication Data:

Jaramillo, Angelo, 1976-
The darker : tales of a city different / by Angelo Jaramillo.
   p. cm.
ISBN 0-86534-534-1 (alk. paper) -- ISBN 0-86534-535-X (pbk. : alk. paper)
I. Title.

PS3610.A73D37 2006
813'.6--dc22

                                    2006022211

WWW.SUNSTONEPRESS.COM
SUNSTONE PRESS / POST OFFICE BOX 2321 / SANTA FE, NM 87504-2321 /USA
(505) 988-4418 / ORDERS ONLY (800) 243-5644 / FAX (505) 988-1025

Dedicated to
Ruth Holmes

What an excellent teacher is supposed to be.
Thanks for saving my life.
I still use the dictionary I stole from your English
class.

Thank You.

Contents

When you get into a tight place and it seems you can't go on, hold on, for that's just the place and the time that the tide will turn.

—Harriet Beecher Stowe

Preface

These stories are but a small wonder into the realm of one young male from a wasted generation. A perennial innocent growing up too fast in a hostile world where the only salvation is self-forgiveness.

These tales are about suffering, decadence, lust, magic, subversion, stupidity, redemption and love. Humans can never be perfect because our imperfect misconceptions of perfection are imperfect. We are nothing more than a highly advanced technological urban nightmare, robust with happy slaves accidentally financing wholesale slaughter and apologizing for it whenever.

Upon reflection I realized that in the past I had done some stupid shit, some horrible shit, some ridiculous shit. This writing reflects the mentality of the way I used to think. This thinking was a reflection of genuine hate. A hate assimilated. Indoctrinated.

I am unlearning.

I am learning like Malcolm X did, to love my enemy. I am relearning not to hate in any way or any form. It takes months to recover, years to heal, and eons to forgive. I was dead, but now I'm alive, only to die again.

It is through suffering and suffering only that we reveal beauty. I can't begin to explain how I suffered for this book. I often dream I could say what I really feel like saying, but I don't think it will get published. Freedom of speech is unfathomable. Even if I thought I could stay arrogant long enough to think I could possibly translate what I thought I might really feel like saying, the presentation would lose it's meaning before the characters appeared on the screen. At any rate, writing is the only thing I can do well, therefore I will stick with it to the terrible end like staying in a bad marriage.

I promised myself not to get too political writing these myths, but sometimes you can't help being who you are, whoever that may be according to someone else and your presumptuous image of that someone. Only the hypocrites know the truth.

Nobody has the right to say what you can say and can't say. My next book will be better. No one will stand in my way this time of writing what I really must feel I should say, even if I don't agree with it.

Our entire world is failing and all I do is sit here writing nonsense. I'd rather converse in silence for eternity, than divulge my sanity today.

—Angelo Jaramillo
Santa Fe

Part I: Death

The Darker Side of Santa Fe

—for Robert and Adam

My father bequeathed to me this legend of Santa Fe that happened sometime around the instant I was born.

A man was torn between two women. One was his devoted wife of twenty some odd years. Like him she was a native Santa Fesino that married her high school sweetheart. The other woman was a newly arrived much younger Guera from somewhere around The Bible Belt. He had two loving children with his wife and a steady job that paid well. Investments in property made some time back were starting to bear fruit. The children were almost on their way to college and retirement was only a blink away. Everything seemed normal, the way it's supposed to be.

Then he encountered her. He met her at The G-Spot where he could be found sipping scotch any day of the week. The G-Spot was a cheap roadside inn on the famous Old Santa Fe Trail. Many locals would hang out there night after night to drink the blues into eternity.

Why he capitulated to temptation he never quite understood. She was half his age and not remotely interested in making any kind of commitment to him. She was a typical transient passing through Santa Fe, unsure if she would see the crimson sky the following morning.

He fell in love with her the first time he saw her. To him she represented the life of failed dreams he was deprived of living. She was sexy, witty, and fast. She was very different from all the local girls. From the first night on they would meet at The G-Spot, share some lies and spirits, and rent a room where they could explore each other's scarred intimacy for hours without disturbance. Her mystery made him crazy.

The affair had been running strong for two years. His wife didn't harbor a clue. Every Sunday they'd attend church together and every Sunday he'd rendezvous with *her* when church was over.

It happened as a magnificent shock when the young Guerra broached the subject of marriage. Two years had passed since her arrival in Santa Fe. She started to take more of a vested interest in him and his finances. She promised him all the joy and ecstasies the world had to offer if he would leave his wife and elope with her far away from everything he knew. The idea haunted him for the next few days. He fell in love with her every second he experienced her pleasure, but he loved his wife. The Church preached fidelity no matter what. His children were old enough to take care of themselves, but still needed a father's unreasonable assistance and advice. Yet, he craved more of the excitement he had enjoyed for the last couple of years. Things like this weren't common in a small village such as Santa. He and his wife came from strong traditional Hispanic Catholic backgrounds. It was not only a mortal sin to do what he was doing, but taboo to even think about thinking about it. In the midst of a mid-life crisis his libidinous ego encouraged him to plunge. His overwrought conscience made him stay.

The gringa began to grow impatient and pressured him more and more every time they were together. Why she didn't leave on her own when he wouldn't give in he couldn't figure out. It didn't matter. His wife was the patient mountain of his existence. The other was the whimsical lust of spring. He thought he loved them both. He didn't know what to do. He had to stay with his wife. A scandal such as this would disgrace his family name and ruin his clean reputation and good standing with the greater community.

Things were starting to change in Santa Fe. Post-Modernization had finally discovered The City Different. People from all over your country started to frequent the old colony. Wealthy Anglo assholes mostly from the east coast, west coast, and Texas were sucking-up real estate faster than a victim perishes from hantavirus. He should know, he was mired in the real estate racket and had sold much of his property to these types. He was becoming a rich man and consequently acting like one. His mistress would not back off. He stashed her in a luxury condo on the eastside of town. She doted upon the spoils he unconditionally offered her. She was growing accustomed to the lush life. She told him every time they met that she loved him so much the angels in heaven were jealous. God would understand and forgive him his transgressions. They were meant to be together.

The days drag. The nights refuse to pass. The household had no suspicions. His family seemed to gravitate toward him more than they ever had in the past. His children appeared happy and his wife professed her love for him by maintaining a peaceful environment to come home to after a hectic day in the world. His heart began to break. He was confused. He started missing work. Several of his business ventures fell through the cracks. Alcoholism was now an imaginary friend that neglected to leave his side. Every night he sacrificed himself to the barstool and every night he came home sobbing. Each time he touched his mistress he could sense the dread and distress only an existential philosopher knows. He and his wife hardly made love anymore. He couldn't remember the last time. He tried to think about his wife, children, and the illusory happy life every time his mistress occupied his fancy.

She had him hooked. He could never stop thinking about her through day and night. She possessed his imagination. Headaches became common. Anxiety was a comfort. He started to gain weight and lose sleep. Life is not as simple as we wish to make it. The external overtook the internal just in time for Easter. Never drink at a bar in Santa Fe during Lent.

When he walked into the G-Spot he noticed an old friend hunched over at the bar staring into nothingness. He had been waiting there forever. They greeted one another and embraced like masculine Chicanos sometimes do. He hadn't seen his friend in a while. He had heard that his buddy had spent time in prison. It didn't matter. It's always good to unexpectedly run into an old familiar face. They talked and reminisced throughout the entire evening. They drank bourbon and vodka like depressed housewives. He told his old friend everything that had been going on lately. He was so drunk the liquor kept drooling out his mouth whenever he attempted to inhale another one. The tears were sliding down his cheeks in torrents. He couldn't help himself anymore. His conscience overpowered him. The friend listened with an obsessive impulse more disturbing than a Charlie Manson rant.

"I don't know what to do. I love both of them. If I go with her, I'll destroy everything I ever worked for. If I stay, I might miss out on the greatest adventure of my life. I'm getting too old to marry again. I love my wife very much, but, I can't get this other woman out of my mind"

His friend continuously looked him in the eye, intensely listening to his confession like an ex-con does when he's sizing you up.

"My children are grown, I have more than enough money in the bank. I don't know, maybe I'm just tired. Maybe I'm tired of this place, this job, this boredom. Sometimes I feel like I can never have enough. I know I have more than any man could desire, but still, something inside of me wants more. Nothing makes sense anymore. I thought material wealth would bring me happiness, but it seems to have brought me more problems than I can handle. I don't know what to do anymore." He heard silence for an awkward breath. The geyser of tears flowed from a deep buried source that had no name. His friend watched him choke back the bile, laughing loud enough to provoke an insulted response.

"What? What's so funny? You think I'm weak? You think I'm some kind of pussy? Not a man like you. Well fuck you and the horse you rode in on. I ain't no pussy! I may be a fool but no more than the dairy farmer that buys milk from the supermarket. Life is hard. It's confusing. You don't know what goes on inside my heart every day. You don't know what it's like to be caught between two women, running a marathon that has no beginning or end. Women drive a man insane. One tantalizes you with the charm of an outspoken courtesan and the other demolishes you with grace of a pensive monk. It's confusing."

He paused as if he had an idea that nobody had thought of before. "I should just kill myself." The drunkenness made the room around him spin. He continued with a strut of bravado and dishonest machismo.

"Yeah, I'll kill myself. I'll kill myself and then I won't have any problems left. I won't have to deal with that gold digging bitch anymore or the arduous staring from my wife's consolable eyes. I won't have to worry about money, food, or sex anymore. I won't feel so guilty all the time. Nobody could tell me what to do. There would be no pressure to accommodate these rude fuckin gringos that come here and demand that I do this and I do that for them. I won't have to feel like I'm selling out my culture in order to survive and take a load of crap from my people. I'm sick and tired of that shit, just sick and tired of everything."

His voice stuttered with every vengeful thought he expressed.

"I could finally live in peace far away from everybody else. People piss me off! I could disappear and tell my creditors to go fuck themselves! I hate this place, this life, this love! No one will miss me. My wife and kids will be taken care of. My girl I'm sure will find someone else. I don't know. It seems so easy, just to pull the trigger and forget you were ever born. If I had a gun right now I'd probably do it. I'd take my own life without giving it two thoughts."

Another awkward silence fell between the pair of lifelong friends. His companero never turned his eyes away.

"You really want to kill yourself bro?" Without looking around the room to see who was watching, his friend brandished a shiny chrome .38 special and placed it delicately on the bar.

He looked up at his friend and without giving two thoughts about it seized the pistol, stood up, walked outside near the swimming pool and blew his brains out, turning the blue water red with his only friend in the world watching alongside him.

Whisper of a Spider

Thirteen venomous spider bites itching like a motherfucker! Four all over my dry skin back, two on my somewhat hairy left leg skinny inner thigh, one huge one in the middle calf of the same leg, two big ass ones on my right leg, two on the right arm, one on the left, and one tingling bitch in the middle of my bumpy scrotum. When I noticed the last one I almost began to panic. But then I just calmed down after an elongated breath and wondered if the spider might have sucked some sperm from my testicles when it created this pimple-looking relic. Never had so many spider bites at one time in my life. And I know they are spider bites because they're bigger than mosquito ones and swell in the inner middle where you can tell that the fangs went in. Chinche bites are not as big. Had them before, many occasions. Especially recently. They itch worse than dandruff developing on a relatively cleansed scalp that hasn't been assaulted by a showerhead and shampoo for over a week. I happened to accidentally scratch a few of 'em in my early morning unconscious hallucinations. On a couple of them the swelling is slowly increasing and the bump is still yellowish, detonating the venom underneath the surface of the skin. You can tell these kinds of bites just took place. Somewhere there's an obese satisfied eight-legged organism frantically dragging its swelled body full of my blood, searching for a hiding dwelling in order to escape my vengeful tennis shoe.

I live with insects. Various insects have been using my body as a source of sustenance and survival. Mainly chinches (bedbugs) and nickel-sized diametric brown house spiders. Occasionally I wake at the appropriate moment to witness a five to eight inch yellow and brown centipede crawling over my blanketed body, staring at me with curiosity. The chinches and spiders are my best friends. They are attracted to my heated blood. My bad blood. They are my only true friends.

It's a sign. An accepted omen. Devious spiritual beings are trying to send an ill-boding message to take over my weak will. Thirteen. Itching like a motherfucker! One tingling bitch in the middle of my bumpy scrotum, one on the left arm, two on the right, two big ass ones on my right leg, one huge one in the middle calf of the same leg as the two on my somewhat hairy left leg skinny inner thigh, and four all over my dry skin back.

The night before I was at the local Med with my pseudo companero. We were up to the usual Santa Fe backward nightlife wayward business: smoking grass, snorting coke, gulping booze, and cravenly harassing potential one-night stand whores sexually, but not successfully. I was at that dimly illuminated smoke-filled shit hole to rendezvous with this pretty-faced fat-assed nineteen year-old and her hot skinny caramel-skinned accomplice. Like every alcohol vending machine, there were bimbo bouncers for cheap hire at the entrance that would repeat what they were told to regarding a certain state-issued photo identification card. Social control, nowhere to go. My pseudo companero and I were both twenty-three so we were allowed access with minimal difficulty. My rendezvous and her skinny caramel-skinned accomplice were both underage, but had obtained fake IDs. God I wanted to bang the accomplice so bad. That evening she was looking hotter than southwestern droughts.

My pseudo companero and I had been there about forty-three minutes and downed two beers each when we noticed 'em at the entrance. After what appeared to be a suspended cognition of suspicion, accosted and despotically detained by the less than intelligent gatekeepers of this bawdy Mideastern tavern run by a short, portly imported Greek, they sauntered over to where we were sitting. I kept licking my lips sociopathically, staring at the sultry accomplice's barren shoulders looking like vegetationless hills yet to be explored. My rendezvous tried hugging and saying "hi" but she didn't exist within my bewildered peripheral vision. I felt like being reckless and rude.

As seconds accumulate and memories expand, our collective frivolous conversation was interrupted by these huge fat fucks rummaging through the gathering crowd, harassing people like if these dudes were employed by the government. I notice everything everywhere at all times, senses shutting down, homeless philanthropists leaving town on the dawns retracting grimace. A good buzz is all it takes to awaken consciousness.

Instinct informed me these dickheads were posing as undercover cops getting ready to pop the next infant crawling back into its mother's bleeding vagina.

"Yo, you and you. You best avoid that big white fucker with the baldhead half-shaven beard that looks like that half-assed entertaining wrestler Steve Austin. Him and his little spic partner are excavating people out of here faster than the British Empire stole artifacts from Africa." I cautioned our female company.

"Where?"

"Over there." I pointed out the swine pretending to be covert portraits, picking on anyone that appeared to be at least one hundred pounds lighter than their obese mud-dwelling farm animal dispositions, or anyone that was engaging in too good of a time. Cops are always the most jealous asscracks. Anyone who would be proud to take orders surely has not the minimalist clue of what integrity envelopes.The accomplice and my rendezvous rushed centrifugally away from my pseudo companero's and my location. Shit.

In a tight crowd of about seventy to eighty people or so, mostly twenty-some year-old alcoholics, the plainclothes pigs were extremely noticeable. I was trying not to pay attention when the big overgrown overfed farm boy cracker finished creaking his neck from an opposite direction. Our eyes confronted each other. Bluish-gray eyes, cold and frozen, reflected my beautiful reproduced binoculars standing in front of me.

"Let me see your IDs" said he.

"Who the fuck are you?" I retorted inside my intimidated head.

My pseudo companero and I immediately displayed our identification cards. We acted like programmed robots.

"This ID is fake" erroneously observed this illegal authority figure after about five to seven minutes of silently meditating upon it like a seminary student waiting to get felt up.

All I could see was his blue eyes slowly rolling blank, exploding out his scabrous eye sockets, oozing yellow-green puss. His redneck skin was expanding in knee-bent intervals. I saw my bulging fist pulverize his graveyard mouth with arrow precision force. I began to laugh in inaudible nightmares as his teeth bent backwards toward his inflamed throat, dripping from a metastasized tongue. I put the .380 pistol up to his right temple and pulled the trigger twice, not realizing I hadn't loaded the thing yet. I shoved four hollow-tipped jackets up his inflated nostrils and sliced his face diagonally with a broken ice cube.

I wasn't sure who he was referring to, but I looked over at my pseudo companero's deadpan face that stared back at me, halfheartedly raised eyebrows, crunched lips, shrugging his undecided shoulders, and then I finally grew some balls: "Who are you?"

"That's not important. What is impor,"

"If it's not important then how come you're here harassing us? If you're an undercover cop or something then show us your badge. Otherwise I'll have no other choice but to regard you as just another quick fix hustler trying to fuck us over for some cash or something. Then I'll be forced to call a real police officer over here to make sure you don't get a chance to indulge you fantastic psychopathic tendencies." The great thing about chotas is that you always know how they're going to respond to your line of inessential questioning. It is not difficult to perceive how the three and a half percent of their brain that uses them doesn't work.

"Watch your language"

He then showed us his badge, all the while turning his shaven head from side to side, making sure the rest of the people in the club wouldn't notice what he was doing or who he was even though he had already approached most of them and arrested three other tenebrous-looking individuals in the presence of everyone in the bar or anyone walking, passing by on the curbside.

"Are you satisfied?"

"Sometimes. When the plasma between my cellular membrane and nuclear distortion conspire to transmit editorial ideas against deficient authoritative delusion." I said.

Upon inspecting my pseudo companero's ID the pig seemed troubled.

"This ID isn't real" he quipped.

"Yes it is!"

"I'm not talking to you."

I halted and glanced at my pseudo companero.

"It's real," exclaimed my pseudo companero with solidified assurance.

"No it's not," shot back the incompetent cop. This dumbfuck couldn't tell the difference between sand and sugar collapsing through his trigger-happy fingers. The cracker called over his spic partner: "Does this look real to you?"

Both expressed an oversimplified strenuous smirk on their confused countenances.

One minute, two minutes, three minutes, four minutes, five.

"I don't know," said the spic.

"Jeeesssusss!"

"You shut-up," the white prick said to me.

One minute, two minutes, three minutes, four minutes, five.

I had about enough of this bullshit. "Excuse me with all polite efficacy. I know that the rigors of a police officer's life aren't always filled with inhospitable gratitude and a pristine woman's affection, but if you will look closely at the magical hologram right there, and at the birth date at the bottom right corner of the card in big black icon lettering, bigger than the other print, you will see that my colleague was born in 1976. Therefore without further miscalculation, you may come to discover after boggling subtraction of an elementary nature has been deconstructed that my friend as well as I are both twenty-three years old. We've been twenty-three years-old for the previous twenty-three years."

Both expressed an oversimplified strenuous smirk on their confused countenances.

"You know what? I think he's right," the spic mused. The white cracker dickhead undercover handed my pseudo companero back his I.D. He was anxiously humiliated. "You two be careful tonight and don't drink too much. I don't want to have to catch you on the street and arrest you for drunken driving."

"Yes you do. That's why you're a cop. That's why you and your five goons just outside the entrance there are harassing everyone. You have no right to do this."

That white fucker just kinda condescendingly glared back at me, brushed up too close to my face and emitted a fascinating odor as he spoke. "Ha! Obviously you don't know where you are living. This is *the* totalitarian police state. We can do whatever we want." And with that he turned his back on us like a good government employee. My pseudo companero and I never encountered my rendezvous or her hot skinny caramel skinned accomplice for the rest of the night. Shortly after we went home separately, each with our hands in our pockets.

Morning next. Decided to write a letter to the editor about what happened addressed to the editors of all three papers in town: two daily, one weekly. I'm pissed, oppressed, defiant, sarcastic, ovulating, and I got fuckin spider bites all over me. Four all over my scabbed back, two inside my inner skinny thigh of the left not-so hairy leg, one gigantic one on the calf of the same leg, two on my —oh fuck Benadryl, I can't take it, the itch, the pain, where is my marijuana?

I got this letter going. Righteous. Haven't written in decades no less than a week or two or four but damn this is some dope shit I'm writing I know they won't print it but I must purge myself of this hate plus I didn't get no pussy last night not that I never do. After writing and rewriting and writing and editing and shaping changing rearranging words after word for syllable punctuation writing and rewriting when writing for half an hour an hour two three and a half to a quarter I'm a keep writing all day maybe a play perhaps a novel or an essay but finish the letter nothing's gonna stop me from writing creating writing today right now nothing another hour to minute to second my brother bombards my creative laboratory asking if I would like to accompany him to a wedding of a friend of his and like the dumb thrill seeking imbecile that I think I am I say "yeah, sure" because I didn't get any pussy last night and I figure you can always get drunk for free at a wedding and encounter plenty of pussy in a self-conscious guilty desperate mood.

"I gotta clean-up"

"Well hurry-up. We gotta go by my friend's house and be at the chapel in forty-five minutes," my brother orders.

"What chapel?"

"Loretto"

Loretto chapel is the local garage for quick marriages. Supposedly the Judea-Christian mythical scavenger known as an angel holds up the infamous staircase twisting and turning to the top level of the chapel. Or the other story goes that some carpenter named Joseph or Jesus or James came tramping through Santa Fe a long time ago, stopped at the chapel and offered to build a staircase with God's grace for a bite of bread and a swig of swank. The staircase now and has never had any nails holding up the crooked structure, supposedly, and its another unbelievable miracle that the local spics believe in. All the same, I always understood Loretto chapel and the obsolete Loretto school as a secret place where nuns were trained to lust after the lord and subsequently get molested by the dominant archbishop. Santa Fe is full of shit like that.

Got ready quick. Half hour. Wasn't dressed for a wedding. Topped with delicate blue long-sleeve thermal material shirt that made my stomach look almost thin in the middle of sweltering summer. Brown Dockers slacks, faded, to cover my crusty anus hidden under soiled gray and white striped shorts. Mountain boots, uncombed hair, unbrushed teeth, didn't even attempt to take a shower, I was ready to get laid.

We drove to my brother's friend's house, smoked some weed with his mother, his Asian domineering hag of a wife, and his three year-old half-breed daughter. It was good ass high-grade shit too. I was feeling fucked-up. We departed shortly after. Got the reggae sounds booming, my brother driving, cruising. The chapel was filled with a bunch of tuxedo wearing suit and tie displaying upper class idiots that stood when they were supposed to and felt and thought that the couple at the altar were making the greatest mistake of their pathetic controlled lives. People only get married because they think they have to. They are following, doing what they have been told to do since they was little. If they only knew that relationships work better without ceremonious utterances of obligation under the scrutinizing eyes of despised relatives, soon-to-be-hated-in-laws, and blood-sucking friends. It doesn't take a cubic zerconia to express your temporal lust. The priest administering the recital looked like he had better things to do and reeked of cheap Captain Morgan's whiskey. I was seated at the back of the chapel in the farthest pew. The worthless disgusting ritual took about two protracted hours of which I had to spend sitting on an unfurnished glossy wooden bench hurting my leaking hemorrhoids squeezed between the corner end and some overly dressed obese middle-aged black woman that stunk of B.O., brandy, and beans and kept saying "um-hu" and "how sweet" every two seconds to some stringy tiny stick figure blonde bitch sitting on her opposite side. Everyone frowned upon me with scorn. I didn't belong there. When do we get drunk?

The reception was held at the Loretto Inn adjacent to the Loretto chapel next to where the Loretto school used to be. The Loretto Inn was another bourgeois playpen off limits to the local native indigent like my brother and I. We attended anyways. One on the left arm, two on the right, and one excruciating zesty vibrating pinch of a tick smack in the middle of my sweaty scrotum.

My brother and I sat outside on some makeshift cheap extended leg table made of hollow steel and plastic wood covered with kindergarten coloring blank constructive paper. Gray clouds were beginning to converge outside above us. The whiff of dewy drift tortured my yearning to urinate outside. There were like five other people sitting with us but I only recognized two of them: this Jew dude and his recently betrothed bleached babe. The bleached babe actually used to fuck my brother a long long long long time ago my brother use to spit in her ugly champagne hair, slap her rosy lips, scratch her kittenish back and cum on her plaqued teeth.

I didn't feel like conversing with anyone. Everyone there was acting like wealthy white personalities. Everyone everywhere in Amerifucked acts like wealthy white personalities. So fake. This is Santa Fake. They all were as stuck-up as my middle finger to such pretentious society. I headed straight toward the open bar and began my intoxication process at precisely 4:23 p.m. Let's start with a shot of Stoli and a glass of chardonnay.

Blaaaaagggghhhh! Sick. The wine tasted like old avocado. I had three glasses by the time we decided to go indoors for free food. We sat at a table with my brother's friend's parents whom we had just smoked weed with earlier before we arrived at the chapel. For about an hour and a half I carried on a burdensome conversation with my brother's friend's mother.

"So what do you think of that faggot George W. Bush?" I said.

"Oh, I don't know. I kind of like him, I think," she idiotically responded.

"What are you fuckin' high?"

"Well, as a matter of fiction I am."

"The guy is a fuckin' joke. He is a shame to humanity's depravity." I couldn't believe she said she liked him. The fucker made me sick. "He makes me sick."

"Well, maybe that is why he is such a good candidate."

Now I couldn't tell if she was fucking with me or not.

"I thought you were a leftist?" I asked.

"No." she replied.

"No?"

"No."

"Oh. Could've fooled me."

"You shouldn't have preconceptions about anyone. Personally I think the Left is lost." How bitter she sounded.

"But you have long hair and you smoke weed."

"So?"

I could tell she wasn't drinking much and probably wasn't enjoying this stupid conversation as much as I wasn't.

"But why Bush. How could anyone tolerate that dumbass." The moron is just a silver spoon cocksucking dunce clone of his crooked ass father. But I guess that's just my perverted brainwashed opinion."

"I'm Republican," she sporadically ejaculated.

"What?" I was bamboozled.

"Yes. I'm a Republican. I vote Republican. I eat Republican. And I defecate Republican."

"That's about all you can do with a Republican. I think I need another drink."

I downed my full glass of cheap chardonnay in one gulp, one breath and proceeded to the free bar for the fourth time. "Give me a cape cod, Stoli." When I returned to the table inside, my brother's friend's parents had left. I sat, sipped my drink, felt my buzz peaking and then decided to walk around the wedding dinner party looking for prey. I met three dumb blonde Texans jiggling their wide hips and stone hoofs on the dance floor and I probably would've been able to take all three of them back to their rooms and run a train had I not tripped twice and fallen over three times while trying to shake my foundation. I was already slurring a bit, spitting all over their images while trying to yell in their ear over the amateur jazz being played by a ready-for-hire three member band next to me. One on one they departed from my presence and I was left alone on the slippery floor staring at the contents of the shape of sweat dripping from my soaked forehead. I needed another drink.

For the next couple of hours I inhaled three more cape cods then switched to Colorado Bulldogs. My brother and a few of his friends were in a dark corner outside, straying from the rest of the party. The crowd had already dwindled quite a bit by this time. Smart people only attend a gathering for an hour or so and leave before the rest of the flock figures out what a fuck-up you really are. I joined my brother at the far end of the outside area and began smoking cigars and more ganja with them. Bad mistake. Do not, and I mean Do fuckin Not smoke weed when you're already trashed on booze. The rush wedged itself between my congested ears. The heat repeatedly circulated throughout my timorous body. My head tightened, my vision condensed, and little voices spoke rapidly around the garden court. Everybody else's eyes were spinning and everybody seemed to have a smile. The crash of laughter became harder and harder hurting my ears. I noticed a woman walking around the yard with a stiff carrot in her pocket, a lamp as a leg, and millions of giant red ants with wings covering her naked flesh, fluttering to the rhythm of moonshine wasted. We were getting blitzed. At least I was. It was starting to drizzle. I was dizzy. Romantic moonbeams perched on Allah's ethereal malversation. Chaotic triangle, diaspora remnants invading city population exploding under half-constructed highways; murder the love, destroy the cure, impossible prosperity awaits my reckoning.

"Another Bulldog barturnder. No what. Actually, actually, act-you-ali I'll stake a better white glass of wines."

The Mexican immigrant bartender just shook his head.

"Wheniver yur reedy."

He just stood there, quiet, contemplative, scared.

"What?" I wondered.

"I'm sorry, but I cannot server you any more drinks."

"What? You're kidding."

"No. I'm sorry." He then turned his back on me and fled. Some fat bitch replaced him and she spoke English a bit better than both of us at the moment.

"I'm sorry sir, but that is the instruction we have received from the bar manager."

"What are you takling about? I came here all the time. I'm regular. I'm a great customer and I'm praying for these dinks. I mean paying."

"This is a free open bar sir."

"Listen here you fat fuckin' cunt. You can't cut me off. I'm a local native resident of Santa Fake. You just will do anything to just git rid off just the local element from this pompous establishment. Huh? Admit it. Don't be silent. Silence is the lover of ridicule."

"Is there something I can help you with?" some porno star country hick looking motherfucker with a gapped tooth wearing tinted eyeglasses and tight sky blue nylon pants interrupted my belligerent lecture, standing behind the fat bitch.

"Are you the bar manager?"

"Yes I am."

"Why can't I have anoter drink? Buuuurrrpppp!"

"Because you've had enough. Make sure you don't give him anymore." He said to the bitch.

"Asswipe! And you too you sell-out bitch. All you do is take orders. All of you take orders." I think I was about to become almost obnoxious. "You're a bunch of fucking whores and slaves. How much dick did you suck to get this gig and how many balls do you fondle to sustain it?"

"Hey man chill out." I felt an icy arm embrace my scrawny shoulders and begin to escort me tumbling swaying legs away from the bar. "They're going to call the police if you don't quiet down." Some tall greasy slicked wop decked out in a yellow-green hand-me-down looking wool suit was the dude trying to calm me down. "Here." He gave me a sip of what he was drinking and I spit it out all over the pants of his suit.

"What the fuck is that?"

"It's cognac. Hey watch out man, take it easy."

"What? You think you're John Gotti or Martin Scorsleezy or some guedo like dat?""

Hey man, I'm just trying to help you. You know, it's not that lady's fault. She's just trying to do her job," he said.

"Yeah, her blow job."

"Ahh, come on. She's actually doing you a solid. Besides, drinking a lot doesn't become you. You shouldn't be drinking so much at a young age. Leave the heavy drinking to the older guys."

"What the fuck do you know becomes me and doesn't? What the fuck you from? You look like you just stepped off the train from some Brooklyn neighborhood populated by shammies still hoping to return to Sicily before the mafia boss cuts off their ear and mixes it with matzo balls or some shit."

"Matzo balls are Jewish and yes I am Italian. Are you a racist?" he casually asked.

"Yes I am. You leftover Euro white trash sons of bitches come to this town thinking you can run the shit telling us local spics what we can do, what to do, and who to do it to. Who the fuck do you think you are? Why don't you just go back to Little Italy are wherever the fuck you from? Get the fuck out of my face!"

"Look brother, you really need to give the drinking a rest. You're not going to impress anybody with such inebriated swagger, especially the women. You also need to watch what you say. You may get hurt sometime."

"Fuck you prick. You don't even want to fuck with me in my hometown. You don't know who I am here."

"Not anybody worth listening to. I was just looking out for you that's all." And with those solemn, sincere words he left me to my ill state of mind. I was infuriated that they cut me off. In all my drunken stupors in every establishment in town I had never been cut off from drinking liquor before. I felt oppressed. I always feel oppressed no matter what. I needed to take my aggression out on someone innocent. I spotted the bleached babe and her Jew dude sitting at the same table outside next to the bar.

"What the fuck is wrong with this world?" I sat right next to her, cozying up, never removing my gawking glare, two inches from the nape of her flimsy neck. "Huh? I feel disturbed. The voice inside my head has grown passive. Blues in winter, blues in spring. To sing in solemnity, desperate hours ravaging my internal being. I see the world. It looks like a neglected dumpster. Must we continue existing as if we're all strangers though we shared identical births that weren't worth the living. Strain, my shriveled colon brings me pain. I am to blame for all the problems we face. You scumbags are all the same. Displeasure with the blessed, no soul to possess. Less than one day ago Picasso squatted on a wooden chandelier, choirboy recitals are not good enough for your irreparable genitals. The sun rays can bounce off toothpaste dotted mirrors when democracy vanishes from our invisible dinner plate, how kind fate can be telling me to kill thee like Columbian recruits into United States sponsored paramilitaries. Abraham Lincoln is not a hero meditating in an unmarked grave; he was a fuckin slave holder that never shaved. You caveman, You whore, You can't defile me any more with your sarcastic balloon openings telescopic observatories metal laboratories making bombs obliterating pigtail communists resisting temptations of tax inflation responsible for my lowlife position sitting here talking to you, you temporal passage afraid to take the equipollent position. Your flat tits look about as voluptuous as a rat's whiskers. Feel the bee pollen soaking my shattered vision of insanity's think tank you fuckin' skank."

"That's it!" The bleached babe squealed in her customary high-pitched voice loud enough for everyone to hear, bringing the amateur jazz being played by a ready-for-hire-at-any-moment glued together band to a sudden halt. "I've had enough, I'm not going to sit here and take your crap."

I began to laugh.

"Oh fuck you! You're a piece of shit. You're an asshole, nothing but an angry asshole. All you do is criticize people and make fun of them. You never take the moment to think that maybe there are some people that listen to you and take serious what you say. What the hell is the matter with you?"

"You fuckin people, that's what the matter is."

"See what I mean. Fuck you! I hope you die. Honey, let's go," she commanded.

The Jew dude followed orders, smiling just a bit.

I kept laughing, having a good time tapping my fingertips on the table. The fat bitch of a bartender overheard everything and was giving me some dirty looks. I felt like killing her. One more drink and I probably would've. Fuck it. It meant nothing to me. They meant nothing to me. All those people and their stupid ways mean nothing to me. The depressed rain is dropping heavily. I am alone fighting a war I cannot win.

My brother trucked me out of there. He seemed to enjoy my fit as well. He told me that he couldn't believe some of the things I was saying to her, right there in public, loud enough for other people to hear me. I told him I didn't give a shit. We left. He took me to Tommy Macaione Park, which was a few blocks north of downtown, and we pulled over in the dark prepared to get more intoxicated. Macaione was this old fart weird ass artist that once got penalized by the City of Santa Fe for taking care of more than three hundred feline cats at his home. As I was preparing the four inch four lines of cocaine, two for him two for me, one for each nostril, I told him that I was nothing special. I didn't possess the body to swoon young girls looking for a muscular time. I came on too strong by being cordial, kind, and deferential. My mind was in the continuous process of being destroyed. Where is the escape? Does it rest here on top of this scratched contaminated CD case of Sizzla singing insurrection? Our revolutionary uprising does not consist of narcotic infatuation. My uncombed hair is infiltrated with lamenting lice doing litigated gymnastics. Combination extortionist slipping a crumbled rolled dollar beneath the seductive plush lips of her imaginary uterus. The underworld has kidnapped me and has yet to ask for a substantial ransom. How foolish for someone to refer to themselves as an artist. My corrosive intellect sweats effluent beads reading Marxist literature upside down planting bombs underneath homeless shelters cuz the fascist impulse inside all of us cannot be reasoned with. We are killers. You, I, the ascending blue spruce that obstructs a withering aspen's lonely chance of hearing the echo of the desolate forest. Animals with horns more horny than Sony Rollins's tapping shoes. As I sit here in the cabin, snorting hope away, the summer snowfall practices wiccan bathing techniques not compatible with motherboard atrocities. I wish I could collect the fervent blood of the Palestinian people on the tip of my acrid punishment and sing a hypnotizing bolero to an Israeli blowen as I violate her horizontal orifice with tremendous thrust. Let us live and search for torment. "What do you want to do and where do you want to go?" I asked my brother.

"Let's go to the Med and shoot some stick. Quit your bullshit. You better not do this or that shit you pulled at Loretto over there or I'll leave you," he threatened.

Sent to hell once again. I rot in the world without a friend. Do not pretend to be my lover if you've never apprehended a four-leaf clover with one hand. We're pulling up to the bar. My brother parks his 1994 Honda Accord LX right in front of the establishment parallel to a yellow painted curb. We had just finished inhaling powder and herb. I am unaware of my presence at the moment. We're walking in the front gate, the bouncer wants to see my ID. Here. Let's me proceed. Through the transparent smoke clouds I immediately lock my blurred vision on this honey sitting alone, back to the bar, right within the frame of the doorway. She wants to be noticed. She sees me taking her from behind with my retina-scorched eyes. Long black silky hair, cocoa flush skin, symmetrical shaven crossed thighs bailing out of a silky pastel colored spring skirt. She doesn't stop staring. I can't look elsewhere. From a distance I can only make out her contours. As I approach her, the details of her façade become clear. She looks Indian, or Native, or whatever you want to call it. Almost mongrel, yet she is hot. Not too thin, not to fat. She has purple red come-on shoes covering her staunch feet. Her feet look good. The green veins bulging on the top part of her feet make me feel like shooting heroin. I wonder what it would feel like for her toes to massage my screaming balls. She's wearing a silk maroon blouse that allows her perky petite tits to protrude just a bit. I stand inches in front of her losing myself in the abyss of her chaotic reflection. We examine one another with our eyelashes. No smiling. After thirty seconds or so I avoid her and order a drink. Upon reception of my Carta Blanca I decide to sit one chair away from her at the bar, teasingly glancing at her from time to time. She looks back at me like if she already knew what it was like to have my discomfort slide up in her. Her lips are robust like a tootsie roll. Her face is a tad pocked but it doesn't bother me. At this state of mind I'd fuck just about anything.

I light a cancer stick, blowing out the first strike of toxic chemicals. I decide to move in closer. The rest of the packed house is oblivious to my lust. "Yatta-hey," I say. "My name is," "I don't want to know your name," she replies. "Well, did you hear that I get paid for sex?" She smiles. My confiscated libido can't withhold the captivating aroma of your suffocating breath. Please listen to my infuriated confession. I murdered the last woman I made love to. She reminds me of you. I loath to filter my epileptic fingers through your smooth hair for fear of pulling it taut, teaching you to submit. You might attempt to widen the gap, ripping my neglected heart shedding liquid ventricles. I have thirteen spider bites poisoning my body right now. I feel you're the anodyne for circumstantial lethargy. How is your psychology? I want to touch your flesh gently.

"Go ahead," she says.

I don't. I wait. "Why are you alone here in this tavern of remorseless souls?"

"Because I'm an unsullied prostitute," she claims. I chuckle with enthusiasm. We both look away for a moment. "How many men have come on to you tonight?"

"Including you about seven. I was at El Paseo earlier with my sister and three different men gave me their business card, asking me to go home with them."

"Why didn't you?"

"Because I was waiting to meet you. I just sucked their pricks collectively in the bathroom."

"You are a countless flatterer," I respond.

"So are you."

"What is your name?"

She replies.

"How come you tell me your name but don't want to know mine?"

She asks what my name is and I tell her, yet, she doesn't seem to ingratiate herself with it.

"What do you think of me so far?"

Considering that I just met you, but based on what you've shown already, I feel I might want to get to know you better. You seem bright, exciting, flirtatious enough to allow you to sit next to me.

This was a bullshit answer for a bullshit question. Any girl that tries to answer that question without spending at least one day with you could care less about the persona searching for ambrosial companionship. Am I handsome? Of course. It wasn't the words she used as much as it was the way she kept looking at me that gave me the confidence to try and pursue her. I knew for sure I would feel her by the end of the night.

We continued to exchange pointless drivel for about an hour in the hopes of solidifying injection. It was almost one in the morning. During our progress she invited her sister over to introduce. My perception of physical beauty on a female is rendered inadequate when I drink and drug as much as I have tonight, but there was no doubting my ability to determine that her sister was extremely ugly. My prey was about 5'6" and slender when she stood up and her sister was about half that height and twice the weight. My temporary companion was older by about two years. Her sister told me her name but I forgot it instantaneously. I didn't like her. She was more aggressive and rude than a Whole Foods customer. She wouldn't shut the fuck up. Her eyes were uneven, her breath reeked stale cigarettes, sour cum stench, and day old uncooked moldy roast beef.

She had pimples all over her face and body, at least the parts that were exposed, some were even in the process of oozing out off-white puss. Her hair was matted, thick, tangled, and greasy, not smooth and clean like her sisters. She had a raspy ass voice. The strangest thing about her was that she had a mouth full of silver teeth, some missing. I asked her what happened to all the ivory in her mouth and she took a swing at me barely swiping the exterior of my stubbly chin with her sharp bright red fingernails. The bitch was lucky I didn't smack her right there. She kept trying to tell her sister that all I wanted was to fuck her and leave her. She was beyond annoying, asking where I'm from, what I do, how much money do I make, where do I live, was it a house or an apartment, what kind of car do I drive, do I have any intentions of marrying her sister and if I did how would I support her and her son. Whoops. That did it. Her son. The whole time the elder just sat there frozen, expressionless. She didn't interject nor refute anything her repugnant sister said. It was like her sister had a spell on her. My temporary companion's vibes were silent. But her sister's were sinister. They felt heavy and uncertain. I wanted her to leave us alone, but when she blurted out that her sister had a child, I wasn't sure I wanted anything to do with either one of them.

Her sister was finally usurped by some tall lanky gringo dude that seemed to know her. Right away she threw herself all over him and began sucking his gums relentlessly. I asked my temporary companion if it was true that she had a son. She said yes, he was two years old. She was twenty-two. I told her that I didn't date women with kids.

"Why not?"

"Because I can't afford to buy diapers and if I want to lick your fingertips I'm afraid that it would conjure up memories of kneeling face down in cow dung for summer recreation."

She said she didn't want to date me but just to sleep with me. In that case we talked a bit more but I couldn't remember what I was telling her. The room was spinning. My body shaking. My constitution was an eggshell. Her sister kept coming by intermittently harassing us and touching her sister in odd places of sacrilege. I kind of separated myself from them, ordered several more drinks, chugged them like an apolitical Irishman, watching four vatos from Albuquerque struggle at billiards on a small barroom .50 cent coin operated dilapidated table. I started talking to this one dude sitting at the corner of the bar. He was with those dudes from 'Burque so I told him that I was moving down there in about a month to attend graduate school at the University of New Mexico. They were all Chicanos. I said I was a playwright and that my material consists of the plight of the Chicano people in the Southwest, primarily New Mexico, primarily Santa Fe, and how we are alienated from our culture, our history, ourselves, and all fucked-up. He didn't seem to take much interest in what I was blabbering but humored me with reluctant nods of disingenuous approval and half-baked smirks. I admonished him to keep a look out for me next year that I would be blowin' up the spot. He didn't care. Every now and then he would glance over my shoulder and check out the woman I had been recklessly seducing. I noticed too that she kept looking at me, sometimes without pause, and wondered if she was obsessed or desperate. I was losing interest in her. Something about her and her familial burden turned me off. I didn't covet a threesome with her ugly ass sister.

At that passing instant this red-headed cat that I had seen around the way a few times, but never really met, came up to me, started rapping with me as if he knew me forever, and even bought me another beer. We were getting along, talking about hip-hop and old Santa Fe meaninglessness when out of the foggy atmosphere he asked me if I wanted a bump. Normally I would have been weary and mostly like declined had I not been so intoxicated and careless, taking him for a possible narc. I answered sure and followed him to the men's bathroom passing my previous temporal companion on the way. In the grimy toilet hole that is the men's restroom at any bar, completely blanketed in half-ass graffiti written all over the stained brick walls with permanent black marker, the red-headed cat laid out two thick ass lines of cocaine for me on top of the toilet's porcelain backstop. I attacked them both like a spoiled prep school adolescent. I almost passed out. I stayed there reading the eloquent restroom literature on the wall: "Fuck You – No, fuck you." "I fucked your sister." "Suck my dick/I would if I could find it." "I made Linda Lovelace gag/ that's because it was so small/ Fuck You." You know, shit like that. Right then I understood the significance of existence. It was so challenging to depart from there. I sauntered back to my bar stool and just sat there, staring into oblivion. My body was tingling all over. I couldn't blink my eyelids. My teeth chattered, grinded, and swiveled.

The bar was closing. My brother said it was time to get out of there. We were on our way out the door when my previous temporal companion, the seductive Indian lady at the bar with the ugly ass sister, grappled my arm and pulled me over between her legs.

"What?"

She didn't say nothing. Just sitting there staring. It was ominous, yet provocative.

"Oh, I see. You want me to wet you down. Is the fortitude of your begging beginning to take hostage of your romanticized savagery?"

Nothing.

I tried walking away telling her I would call her later even though I had never obtained her telephone digits.

She didn't let go. Her grip became tighter as she squeezed every molecule of confidence out of my drenched pores. My spider bites stopped itching. I didn't know how to react. She tried kissing me, tugging my stiff neck toward her dehydrated lips but by some unnamable whirlwind I was able to resist. My brother crept back inside through the doorway and insisted we leave now or threatened to leave me there helpless and vulnerable like a snowflake two inches from the ground.

I wanted to leave. I was trying, halfheartedly. I had already made up my pixilated mind that I just wanted to go home and sleep off the drug and alcohol abuse. There were no moments left to celebrate, nor energy to frolic. Two in the morning. It was time to crash. My body knew it, I knew it, but my cock was defiant as it grew and grew and grew and rose and hardened as my re-united temporary Native companion began to fondle my testicles right there in front of everyone. I was frightened of being fearful of fear.

"Later bro, I'm leaving," my brother said. "Make sure he gets home and try not to abuse him too much."

"Don't worry, he's safe with me," the Native retorted, holding on to my waist ferociously like if she was trying to prevent renegade hyenas from stealing her plunder. Every time she spoke her voice sounded extremely monotone, without zest, personality, or life. I didn't feel safe in her clutches but her bony fingers felt so tender cupping my shrinking balls. Her sister with that tall gringo dude joined us and had figured out that all four of us would go back to his place and get to know each other a little better for the remainder of the night's morning. She even gave me permission to fuck her sister. My temporary companion smiled with zombie lustre. Those four vatos from 'Burque were watching us intently.

"You know what," I began, "you should give me your phone number and I'll call you later on. I can't go right now."

`"Come on, please," she moaned.

She gave me 'the look.' It is very difficult to describe 'the look,' but it was that fuck me look. Not a swinging dick in the universe can resist it. Women know how to wield that shit at will. I could already picture myself shooting sperm all over her face.

"He won't call," her ugly ass sister chimed in.

"Just come with us, please. I promise, you'll get what you want," the Indian lady kept begging and soliciting me like rookie Mormons. This was very difficult. I felt like I was in a big city like Chicago for the first time, alone.

"Hold on one second, I'll be right back. I just want to catch my brother before he leaves."

"He won't come back," her sister said. The Indian lady released me, cocked her head diagonally and pouted with her lower lip extended, rubbing her spread thighs quick enough for me to recognize she had no panties on. This world is confusing and unfair.

Thirteen.

I'll never know to this hour why I didn't go home. I was exhausted and totally out of my mind. Almost half crazy. Walking out the entrance I had no intention of returning. But I was tempted. I was horny. My attitude toward women at the time was all wrong. I saw them as sex objects and I thought that was all I wanted from them. In some stupid ass way I kind of convinced myself I was some kind of player. That seems to be the theme for males of the last generation. Fuckin' television, industry, and hip-hop. I deserve to be punished eternally. Besides, I wanted to fuck as many different varieties of girls as possible. All kinds of ethnicities. I now had a chance to fuck an Injun. I needed to fuck an Indian. I wanted the squaw.

When we got to my brother's car, I stopped. I looked over the rooftop at him and told him that that Indian broad wanted to fuck me. It wasn't a figure of speech and he knew it. I was cognizant enough to realize I had two condoms in my back pocket that I picked up from the clinic after the last time I was tested. That gave me the confidence to venture back into the bar. I should've known better. My intuition wasn't in it. I told my brother I'd catch up with him later. In a month I would be out of Santa Fe and on my way to graduate school in Albuquerque. In 'Burque I would meet way more women than I ever have and far better looking ones than the one I was about to defile. My intentions were to screw as many of them as I could. Right now I was desperate though. I hadn't had sex in a long time. I didn't know what I was doing.

Who needs a woman when you have the early morning red sky? Who needs a woman when you possess the knowledge that one day you're gonna die? I wanted the woman. I wanted the excitement, the danger of a one-night stand with some whore I just met and would never know. I wanted to have sex with the unidentifiable. I wanted trouble.

When I got back in the bar, my previously re-united Indian lady companion was sitting on the stool she had been on all night and those four vatos from 'Burque were surrounding her, all up in her shit. One dude kept trying to grab her around her acquiescent hips but she immediately withdrew when she saw me return. I sat on the stool next to her and she stood up, leaned between my legs and put my arms around her stomach. One of the guys from 'Burque kept begging her to go hang out with him and his friends but she refused. He suddenly gave up. It was apparent who she was going to disturb that night.

Her ugly sister and that dorky gringo she was latching on to asked if we were ready to go. My temporary companion and I walked out ahead of them. Walking down Galisteo toward wherever their car was we noticed her sister and that dork were nowhere in sight. Impulsively I launched my temporary companion into a corner of some next-door store merchandising dead sheep's skin and began kissing her violently. She loved it. She clutched my head, pulled me closer and started moaning. Before I knew it my fingers were sliding in and out of her moist universe. It never really did quite rain. Anybody walking past us leaving the Med or across the street leaving another dumpy bar received a free soft porn freak show. She kept breathing hard on me, telling me to put it in her. I wasn't that out of it, though God knows I wanted to. I just kept fingering her, making her cum, dripping all over the sidewalk. When I finally removed my fingers and sniffed them, her intensity didn't smell too bad. I made her lick my fingers.

Her sister and her catch passed by so we decided to follow them, never letting go of one another. When we got to the end of Galisteo at the intersection of Galisteo and Water Street we met up with that redheaded cat and some other dude. Then these three other guys approached us from across the street. Two older men and one younger fella. They were all stupid Hispanic locals. The young guy seemed to be familiar with the ugly sister.

"What's up? What the fuck you doing with that punk?" the younger gentleman asked.

"Nothing." The ugly sister had no problem abandoning the gringo and threw herself all over that other guy.

"What are you looking at punk?"

I just love my people. The gringo looked at his shoes and couldn't quite figure out what had just happened. He wasn't about to put up any kind of resistance. Apparently one of the older men was the father of that young asshole that the ugly sister now had her body wrapped around. All were talking shit to that gringo, threatening him with the end of his existence, especially the ugly sister. It was fucked-up. As he was backing off a dark blue Bronco SUV pulled-up. The other older man that I noticed just a second earlier with the father and son was driving. The family duo opened the doors and told the ugly sister to get in. They said that her older sister and I could come along as well. The older sister asked if we were still going to her car. She didn't seem to trust these new faces. She seemed unfamiliar with them. But her ugly sister acted as if these guys were her pimps and she had made a big mistake getting caught with that white dude and she better not make a bigger mistake by refusing to go. I had never seen these guys before. Everybody else was starting to get into the bronco. My temporary companion and I stared at each other for a second. I didn't have a clue what was going on. I really didn't want to go. The tall gringo dude made one quick attempt to take the ugly sister by the hand before she got into the car. The younger dickhead (he looked like an overfed pit bull terrier) pushed the gringo to the ground and spat on him. We jumped in without any fuss and the doors closed like prison cell chambers for the first time.

Thirteen. The hard luck number. The two on my somewhat hairy left leg skinny inner thigh throbbed in unison underneath my five-year old slacks; the one on the left arm exploded, gushing metaphysical oxygen around the pink hairs on my arm; the one huge one in the middle calf of the somewhat hairy left leg skinny inner thigh grew legs, lifted itself, searched for a spot closer to any ankle, attaching itself with circular teeth ensconced in a potato sack; the two big ass ones on my right leg shot silk across to the two on my right arm escalading drum pipes blinds holding canes staring on grounds drenched in feces shooting barbed-wire bullets honking pandemonium never heard listening to Matisse's fervent brush strokes make love to crocodile babysitters; the four all over my dead skin back scratched the senator's daughter wishing the Roman Empire fumbled business setbacks beautiful noise boys and girls come follow me to the Halloween daytime parade tickling Jesus' bare feet kissing lizards worshipping decapitated rooster heads reciting Rilke's final moment of isolation; and the one only the one all over in one to one as one with one inside one out the one in the one all over one around one above ground one touching one licking one poking one making fun of one with one without one there'd be none but one is one when one becomes one underneath one digest one digress one leaving one for one much better than one someone anyone done one fun one gun one down brown cat one alone one alone one alone one alone one obsessed with one one in the graveyard one to one in one out one on top of one in back of one lazy one crazy son of a gun one bitch one whore one dirty one one more time one - one tingling motherfucker in the middle of my bumpy scrotum.

In the car I couldn't help but feel her clean-shaven thighs for the whole ride. Pride aggrandizes when I smell crisp skin. The others paid us no mind. We sat on the left side of the back seat next to the left rear window, she by the window, I in the middle. We stared toward the front windshield. I sneaked my index fingers sneakily under her skirt feeling the undulating apprehension. Felt good, supple and sweaty. I was ready to embark with no destination. We finally arrived to some strange house near St. Michael's High School. The driver said it was his chante and we dismounted. My fingers were sore. The rear windowpane next to my temporary companion was fogged.

We got into the house and there were all kinds of expensive furniture and art decorating the marble floors in upside down tundras gloomin' with recently shined alcoholic tenacity. I'd describe the décor but I don't know shit about décor and besides I deplore those individuals who can give you every detail about material objects, their history, and insignificance. There's no intelligence in materialistic infatuation. There's no intelligence in bonding yourself to this shitty world with it's shitty preoccupations. Besides, writers that describe too much suck dick like my temporary companion was telling me she wanted to do all through the ride on the way over here.

We were in the house, in the kitchen. The father of the little runt pit-bull looking asshole, a small little short portly scumbag, was carrying a case of Heineken brew, and we in the kitchen making introductions. "Hello I'm this guy's dad," he tells me. I met his son and the driver of the Bronco and they turned to my temporary companion. "Hi, I'm Officer Something or Other and you are."

What the fuck did I just hear? Officer? Am I sure I heard correctly? This motherfucker was a cop. I thought my substance abuse inducement was confusing my thought process. "And this is Officer So and So." No fuckin' way. "You guys want to do a couple of lines?" the newly introduced swine asked. No fuckin' way! I can't believe I was being asked by a police officer to do a couple of lines of cocaine with police officers. I thought I didn't hear correctly. It's a set up.

I didn't respond. I stayed silent as first graders on their first day of school. I didn't trust these punks. It's gotta be a set up. I dealt with pigs last night and I want nothing to do with these bastards right now. I had to get out of there. Where am I?

My temporary companion and I immediately made our way to the open spaced living room quarters, sat comfortably on the couch and started feeling each other up. Everything between a man and a woman is mistrust. We are just animals trying to be transcendent independent of ludicrous shambles perpetuated into deep thoughts. I wish there were better days than the ones I am living. I touched her, she touched me. Somehow the tremblings inside us never escalated into romantic feelings of absurdity. The driver of the Bronco passed by at one instant and informed us that several rooms existed in the house that could confine us to closed quarters outside other's glancing inelastic collision. Then he disappeared for the rest of the night.

My art is all I have. My art is a woman I can seduce without resistance to insecure notions of psychotherapy. I suddenly attempted to escort her to one of those other rooms, my crotch she cupped with five fingers, my fingers smelling like her rotten aroma, a coma I wanted to put us in. I am angry with saliva all over me. Institutionalized with lust capturing everything. We were alone with each other while others remarked on the high of each other witnessing the other watching other one another as the other referred to someone else except this other person while together we stopped and confronted the turquoise as it lectured the practices of safe sex intoxicated limbo libido drenched in showers of remaining teardrops.

"No," she muttered.

"Okay."

We embarked back to the sofa. Right hand and index finger lodged into her diamond remaining satisfied for the time being she with her hands down my pants we sat still dancing motionless the vibrant dimensional numerous paintings on the wall spoke to me and carried conversations about how the night is not offensive to the believer in underworld destinations. Distorted portraits of elusive personages I'd never encounter outside of enraptured utopia. We could hear the others in the kitchen snorting.

"Come on," I forcefully whispered into her waxen ear.

"No."

The sticks clap, counterfeit dollar bills elapse, computer dementia happens when you've spent too much time inside the house all day. I wish somebody would say what I need to do. We kissed and tongued and touched and tickled and felt and clasped and gasped for air as we compared our pubic hairs with the delicacy of a French bistro chef's intimacy. Nothing's gonna happen my way unless I say it shouldn't happen. What does this woman want? I sleep naked thinking of you. What I want to do to you has nothing to do with who you think you are and what you could never be. The scratchy blankets and sheets cover my emancipated inquiry as we seem to suppose that the other is better than one or the other. Bizarre vibrations pass through your mansion of pretentious delicate shell covering your vagina in my half opened mouth. Nobody cares about our melting imitating Balzac condition.

"You guys want to do some coke?" blazed into the living room her grotesque sister with dilated eyeballs.

I shook my numb skull no looking at her with half-opened eyelids and my temporary Native companion responded accordingly, following my lead though I could tell she wanted to do some because after her sister retreated she unassumingly asked me if I was sure I didn't want to do any cocaine because there was plenty of it around and I didn't have to pay for anything. No way I was doing cocaine with a couple of pigs and probably pig informants. But I stayed there all the same.

Her cantankerous sister came back and asked if we wanted to do coke again, this time persisting after I said no twice. "Are you sure, are you sure, are you sure, sure?"

I wouldn't give in. I felt these people were trying to set me up because anybody that knew me in town knew I was affiliated with cokeheads and drug scenes. Early on in anyone's drug career in Santa you get put on a list. I felt I should get out of there. But the Indian lady had her lotioned hands all over me so gently I couldn't help but think like a man.

A few more moments and the dishpan would be clean.

Stand up. Walk with me. Behind her silhouette shaking tremendously uproarious I guide her toward a room. The room is connected with a central bathroom that leads to another bedroom. The bedroom is posh. It has a tropical ambiance combined with a revolting southwestern motif. The bed is neatly made, taut bright colors of orange, striped yellow, and moss green form an abstract image of fire consumed by serenity on a cloud puff comforter. I notice two large bay windows looking out to a back or side yard as I toss her onto the bed. She giggles like a deathbed patient in an unsanitary infirmary molested by the nightshift nurse. I turn the lights off and leap into fate's malfeasance. In darkness we find each other's nervous limbs. In darkness we see nothing. In darkness we become the living fortitude that most people fantasize about. I lift her skirt and try to lick her. She utters no and lifts me for a detrimental kiss. Her lips are moist. Her kisses are brief. Her hair is as wild as springtime wind.

Her body necrophilic in a *Blue of Noon* narrative sort of way. I kiss the future away. The passion is intensifying. I'm crying in my dreams. Dying for my infatuation. I'm reaching for the condoms in my back pocket. Two of them. I pull one and pull down my pants and pant. My shlong is half hard and heartbroken. My scrotum is tightening. As I rip the package open she whispers "hurry" all the while fingering herself with her left hand and twisting her left nipple with her right hand, index finger and thumb. Brain damage. I roll the rubber on to my almost erect phallus and psychotically try to force the covered worm into her tunnel. It won't go in, it won't go in, it is not hard enough damn it. I've dealt with these kinds of circumstances a million times. I don't sweat it. The condom eventually rips and my penis falls limp. Shit.

"Do you want to suck my dick?" She shakes her head from side to side and my pride is spent for the evening. Shit. Thirteen spider bites itching like a motherfucker! There is nowhere to hide when shame sets in. Try it again. Pull the second sheath. I jerk and I jerk and I jerk and I jerk my flesh pipe but it won't get hard. I think the booze and coke is setting in. I can't get any blood to flow to the shaft. Shit. I purposely tear the contraceptive in the hopes of demoralizing myself. I've decided I don't want to have sex right now. I'm scared. But I do, I do, I do. Dilemma. Quandary. Predicament. Decision to make that will affect me for the rest of my life to live like every decision to make. I roll over off her and lie there in awakening dampness covered in frustrated sweat. I make a dash for the light switch. She's sprawled out in wreckage consisting of frazzled hair, torn blouse, and one shoe on. She looks at me with neither disappointment nor enjoyment nor regret. I lie next to her and try to carry a conversation but all I can concentrate on is my shriveled penis and this unfathomable desire to penetrate her loins. She looks so fuckin' good.

Thirteen bites!

For a while we just lie here, talking about things to forget. I've lost my motivation. I'll never have the chance to fornicate on coke. I should snort some cocaine next time I'm with my girlfriend before we engage in sex. Can you imagine the stamina? I'll never get to fuck on coke. Damn it! This opportunity is out of the question. No way am I fucking this whore that I don't know without protection. I've done it before and it scared the shit out of me. I didn't recover for months, almost a year or so. You never really do recover. It is not worth the agony. A one-night stand is not worth it. Not in these apocalyptic times. I might as well pull up my pants and think of a way to get home. But wait! What is this? My cock is moving. It's grown just a bit. Her naked thighs and the smell of dead blossoms entice me. She is hot. I can't pass this up. You must. No, I can't. You don't know her. You don't know where she's been. So what! Life is to live. Gotta take chances if you want to experience excitement. Besides, life is about decay and here in The West decadence is a virtue waiting for peer approval. Who gives a shit! I don't plan on living past thirty. Do it, do it, do it, do it. No, I can't. You'll never get the chance to fuck on cocaine again. Kiss her, just kiss her. I want to fuck on cocaine. I want to fuck an Indian. We're kissing. She is so soft. Her skin is fuckin' smooth and her body is so tight. My dick is growing. I already know I'm gonna do it even though I know I shouldn't. I don't plan on living past thirty. The lights are beaming and if anyone wants to receive a free amateur porn show they can easily view us from the uncovered bay windows. I think someone is out there. It feels like a pair of eyes and a video camera are watching. I think the driver of the Bronco is out there, watching us through the bay window. I'm not even conscious of this. My mind is turned off. The adrenaline is taking over. We are getting into it. I'm feeling her pussy and it is very moist and hot and ready. My dick isn't that hard but hard enough. I don't know what to do though I'm doing it already what I shouldn't do to do it I know I'm doing what I don't know I should do. I push myself up on top of her, inhale, exhale, and stare into her blurred expression. The moment of truth is the moment everything stops. The fascist impulse inside all of us cannot be reasoned with.

The finch still sings in the early morning. The dawn still protrudes lavish colors of red, pink, and fire when the night covers the earth. There is still a perceived drought here in my hometown. I haven't touched a woman in two and a half years. Music is alarming, catastrophic harmonics permeating what is inside the paulo duro plant. My black cat crawled on me and rubbed his claws of his front paws on my chest and belly. I stare at the bare carved vigas in my room lying on my back bare naked. I have no concept of what I just did or what I am to do. My black cat consoles me. He is the only one that can heal me. I've invested half my soul in him. He is my protector. I am not healthy in the brain. I feel like killing myself. I always feel like killing myself. There are not enough creative writers in the universe to describe the chastisement I punish mortification with.

In her car I kissed her for the last time knowing she was not wanting me to go. Her lips are chapped. I touch her thigh and feel like doing it again but by this time I'm all out of courage as the dope wears off and reality returns.

She gives me her phone number. I tell her I don't have a phone. Drop me off at a house on my street that's not my own.

I see a picture of her infant son on the sun visor. She's driving me to my designation and I feel like telling her I live on another street so she can never find me just in case she decides to look for me later on if I got her pregnant or something.

We're dropped off by the cab downtown not to far from where I live. We should have come here first. Where was I six hours ago? I had four opportunities to walk away.

The sun has not risen above the eastern Sangre de Cristo mountain range; yet, light is unfolding the mysterious nature of the city's cicatrization.

The cab is driving along a road I am unfamiliar with, the driver silent as summer late night weeknights. I am unfamiliar with the woman sitting next to me holding my hand and resting her head on my shoulder as I look out the rear door window wondering where I've been, where I am, and where I will end up tomorrow. Life will continue. My dreams of dying young do not seem plausible anymore. I'm wasted.

I didn't have to go out with my brother when he first invited me.

As we leave the house I walk up the dirt walkway to the cab and almost trip at the top of the climb and barely hear the cop father holler "watch your step!"

The little pit-bull looking runt says he'll get his dad to call us a cab as she and I sit on a single chair in the living room watching some newly arrived muscle bound young brown male wired on cocaine do handstands and somersaults running around the house constantly and every once and a while reintroducing himself to my temporary companion saying he's never met her for the fourth time in less than an hour. Reminds me of when I used to do coke almost every night.

I should've just opened the door and stepped into the car.

I'm out of smokes but still insist on carrying an empty pack of Marlboro Lights in my shirt pocket, listening to the crumple of the cellophane wrapper. I'm just a fuck-off in a world that takes itself too serious.

Didn't have to jump in the Bronco.

She is dressed without panties. She can't seem to find her underwear. I swear to her that I didn't steal them. Her sister pulls her out of the bedroom, slams the door in my face. I finish buttoning my pants.

I wash my cock in the sink of the bathroom that separates two rooms when the little pit-bull looking runt walks in with just his shorts on, says what's up and takes a piss in the toilet.

I'm standing here naked washing my prick with thirteen swollen red spider bites all over me. The reflection in the mirror is one of self-destruction absent the commitment.

I could've walked away and walked home.

We lie there together in silence. The only words we exchange are when I tell her, "just so you know, I've been tested for HIV and STDs and I'm clean." She responds that "it's a little too late for that." I ask her twice if she's ever been tested. She is silent. My paranoia prevents me from ever having a good time.

"Stop. Stop. Get off!" she grunts. I'm fucking her faster and faster trying vaingloriously to make myself cum.

"Stop. Enough. Stop!

She is crying

"Wait. I gotta cum, I gotta cum."

She is crying.

I can't even feel the pussy no more much less my dick penetrating. All the sweating I've done has dried-up. She is wasted. She tries to push me off but I keep pounding until finally I feel the sensation of release and hardly any cum comes out. The orgasm doesn't even last one second. I've just experienced the ecstatic sensation of disappointment. I guess fucking on cocaine and gallons of booze wasn't a good idea.

Shit.

"Stop. I can't." She's wailing as my dick is rock harder than a baseball without a stitched leather cover.

"You want me to stop?" I ask.

"No. Keep going." She starts to scream aggressively.

I stop. Push up off her and stare. She pulls me back down and starts biting my neck. I start gyrating again. She cries and wails. By now we are into our second hour of straight fucking. We had one brief intermission about forty-five minutes ago because she was tired and couldn't stop sobbing but we started up again within five minutes. My dick was real hard all the time and not once went limp. I knew I would have crazy stamina. We did it every way. She must've came about a dozen times. I wasn't even aware if she did or didn't but I could tell she was into it. At one point I heard this weird banging on the wall and felt it was not coming from us. We were rocking the bed but the banging seemed to have come from another room. When I would pause, the banging would stop a few seconds after. When I started again, the banging followed a few seconds later. I heard laughter and trees whipping the roof. I heard the cackle of a witch zoom past my sideburns as her hands scratched my back and her nails carved my shoulder blades. She broke blood. We fucked rougher and mightier than horses. The banging. The eyes upon our bare bodies. We bounced up in the air off the bed, levitating in defiance of Newton's presumptuous nature. The cackle was louder. Her screams were soft. A tiny baby dragging its umbilical cord looped around its neck crawled to a corner of the floor, crossed her legs and played with a dead rats broken neck. I could hear the pigs in the kitchen snorting their omnipotence, laughing uncontrollably. There were knocks on the door, shadows on the roof, doorbells ringing endlessly, fingertips protruding out the mattress tickling my spider bites. The eyes outside. The banging. A rooster began to bring the sun up. It was still dark. Her eyes turned pitch black. She wouldn't remove her fixation from my face. She smirked with deep black dead eyes. I envisioned a deer being butchered with broken sticks by dwarfed forest people wearing feathered headgear as a plucked eagle talked slowly about the future. A shot rang. The banging. There were more guests in the house. More noise. Louder. Doorbells. More eyes. The eyes. The eyes of love and karma looked upon me with regret. The rooster's call. She was covered in my sweat and blood. From time to time she vanished and I was left alone rubbing up against the dry sheets popping off the mattress that we broke when she returned. She would smile then go blank. I heard thunder outside. I saw her turn old then into a young girl. She completed twelve life cycles before we finished. She groaned, flashing like a still photograph with every thrust. Lost children paraded around the house chanting playground hymns, ringing church bells. A bonfire inside the house. Paintings I saw out in the living room were now inside the bedroom. There was a knock on the door, laughter in the kitchen, banging all around, odor of death everywhere and several pairs of eyes upon us. She was still crying.

In the Southwest, particularly Santa Fe, many fake-ass gringos feel the Indian is some enigma or some shit. White people are so infatuated with Indians here that many of these individuals claim they have Indian blood in them. The gringos dress like them, although in their own Western anglo/saxon exploitative way. They wear the Indian's jewelry that they sell on the Plaza, and they market their art for all the other gringos that have never actually seen a real Indian. That's what Indian Market is all about. A lot of tourists come to Santa just to behold an actual living Indian. I've even known a few gringos that have gone so far as to call themselves a shaman. To the no culture ones, the Indian is some mysterious being with supernatural powers that calls on the spirits of the spirit world to intervene in the running bulls bath of the shadow's unforgiving will.

To me, the Indian, or Native or whatever you want to refer to them as is just another piece of shit human being. They don't possess any more supernatural skills than the man who leaps from a forty-story building thinking he can fly.

But that night with her, who was some Native from some people or pueblo up north, was strange. Too many unexplainable things occurred and there were too many moments where I could've prevented it all. By far this event has fucked up my life more than any other experience or person I've experienced has yet to do.

One night.

My father has always told me that I am the type of individual who can work hard on something for days, months, and/or years, build something for the future, and then fuck it all up in one night. I was on my way to graduate school in two months. Two months later I would have my choice of beautiful women to bother. They were just a sex object to me. Two months later I would be free from Santa Fe and it's tendency to trap a local in a self-destructive cycle. Two months later I would have the opportunity to start working and flourish in something that I love.

Thirteen spider bites itching like a motherfucker!

I should have seen the signs from the night before. My spiritual prowess is weak. I do not possess the discipline to exercise my will power and refute temptation. Temptation of the flesh is the worst by far.

Thirteen, the hard luck number. Four all over my dry skin back, two on my somewhat hairy left leg skinny inner thigh, one huge one in the middle calf of the same leg, two big ass ones on my right leg, two on the right arm, one on the left, and one tingling bitch in the middle of my bumpy scrotum. When I noticed that one I began to freak out. That one was the omen. The one on my balls.

When I noticed it I knew that I definitely should not even attempt to engage in sexual activity, if for anything out of embarrassment. It was because of embarrassment that I went through with it.

Thirteen. Thirteen. Like a motherfucker.

Two months later I notice something.

Contributing to Genocide

Working as a greasy busboy at one of Santa Fe's long-gone classy restaurants was one of my greatest experiences ever. Besides cleaning up the crumbs and the half-eaten food that doesn't quite make it to the slobbering mouths of overweight creamy elitist pigs, once in a privileged while one of the three or four minority bussers on shift any one night would get to be the lucky one to close up the Neo-Californian crappy restaurant. The most convincing aspect of the midnight propaganda to persuade some shmuck that closing-up was the shit was the excuse that the closing busser makes more bucks. Although this was entirely not false, it was also entirely not necessarily untrue. Nevertheless, one night in particular I was one shmuck that didn't mind sweeping the floors and picking up the multi-colored table candles for as long as time would not allow.

It was an average closing. All the customers were gone. The two closing whiteboy waiters were in the back room counting up the nights booty, pocketing just enough to convince the others that everything was legit through the use of sabotaged mathematical equations that didn't equate to much except scribbles and stringy drawings on the cardboard back of soiled waiter tablets. I was watering the water starving plants outside on the window terrace which was more like a one person balcony. It was late. I don't remember the time. Sometime around really dark. The dried-up cracked leaves of the plastic looking plants swayed with every sigh of the late evening's boredom. I was just about finished with my final task when in walked my brother. I met him halfway in the main dining room area and he had this look on his face like someone defecated in his mashed potatoes. His fingers shook along with his incarcerated pupils surrounded by burning red eyes. He was jumpy. Real jumpy. I had known this fool a long time and viscerally I apprehended the murky vibes that can make you sob silently twice and a half. Bad vibes means bad moments.

What's up I said and he asked me if I still had the gun on me that I used to carry and I said yeah how come and he said he'll tell me later how much longer do I have and I replied I'm done so let's go he responded and I took off my greasy busser apron walking briskly to the back kitchen to punch my card, gather my shit, walk back out to the main dining arena but stopping briefly to cop a slice of bread and butter and a snort of some wine in a water glass left over from the bottles confiscated by us bussers when the elitist patrons were too stupid to finish them utterly. I reacquainted myself with him again in the main dining area and we headed out the front glass doors with fake gold trimming. Down the only escalator in town I thought to my other self that tonight seemed unseemly like tonight. I was scared. More frightened with every step into nowhere. We got to the bottom of the escalator that only moves upward and I had to find out.

Whattaya want the gun for?

Dude, while I was standing outside in front of the Anasazi this pinche primered lowrider with like four or five spic wanna-be gangsta asses was driving by and they slowed down where I was standing, mad-doggin me so I was like 'What's up?' and the driver starts throwing me a finger and the rest of the punks in the back seat start yelling out Hey you fuckin' pussy, what the fuck are you looking at bitch? You wanna die? and then they kept yelling and threw shit at me as they drove off slowly still throwing me a finger and I was like fuck that shit bro I'm not gonna let these pussys dis me so I took off my fanny pack and started running after them. Obviously I didn't catch them so I said fuck it, I'm almost out of work, I'll get my bro and we'll find these fucks and then we'll see what's up.

So you just got out of work or what? He said yeah and asked me if

I was down to find these putos. I casually retorted sure, I was just about done, just give me a second. We got to my piece of crap vomiting blue colored 1984 Oldsmobile hand-me-down repeatedly after repeatedly after and after. The car was adopted by me after my older older blood brother decided that it had broken down on him twice too many times always in problematic situations that were uncalled for. This Oldsmobile couldn't hit 30/mph in one hour, even if it could enable the speedometer to top 27/mph--ever. It was a piece of junk envy. At the car standing outside in the starry dark late early evening we glance at one another for an eternity lasting no less than forty seconds. We open the doors simultaneously after I unlock the driver's side and enter the rest of our young adulthoods that haven't quite begun yet. As the ignition strikes, the thunder of the engine wheezes, the clank of the corroding pistons plummet, the motion of force facing gravity sends a riveting twitch up my pinching anus, and the night remains as silent as an overpopulated monastery.

I think they're still downtown. We'll just cruise downtown a bit, see if these punks show up.

Well, here I was, here we were, getting ready to do who knows not what looking for some spics to fight with. Same shit forever. Spics fighting spics, only this time it's two wanna-be self-proclaimed upper-crust spics that look white in the lamenting souls of our subjugated brown brothers. My brother is not himself--ever. He's just as dark or probably darker than these idiots. Aghhh, we won't find them. I hope we don't find them. This is how my senior year in high school begins. Fuck it!

Streets started to look like golden holograms because of the veiled street lamplights suckling down to the grayishblue pavement. Everything moves so slow. A clear night, filled with radiation.

The gun is under this ripped-down drivers seat attached to the passenger seat. I stole it from my father's desk like exemplary young males in your country are supposed to do. Article II of the Constitution of Crap has nothing on me 'o my. 357 Smith & Wesson snub-nosed revolver. Black steel. Heavy as a broken heart. Loaded like nostrils and sinuses full of coke. Six hallow-tip bullets ready to pierce an artery or a black lung or a neck bone or an empty skull.

Was I ready to kill somebody?

Or at least be an accessory to murder or attempted murder. I'm sure my bro ain't gonna let me be the one to have all the fun and bust a heater. And believe me not, with a .357 you just don't injure a motherfucker, you blow a hole in him the size of the grand canyon if it was never created and subsequently discovered. Murder is for everyone.

Hey is that them? Wait up bro, slow down a little. Is that them? We saw this gray primered piece of shit cruising around the plaza. I pulled-up behind them like tailgating and I just hate to tailgate. Tailgate those fuckers. Oh wait! Wait, wait. I don't know. Is that them? What do you think? How the hell should I know? I'm just your demonic chauffeur, your little chulito Wait? Sssshhhhhhh. Shut the fuck up! No. That's not them. They had different rims. Those rims are solid chrome. See? See how those rims are solid chrome? Look. I looked. Yeah, those pussys had more like spikes inside the shaft of the rim, you know what I mean? Nah. That ain't them. Keep cruising.

Like a black and white Siamese cat wrestling, my decapitated brain kept melting and licking. The heart that once was an organ halted the seizure. Invisible breath after breath, the dirty windshield washed in contaminated frost. Lights constantly everywhere in this mini-urbanesque nightmare. I could feel the front wheels wobbling sickly and the rear ones depressing on the rippling concrete of a street. The Oldsmobile was neither old no more nor mobile ever. It shook faster than a vibrator trapped inside the box, never to escape into an abandoned soggy cave, plugged into mediocrity. Time yawned for a long moment that couldn't pass. We drove around the derelict streets looking for people I've never seen before nor never will meet. I kept reminiscing quietly about our relationship and how we grew up together. How we used to fight and reconcile. How I followed him everywhere around everywhere--sometimes him being frustrated and slowly becoming upset and perhaps putting me in the spot for a sec ridiculing me whispering to his so-called friends, telling them I couldn't be independent ever because my frail love cared too much for nothing but not about anything. Feel the sizzling cymbal crash while your clapping hands steal a stash of sleep. Never letting me down. Never ostracizing me. Not that the handle is hot when the kettle of tea settles, but the sun rises in the west while we're not looking for hope anymore. I felt like Trotsky in his last days coveting the moment Raskolnikov would swiftly grace the back of my head with a rubber ax, ejaculating an avalanche of trickling purple-red dark blood down the nape of a broker that pawned her last birthright on a late Mexico evening.

The night kept moving as fast as it did slow. My bro always looked out for me though. He's the one who taught me the intricacies of partying like a ready-made fool. He's the one who fought for me when I ran away from a bully faster than a bullet from a barrel. We were asking for trouble that asked for it first. None the wiser less, she that asks for it first is she who receives it second to last. I was feeling guilty already, responsible perhaps later.

An agonizing hour had run past our idyllic visions faster than Hermes on hot coals turned upside-down. Nada. This is so stupid. We're not gonna find these morons. Start cruising up Cerrillos Road. We'll drive up and down a couple of times and if we don't find them, fuck it, we'll just go home. Leaving downtown, perhaps for good, I hit middle-high-low gear pursuing a visible ghost of my life never lived. All cars look the same. Feel identical. Nothing. This is for the better, if not for the worst. My brother is silent now. Lips pursed tight, twitching. His obsidian eyes staring farther into the dark tunnel of the early morning night. He's disappointed, I can tell. He must really be pissed. I know he is capable of killing these rodents if we find them. At this sacred second we're smoking ganja, passing it right to left, forth to back. The raps is swimming in my shocked brain waves like spilt nuclear waste in a brown ghetto slum with narrower streets than a gringa's chicken-plucky legs. I feel like we're in one of those 1990s black gangsta movies directed by the Hugh's

Brothers or John Singleton or maybe even in some unfortunate Dr. Dre music video, promoting your country's virtue of unrestrained, genocidal violence. Nothing is too much to handle. Thank the absent Lord I'm drunk and stoned.

Ahh forget it. Cruise through the parking lot of Allsup's and if they're not around there than we'll just say fuck it? Okay?

My brother finally came to his self-centered senses that are never there. I was more than obliged to commit this pattern of salvation. The Allsup's on Baca Street used to be one of the very few monuments of vengeful corporatism that the remaining spics in town get to commingle at and fallaciously exercise their non-bestowed non-existent claim to assemble freely in front of the eyes of the butcher. Passing through the shortcut that was the parking spot, I spotted nothingness. Thank the God that's never around. I was about to turn right onto Baca Street and head toward sanctuary when a low-riding primered pinche looking automobile with pitch black tinted windows, including the front windshield, came trollying right in front of us. I'll be fucked by Asian dominatrixes, it's a fuckin Oldsmobile too. Time froze again as it always did. The rims inside the tires had chrome spikes.

That's them! That's them!

Wait bro, don't get out of the car.

They paused in front of us, rolled down the passenger window and one thin, really young pale-looking cockroach placed his fragile upper body out the window and began to throw fingers and yell multitudinous unpleasantries in our direction. I swear these bitches couldn't have been more than fifteen to eighteen years old. My brother tried running after them, but they peeled-out and blazed down the street into darkness.

Get in! We'll chase after them.

Down the blanketed street I reached under my seat and lovingly grasped the pistol grip pump of my daddy's .357 and gently placed it into the sweaty palm of my brother. I just gave him the holy approval to do our stupid Creator's work. Needless to not say their Oldsmobile was fixed-up therefore faster than my piece of shit Oldsmobile. We headed down one-quarter of a mile to the mandatory slow-down decline. Fifteen mph lights were flashing for the slow turn. Not even Richard Petty could make this turn faster than 21 mph.

On the left side of the road there was an infiltrating gringo male who happened to be riding a bicycle in the diminishing gentrified barrio at one in the morning. The wanna-be gangsta vehicle in front of us halted. Break lights beamed bright red. I had to slow down in order not to rear-end them and end all our lives. That same vato that stood out of the passenger window in front of us stood out once again. He talked some shit to the bike rider and launched a 40 ounce bottle half full of St. Ides at the man. I saw the bottle crack on the head of the rider and he tumbled off his bike into the bankment off the jagged angle of the concrete. The dudes in the automobile we were chasing started yelling and celebrating as if they just won World War III. That pissed the benevolence out of me. In the incinerating mist of all this present mess, I still occupied enough vacated space in my freezing heart to feel some sense of worthless compassion for this misplaced chap. I felt the symphony of oppression. After witnessing the brutality of the act, I understood for the first and last time the beasts of unwarranted aggression and violence your country has conditioned us colored minorities to be. I felt sickened, and yet justified. Even though it was unwarranted and unsuspecting, he shouldn'tve been there. These guys had the right idea but the wrong methodology. I don't even think they were capable of understanding the significance of their act. What a triumphant moment for us all. The fucker had no business in our neighborhood, especially riding a bike at one in the morning while we're trying to kill each other. My sympathy didn't last too long.

They stopped.

Congested lungs from smoking too much weed could be heard on opposite lines of the front. That punk bitchmotherfucker that pitched the bottle was still sticking out the passenger side open window and spitting mad shit.

My bro protruded above his passenger side automatic rolled-down window. An Aztec Apache standoff ensued. Frozen rage sweltering inside each of the dead spirits. A portrait waiting to be painted.

What the fuck motherfucker, you wanna talk shit to me you fuckin pussy ass! Why don't you get the fuck down and we see what's up. You scared bitch! Let's see how bad you really are you punk ass!

As he was reciting this inappropriate speech of sentimentality, the gun swung delicately between his swollen thumb and rigid index and middle fingers of his left hand, still hanging inside the interior of the automobile.

I shitted. I wasn't scared nor nervous, but I shitted. Time didn't freeze but it didn't even exist. All I could wonder was what do we do if they die? What happens after the bullet shatters the epidermis, penetrates the breastplate, the cranium, the timid nipple? Am I supposed to feel jubilant about killing one of my own? About killing myself? I imagined open meadows filled with chamisas releasing itchy pollens, loose twinkling leaves resembling overgrown dust particles that I couldn't breathe. I couldn't breathe. Death died. Life vanished before the trigger could be pulled or lifted.

I love you brother. You have showed me uncompromisingly what strength does to love. On your way to prison flash an ignored sign of hope so the rest of us self-righteous survivors may continue to live as we have wept. Pass the gun to me after you're done so I can aim it at the supreme target of desperation. Escape existence towards redemption. I am the road kill lacking resurrection.

Boom! Boom! Boom!

That primered Oldsmobile blazed out of there faster than an imagined Ben Hur chariot race. The skinny vato talking shit one second earlier slithered back into the car quick like a prairie dog being chased, leaping quickly down the dirt mound.

Everything happens too fast when adrenaline permeates your trembling arteries. In the fake ass movies a gun shot sounds like a firecracker popping. But in this shithole reality that doesn't even seem real, you don't even really hear a sound. It sounds distant, a far off surrounding one big BOOM and then your ears start ringing and are turned inside out and the air smells like sulfur. I saw the lightening discharge from the barrel of the gun flicker three times, but I couldn't tell if that dude that my brother was aiming at was hit, shot, or burnt. Once their car started moaning my bro harked to punch the pedal and chase them. They took off. About one hundred yards down Baca Street they made a right turn onto a side street, Sierra Vista, and I was almost able to catch-up with them.

Boom!

My bro had popped another cap and by the time we made the turn, the primered lowrider was not in sight. They had hauled ass out of the neighborhood.

Since going after them a second or third time was out of the question, my bro and I decided it would be best to go home and chill. We weren't that far from our house so I just cruised cautiously, keeping a lookout. There is nothing more exciting than hunting a human, trying to kill one of your own. All I could think about for the rest of the night was how my brother and I used to be close.

Imperial Road Kill

You shouldn't drive drunk. I popped another miniature of Stoli and finished rolling the joint. I smoked the entire *leno* before my city league basketball game. City league basketball is for losers, has-beens, wanna-bes, and runts. I am all four on all fours. My other brother showed up about ten minutes before our game started. "Are you ready?" my other brother asked. "Fuckin a!" "Are you ripped or what?" he asked again. "Not yet." "Let's go, our game is about to start" he urged. I threw on my sweaty unwashed #20 black and gold petrified jersey, shifted my cock in my silky hanging baggy shorts and downed one more miniature of Stoli before driving to the game. I had a good buzz going. My other brother never wants to drive in the same car or someone else's car so he took his own and I hopped into my 1987 Volkswagen maroon piece of shit Jetta. I loved that car. We turned right on Paseo de Peralta from St. Francis Drive coming from West Alameda which is the first main vein you hit coming down Bob Street. My other brother on the left lane me on the right. "Hey! You wanna race scumbag?" My other brother just kinda half grimaced then got serious watching the road maintaining both palms on the steering wheel though no one was in front of us. I was howling relentlessly sticking my curly hair headed head out the driver's window yelling and hollering and talking shit drunk like someone that's actually from Santa Fe. "Let's race bitch." Started revving the engine shifting gears a madre flooring the pedal determined to outrun my opponent though he was not moving any faster than he was when he first turned onto the street. I thought I was in high school again cruising my first hooptie around Airport Road romping through unpaved sand lots hilly hitting bottom damaging my shocks and undermining the age of a short-lived 1979 Ford LTD scrap of plastic metal before I burnt the engine because I forgot to put oil in it. I was way ahead of him across DeVargas Mall approaching that crosswalk everybody was getting killed on recently crossing that part of Paseo de Peralta across where Albertson's used to be when there was no crosswalk there though there's one now. The reason so many pedestrians get killed each year crossing streets in Santa is because there are way too many vehicles snaking across the overcrowded city that's not so different. Perhaps it was the liquor inside my belly or the smoke betwixt my brain but I think it was more the names of the street I was driving on and the mall I was passing because I sure felt like a Spanish imperialist bastard. I was acting like the first Spaniards that arrived here in New Mexico looking for a Native to excruciate. In my steel horse accelerating sixty, sixty-five, seventy, seventy-one, seventy something in thirty-five mile per hour speed limit zone about fifty yards in front of me I see these figures as small as green plastic army statuettes with the mantled feet running from the opposite oncoming side of the street to the median crossing the median running across not looking both ways like we were supposed to be taught in elementary school running with one solitary body straggling behind the crowd. I slammed on the brakes knowing I didn't have enough length or space to stop the vehicle in time. I turned the steering wheel as far right as I could, screeching the pavement below all the while the straggling being is still running hop scotching his ass right toward me I knew I was going to hit him, I'm going to hit him, I'm going to hit this fuck. Oh shit. I bounced on the curb and his growing image and oncoming constitution zoomed past my eyes. Slam!

A suffocating panic obsessed my nerves. Adrenaline consumed me. I hit the fucker, running over him. My life is over. My life is over. I'm going to jail and never getting out. Should I keep going? I stopped immediately and ran over to the dude on the ground already getting up wobbling, staggering to his upright, his friends that dashed in front of him looking back at him and laughing. "Are you all right bro? Are you okay?" I wondered out loud. "Hey bro, do you think you can lend me some change so I can buy some beer?" He barely was able to pronounce this monosyllabic solicitation. He was drunk, smelly, with greasy hair, an Indian, and most likely homeless. I almost laughed when he said this to me but the adrenaline pulsing throughout my stiffened, shaky limbs prevented me from relaxing and making a joke out of the situation. "Are you okay bro?" I asked again with a slight unabashed chuckle. "Hey, can you get me some beer bro?" he repeated. I couldn't help but laugh now but there was no time to hang around too long. I noticed he was on his feet walking, sort of, so I patted him on the shoulder told him I couldn't help him with change to purchase beer, heard his friends talking some shit to me as I hopped back into my puttering Volkswagen and got the fuck out of the area before any potential witnesses could identify my automobile or myself. On the way to the gym I realized he must've hit the side of my car in the front and swiftly fallen down due to the impact. Luckily I had one more miniature of Stoli on me. I downed it before entering the gym. That night I played the second best basketball I've ever played in my life.

Solitary Trip

An eminent feminine's voice slowly sashays through the shadowed corridors of an empty house. He'd just digested more shrooms than he should've it took about an hour and a half dozing into the dream out of death into sleep grasping breath cricket's feet chippering chiding reminiscent screeching outside villainous stranger searching the premises with a singular flashlight calling out the name of his lost dog the sound is too audible but the name unheard of he won't leave lying back with a glare of radioactive television airwaves highlighted shadow giving away the awareness of a soul sold on the second floor the light of flashlight dances arrogantly the channel changer automatically turns the television off then on off then on watching *The Yellow Submarine* because he thought it would be a good idea two voices waltzing together inside outside around the foundation of the house empty inside the dream visions of a tired body lying on a ruffled bed half-naked man sleeping with eyes open unconscious it took almost an approximate hour for the shadow to approach him configuration of a feminine disposition with long white hair but no discernable features to record she softly whispers that she'll leave whatever item of paper she possesses in her right palm she smiles carnivorously placing it over his enslaved awakened eyes snoring nostorum panamina batstatu con du forlium sendaanfren amon daaaaaa he eerily sings an uncontrollable demon indoctrinated aria like a molested catholic choir boy eyes pasted open the paper vanishes through the brick floor he repeats a similar enchanted harmony the stench of skunk suffocates the slowly widening chamber making him sick through his nostrils instantaneously into the dream rising out toward reality the stranger outside blares his headlights and calls for help hello Hello hello hello Hello Hello hell is a place on earth anyone can find internally the heat images of Blue Meanies on the screen become brighter twisted coral shaped transmogrified figurines parading while the wind blows secretly horns spit high drums cacophonous the violet lights flickering violently the out of tune melody cautionary premeditated steps slammed delicately on the wooden steps leading to the third story derelict he screams inside mouth soaked from dehydration tongue bleeding ferociously the experimentation of human existence cannot survive the innate destructive proclivity to erase memory by means of endeavored failure the seductive voice feminine consoles his heat rash dripping freezing water droplets from her slashed fingertips soothing vocal element hidden away somewhere in a pitch-black nightmare he decides to switch the radio because it seemed like a good idea lying back on his bed in his room listening to the *Mule Variations* of Tom Waits' baritone voice become deeper and slower in psychiatric ward gloom coldest room in the house a dead soul visited his mother while she mourned the passing of her father staring uninterrupted at the vigas holding up the roof for decoration the knots and cuts and holes in each individually unique viga begin to move countenances horrified transfigured mutilations appear then vanish some strut while others laugh and some look sad as one bewails the others moan while others dance gloating teeth abysmal eyes everything begins to move too fast the images on the screen sounding louder and high-pitched voices speaking become marbled juxtaposed with the man outside laughing flashing his flashlight on then off the prostrate body cannot question he is haunted but his body won't move the faces on the vigas approach his gaping eyes and he starts to smile a bit he welcomes death those kinds of dreams that seem so real like you were alive awake and you could sense everything in the dream with the power of your senses you could smell certain aromas you can see what your thoughts project and even conjure and construct certain images on spot without any seconds to pass you can hear what isn't heard you can touch and feel tenfold solid smooth rough thorny soft you itch you're sore you cramp you feel yourself jostle in bed but you are standing and then falling then walking upright to an unknown you are stalked but this was not one of those dreams this was not a dream if it were a dream he would have control of what was happening inside his head and around him outside in the front and back yards the summer was dry and the night was cold dead silent but he heard the pattering of raindrops slam heavy the light wandering around outside now moved upstairs to the neighbors yard him still calling for his lost dog peeking through the walls the lights shining through the windows behind him lying on the bed infatuated with his new friends extending from the vigas above carrying conversations with them though frightened by the responses received a dog barks sardonically Tom Waits starts to sing to him personally addressing his every aesthetic sunshine the pleasure combined with reverberating gong resonance repeating the same words over and over again about a man wondering what his neighbor is doing in there the paranoia more intense than a fanatic attempting to make contact with outer space aliens that don't exist except in the mind of a lunatic he throws himself off the bed punches the power button on the television it was too much for him the eyes of the cartoon characters on the screen would sparkle and explode the blue and white images on the television were no longer confined to the set the scenery never changes Tom is becoming sanguineous he ran through the house on all fours slowly shredding the rags beset upon his goose-pimpled hide the brick floor had waves and he couldn't remember which room he was headed for though he has lived in this house for over twenty years many times he deliberately blindfolded himself to see if he could make his way through the house without any assistance but now it was precisely his vision that hindered his progress he kept stopping and stooping and crying screaming out for aid to help him through this house and floor and roof and walls that were moving and breathing and growing and condensing on their own he didn't recognize his home anymore the sweat soaked the floor below as he paused to think sitting naked against the off-white serpentine adobe wall wrapping his skinny arms around his bare knees twisting his neck from side to side holding a .38 caliber Smith & Wesson between his perspiring palms it just appeared there absent an origin with the barrel headed towards the moon you know you've lost your mind when the ground feels like air there is no equilibrium running through the house fading into blackness dazzled by the extreme brightness of the light he madly ran through every room he could locate in order to find a telephone either he'd manage to call someone and hear a familiar voice or catapult his soul he managed to contact the police department through emergency assistance it took what seemed four hours to press three buttons and they sent a patrol car over to investigate the entity outside with the flashlight looking for his lost dog lamenting for help wandering around the neighbor's yard then his own then the neighbor's again then his own in the front or the back or the west façade and covering the east it took more than an hour for the patrol to arrive even though there was a sub-station less than three city blocks away the patrol car drove up the street and left without interference maybe there was no one outside he fell exhausted to a plush chair giving-up hope for any kind of assistance existence is something you must accomplish alone the pavement streetlights outside through the stretching windows on the middle floor calmed him for a second little hummingbirds die in a greenhouse because they panic his heart was hurting clenched tight short breaths sweat dry body chilled eyes so dilated he couldn't see the brown on his pupil any longer the city lights outside were flashing rapidly hurting his eyes like police lights in back of you when you get pulled over the flashlight was still wandering the man now started to call him by his first name a voice feminine touched his spirit with apology he opened the doors to the back yard dashed outside and found his breath tear through his lungs in the form of thick fog the stars above were moving around the vacant sky disorganized it was excessively dry and torpidly hot realizing it never did rain he rushed back inside the house your own fear is the devil's only shield outside he heard nothing but the pulse of crickets and the tickling of the calm summer wind inside he found a bathroom flipped on the light shocked to discover a body in the mirror severely pale with long gray hair and wrinkles over his once youthful skin he witnessed himself age decreasingly red blotches appearing in sparse records over the face like perioral dermatitis the reflection embodied sorrow the young man turned on the faucet and stared for hours at the mercury precipitously drain the pain of tomorrow resides in a wish today is more frightening than an unused imagination upstairs a child was sleeping with eyes pried open to witness the shadow strip bare laughing at his own precariousness fascination is the pathway to a utopia demented the child cries for protection but his mother took the hand of the mutilated carcass upon the last visit and followed it to nothingness being is the communal burden alone in a ritual a hawk floats above the sunlit depressed desert wings spread wide soaring without effort for miles hunting for that child lost to the world he saw her again this time she aged corroded flesh comb bristles for hair and tormented black eyes complementing a devious smirk she walked towards him at the bottom of the driveway her two dogs jumped out of her yard and tried to attack him the dogs stopped short he yelled vulgarities at her and chided her for her disobedient dogs she smiled still one hand on a cane concocted from human bone hunched over forever there was black magic stalemate she vanished into air and he found himself in front of a bonfire he saw her again in the same place in the same situation he was young she was old he yelled something charmingly violent to her told her he was not afraid of her he knew she was a bruja but her power was not as strong as his she smiled frozen sunken eyes twitching and she vanished again laughing. He felt something grab his leg and woke up screaming.

Nobody Speaks Latin Anymore

Tiny tramp with malevolent intent giving me a pair of red silk underwear for Villian-tine's Day. She wasn't even that attractive: skinny frame, dry thin attenuate hair with split ends all over the place, squinty eyes, chafed off-pink flesh, dented shoulders, negro lips, donkey teeth, and a proboscis that curved upward at the end. She was working at this leather shop in the Villa Linda Mall on the south side of town.

My boy and I were just chilling one day when I told him, "hey let's go to the mall and visit what's her face to see if she'll hook us up with some merchandise." "I'm down," he encouraged.

We got to the mall strolling stoned on herbals because we had been drinking all day. Inside the store there's multitudes of mostly black and a few dark brown items made of leather. There's tons of jackets, there's backpacks, purses, purses with strings, pants, bracelets, biker bracelets, bracelets with spikes, caps, chaps, hats, scarves, gloves, lots of gloves, shirts, blouses, knife holders, and other miscellaneous crap made out of leather or looking like leather. The store was a haven for masquerading sadomasochistic queers. She is flirting with some young punk whiteboy at the front counter where I take notice of the cash register unattended. Annoyed, I ignore her and me and my boy immediately go to work browsing as if we had no business there. One of her fellow employees is finishing helping a customer then commences to act like she's folding clothes, peeking at us from time to time like a Korean owner of a liquor store. The shop is small. We didn't know if there were surveillance cameras hidden or not. There's a cool ass leather derby I spot and covet. The pussy whiteboy leaves. I approach her with arrogant charisma. She smiles, looking stupid as I think I can have it both ways, coitus for free and something else.

"Hi," she squeaks.

"What's up? You looking rather sexy today."

"Hee, hee," she giggles like an eighth grader puberty blush.

"You know, we've been to the outlet stores, the other mall, Hastings, and other places and picked-up a few things. I'll give you something if you give me something."

"What do you want?" she stutters trying to be seductive.

I whisper, "I want to eat you and a jacket or two."

"I can't."

"On both or one of the other?" I retort.

"I can't," she regretfully repeats. "I can't give you anything. My boss will be back soon and if he catches me he'll be mighty pissed. Hee, hee."

"Who's your boss?"

"The owner." She was sure of that at least.

"Did you know that the owner's insurance company covers any stolen products and/or merchandise. He'll probably make more on the insurance than he would've on a sale."

"I can't. I'll lose my job." She almost seemed serious.

"Come on. I promise, if you let us take something and play it cool I'll take you out and psychologically molest you like you've never been swooned before."

"Stop it," she smiles, turning away.

"Come on. Please."

"No."

"Pretty please," I beg.

"No. I can't."

"Then I'm gonna take something anyway and there really is nothing you can do about it."

"No don't. I'll lose my job," she pleaded.

"No one will find out."

"My co-worker is watching us."

"That's okay. I like it when other women watch. I'm going. Don't look."

"No don't." She reaches over the glass counter and grabs my sleeve, trying to prohibit my movement. "I'll call security if you do." The sneaky decolorized cave specimen.

"You wouldn't do that would you?" I presume to wonder.

She pauses. Smiles sinister. "No. I wouldn't. I might. I don't know. You have to go."

"No."

"Please! My boss will be back soon and I'm sure she'll tell him what you guys are up to." Her co-worker was watching us with intense curiosity like a five-year old watching some pedophilic Disney animation work.

I poured into her devil blue eyes and realized I wasn't getting anywhere.

We waited too long. If you're going to shoplift you do it right away real smooth breathing without effort. We were there for forty-five minutes before we took anything.

She wouldn't agree to go home with me nor to hook us up with any jacket. She did however inform me that today was payday and she knew that her co-worker had cashed her check and the cash was stashed in her purse in the backroom. I told her I couldn't go back there because I was not an employee and only employees were allowed back there. She said that there was a bathroom back there and she would take responsibility for allowing me to use the facilities as long as I gave her half the loot. I announced that I needed to take a piss loud enough for her colleague to overhear our conversation do I have her permission to use the employee's restroom to relieve my bladder of course she responded.

Racist little trollop.

I sauntered to the back, walked through the door, closed the door, locked it. The room was caliginous inside with a single exposed 40 watt light bulb stuck in the center of the peeling plastered ceiling displaying painted black walls and a few empty to half-empty boxes tossed here or over there. I began searching for the purse. I found the imitation black leather item under a cheap plastic pullover, unzipped it, tossed a few things around inside the bag and discovered a white envelope with a bank logo on the front, ripped the top of the envelope where you lick it and found one hundred and sixty-two dollars and some change. I placed the cash in my pocket, chewed the change then tossed it somewhere on the floor and threw the bag back on the floor exiting the room.

As soon as I walked out the chick I was stealing from locked her eyes on me like a jet fighter locks a target in a dogfight before the missile is released. Her judgmental squint made me feel less than innocuous. She headed toward the back room.

I grabbed the leather derby I wanted, put it behind my back, told the miniature conniving slattern on the way out that I would call her later, gave her an incredulous acknowledgement, and walked out with no buzzer going off. My boy got away with a backpack.

I spent the money right away, wasting it on clothes I didn't need. It wasn't like I needed the cash. I was dealing drugs at the time and making quite a sparkling nickel doing it. I just wanted to steal something. I had to steal something and there ain't nothing better to steal in the world than loose cash. I used to steal all the time in almost every kind of business in Santa. Kleptomania is an art rarely practiced to perfection. I stole so much shit in my lifetime that years later when I retired from shoestring thievery for some stupid reason or not another I discovered myself in church one day at the St. Francis Cathedral downtown stepping toward the confessional. Entering it I think for the first time in my life kneeling down on the maroon velvet pew the screened door across my face slid open forcibly and I really didn't know what to do so I asked the priest what to do and he ordered me to do this and say that and make the sign of the trinity and confess. I told him about every shitty thing I ever did from fighting to cursing to lying to dishonoring my parents to blasphemy to worshipping idols like the kind of gloomy candles you purchase in a grocery store to cheating to vandalizing to stealing to masturbating to fornicating and all the different women I fornicated with. He didn't seem too interested in my hour-long confession until I got to the last three. He wanted to know how many women I had been with and how many times I fornicated with them. Before that, though, on the stealing thing, he recommended that I return everything I stole to the proper owners. I informed him I couldn't do that because I had either already spent all the money I robbed or sold the items I stole or lost them or secretly I just didn't want to give them back. Besides, it was a stupid recommendation. I was wearing a sweater and some jeans I had boosted from the outlet stores at the end of Cerrillos Road and I wasn't about to leave the confessional totally naked even though I'm sure he would have appreciated that since he was more preoccupied with my sexual encounters than anything else. I was seeking redemption from a dirty old man. I never went back to church but I did continue stealing. Even today every then and now when I'm hired to work in a retail store that is owned by some rich white bastard I make it a point to learn the system as much as I can before I embark on a free for all of cheap goods that were made by some poor peon in China or North Korea or Mexico or Taiwan or some third world country that hosts sweatshops and slavery. I find more redemption doing this than baring my soul to some perv in a cassock.

Capitalism is the perfect crime, forcing us to whore our humanity for money that doesn't exist except inside the vainglorious misconceived perceptions of value invalidated by existence and extremists. To be successful in a world revolving around money you have to steal without getting caught. You must prey on the weak, the unsuspecting or the perceived innocent to secure your fantasies and satisfy your desires you are unsure of. Working eight hours a day for anything less than twenty dollars an hour while the price of transportation exceeds your annual income, while the price of healthcare surpasses the price for contaminated hormone injected processed food that makes you sick before you attain the age of wisdom to understand how disillusioning life is because humans make it that way, working that way for that much is filthy. I don't care anymore. I take what isn't mine and make it mine. And I didn't have to kill for the cash I liberated like celebrated politicians or oil executives do to secure their foreign interests in lands where oil reserves lay beneath the corroding crust of earth that belongs to no one.

One week later I get a call from the slut's mother telling me that I need to return the money I took from that chick because the boss is threatening to terminate her daughter's temporary employment and "call the police in on this one," as she puts it, if I don't return the money I stole because she knew I stole the money cuz her daughter saw me and a friend of hers and the chick I stole from saw me. I said I didn't steal the money I don't know what she is talking about and rammed the phone down. She called back later on that evening and happened to catch my mother on the phone while I was out. She told *her* version of what took place and suggested that perhaps maybe we can sit down together cuz after all we wouldn't want this to embarrass our family. Needless to say my mother was taken by surprise and not very pleased.

That following weekend my mother, the little fiend, her mother and myself agreed to meet at the food court in the Villa Linda Mall. My mother and I sat down first and a few minutes later my nemesis walks by with her guilty carefree eyes and her mom on her side.

"Nice to meet you. I'm so sorry it had to be under these kinds of circumstances. I hope we can agree to resolve everything without involving the police. You know, this is so unfortunate. My daughter has been working there for almost a year and she doesn't need to lose her job because your son stole from that girl."

"Wait a minute," Mom interrupted. "I want to hear her side of the incident before we proceed any further."

"Have you talked about this with your son?" The other mother patronized my mother.

"Yes I have. I heard what he had to say and now I want to hear it out of her mouth before I listen to anything else. You know, my son is not the only guilty party sitting here today." I certainly was not about to not confess to my mother.

The stunted harlot's mother was stunned. Her scheming daughter smirked with unapologetic caution.

"Well," her mother somewhat ordered inquisitively.

She glanced at her mother, then whispered, "Why do I have to say anything? We don't even need to be here."

"WELL," her mother seemed a little more dauntless.

She waited, looked briefly up at me with her rhinoceros horn of a nose and smiled, then immediately dropped the smile, glanced swiftly at my mother then gazed at hers and finally opened her mouth.

"He and his friend came into the store looking for trouble. I go to school with both of them and I know how they are. He came up to me and asked me if I would give him something like a thousand dollar leather trench coat. I told him no, but he kept insisting on it. He wouldn't leave and then he went into the back room while I wasn't looking because I was helping a customer. I don't know what he did back there but the next day the mall security comes over and starts asking me a bunch of questions in front of my boss. My boss was really angry and threatened to call the police and have me arrested if I didn't tell him who he was and what had happened." I thought I almost saw water in her eyes but I think it was more like an exultant gleam.

"And then?" Mom interjected.

"Now wait a minute," her mother breeched the interaction between her shyster daughter's misinformation and my mom's motherly wrath. "I think my daughter has been courageous and generous in her presence here today. All we want is for your son to return the money he stole from my daughter's friend."

"She's not my friend, Mom. I'm not friends with that Mexican."

"Sweetheart!" her mother feared.

Both Mom and I stared down the petite bigot until her eye sockets were swimming around the grouting on the tile floor.

"I'm sorry, I don't know," her mother began, ingenuously.

"Now look here!" Mom started. "I don't want to be here anymore than that little bitch does."

"How dare you."

"I dare and I don't give a shit. That little bitch is a liar. Yeah *you*, you little bitch. Sitting there smirking the whole time acting like she's innocent while you're there defending her like she's some recently anointed saint. I know that she told my son where the money was, whose money it was, and how much was in there. I can only appreciate my son for not being stupid enough to share any of the money with her like she wanted him to. Now I'm not defending either one of them. Both of them were wrong and both of them should pay."

"Well I can assure you, she has already received ample punishment for this."

"What, a week vacation from school while you and daddy drive to Utah for some Moron ceremony. No. That bitch will get what she deserves later on in life. I can tell. You have a load of problems with that one there and if you ask me she's not worth the pair of shoes you walked in all the way from your car in the parking lot to this food court. My son regrets what he did and is willing to return the money to the owner. We're going over there right now and after he does it I don't want to hear from either of you anymore. You got that?" Then she turns to me, "and if I was you, I wouldn't talk to that little whore at school or anywhere else. Stay the fuck away from her cuz she'll get you in trouble again." My mother had a way of putting things in perspective. I don't think her mother, nor anyone else for that matter, expected my mother to speak like that. The meeting surely didn't go how her mother might have desired it to. She sat there shocked into immobilization as my mother and I stood on our feet, pushing the chairs back and sliding on our way toward dubious atonement.

In the store she stood there, working effortlessly the way a giraffe grazes, dark skin, foreshadowing hair, not noticing our presence. I hesitantly made my way towards her. She was definitely Mexican as the bantam white supremacist viciously observed.

"Hello."

"Hello," she answered with calm, welcoming grace.

"I'm not sure if you remember me or not." My eyes searched for something other than her face to focus on.

"I remember you," she said with nonchalance. "You're the friend of my co-worker. You were in here the other day."

"I came back because I wanted to return the money I took from you."

I desired to get this over with. Her face shined appreciative as I handed her a blank envelope.

"Oh, thank you so much! I'm so sorry things turned out this way."

"It should all be there," my mother interspersed turning to me with authority. "He wanted to return it to you face to face before the police were brought in."

"I wasn't going to bring the police into this."

"You weren't?" my mother and I asked simultaneously.

"No. It was my co-worker's mother that called the police. I don't want nothing to do with police. Where I come from you can't trust them. All I did was ask her who took my money. I thought it was her, but she right away said that it was you, then she called security, the boss, and her mother and then the police. I'm sorry it caused so much trouble for you. I didn't think you would take it. I thought she did because she's done it before. And I need the money. I have two little daughters at home and it is very difficult to take care of them on your own. This is my second job. I have to work two jobs just to pay rent and save money to help support my parents back in Chihuahua."

She and my mother continued a lengthy conversation and I got to find out a little bit about the person I had just robbed. She was Mexican, roughly twenty years of age, from the impoverished whereabouts of

Chihuahua, barely arrived in the States a few years back after spending almost two years in Juarez earning the money she needed to pay some coyote to cross the border. The first time she tried to cross, she was ripped off. That's why she stayed so long in the infamous border town. Her journey into the States was gruesome. She spoke broken English with a sweet, soft pitch and an air of easiness. She was calm, mature, and respectful. While she spoke of her struggle, I began to hate myself. I felt sick and I didn't desire to feel better. She had forgiven me and I don't even remember her name. She had forgiven me. I thought I lived in a world of bitterness. But she had forgiven me. I thought that nobody was capable of forgiveness and I had every right to infringe on the rights of someone else without a con-of-science. I'm not a moralist, but I don't think I ever quite felt like literal shit until that moment. Had she not forgiven me I wouldn't have cared about what I did. Peeking at her relaxed disposition from time to time as she spoke with my mother, I realized I had robbed from my own. They struggle for daily life a million times more than any of us spoiled bitches could ever begin to think to imagine. The only reason Mexican immigrants are willing to leave their homes and their families is because for years the United States has been trying to annex Mexico as one of its own possessions, or assets, and as a consequence has totally wrecked its economy and undermined any chance for genuine democracy to occur there. They are the labor force of the Southwest (moving into the Midwest) of the United States. They are the ones who pick the produce in the hot sun all day earning cents for every pound; they are the ones who wash the dishes for high-end fancy restaurants and the not-so-appetizing eating places; and they are the ones who deal with the white man's filth in the luxury and cheap hotels.

I felt the worse I'd ever felt. Not because I took something that supposedly didn't belong to me, but because I had robbed from a brown, hard-working honest woman and her children. I had robbed from the poor. I should either have been shot to the dirt by a firing squad in public view, or I should have been honored as a successful Amerikan businessman. It was the worst thing I have ever done in my life. By far it is the worst thing I have ever done in my life.

She forgave me.

I will never forget what I did.

I will never be able to forgive myself.

Fruit of a Poisoned Tree

I had her on top of the plush headrest of her foster father's silent grape colored favorite chair. I can't remember how I hoisted her up there in that position.

I was twenty. She was seventeen. She was illegal, but I was barely three years her elder and she was sultry at the time before I discovered that she was a major puta in this small city. I met her at the Boys' and Girls' Club. She would glance at me from time to time with come-on eyes allowing them to stroll along behind me as I passed by her guilty desire. I moved in and moved on in no time. After talking to her the first time, in the midst of conversation she revealed her half identity to me. When she told me she was "born/again" I almost puked and stopped talking to her right then and there.

I showed up at her house, her parent's house to be precise, and the front door's unlocked. Her parents were not around. Her parents were the brainwashers of this curious sacrament and more born/again than Judas. She used to always try and show me the errors of my waywardness and preach the Gospel. She even attempted to talk in tongues one time. I responded with my own.

She was standing there wet and dripping, hair plastered to her face, in a white stolen hotel robe with her bare feet looking like some deep tropical forest copper tone naked native you used to find in the pornographic photographs of *National Geographic* in the old days. I didn't hush a syllable. I took a giant step for atheists when I slithered my arms around her waistline, kissing her neck twice softly. She kissed me back. I had my fingers fondling her nipples. She was hot. Her flesh was softer than the inside of a pillow. I maneuvered her hips onto the top of the plush headrest of her foster father's silent grape colored favorite chair. She started leaning back moaning before I saddled my dirty tongue into her holiness. I couldn't believe it. She didn't smell at all. It was refreshing, yet disturbing. I personally thought this chick was possessed by some malevolent spirit just by the way she would look at me. I believe Christians are doing the Devil's work. Nothing but evil emanates from Christianity. From the Crusades to the Inquisition to the acquisition of this place, superfluous with those 70 million backward redneck cult members more dangerous than any Arab. Even Tolstoy asserted that Christianity and the church of Christianity, whether Protestant or Catholic, has nothing to do with the teachings of Jesus Christ himself, whoever he might've been. I can't stand born/again Christians. Instead of reading 'freedom of religion,' the First Amendment of the U.S. Constitution should read 'freedom *from* religion.' These assholes telling me I'm evil cuz of the words I choose and a woman's choice. And they're the worst hypocrites and extremists. The war in the Middle East not only has to do with oil, but also has to do with religion. All religions should be banned.

We were running out of time. I got to lick a few times like licking an ice cream cone before the poorly placed scoop falls off the cone onto the unwashed floor. Her vulnerability tasted like caramel without the aftertaste. I'm not even sure how she was holding herself up. All I could think about was the times she used to pontificate about the necessity for abstinence and that you should give yourself to the Lord instead of to the temple of the flesh.

Headlights appeared in the late haze that a screen door gives off when light is reflected off it. "I thought you said your parents weren't coming home," I scolded her, tossing her over the chair doing an inverse somersault landing on her feet, toes clutching the carpet. She sprinted to the back room leaving a trail of water drops trotting in her stead. I had just finished buttoning my fly when her father walked in steamier than a cooled clam. He didn't say a word to me, walked straight toward the back looking for his daughter, calling out her name ready for the reprimand. The mother politely asked me to leave.

I took his daughter out one more time after that incident and the fucker ended up calling the fuzz on me. We were out eating at a pizzeria with some other fake church friend of hers. Eventually her friend left. We had nothing left to do but fool around. For being a born/again Christian she sure loved to tease the cock. She told me once that she had participated in a snuff flick where she witnessed her boyfriend at the time enact the climax. She was a lying dog in heat.

In the back seat of her car around four in the morning I had her shirt off, her pants unzipped, and her hand on my manliness.

I see this flash of light that looked like it came…shit, I knew where it came from. I always know what that kind of light flashes like. It was a police searchlight or spotlight that they have on the side panel of the cars. The windows were steamed up. There were sounds of footsteps moving up the dirt driveway. The born/again Christian buttoned up her blouse and adjusted her skirt just as the cop was knocking on the car window. He shined his flashlight in my face, asked who we were and what we were doing. I told him nothing. She told him everything. He informed us that her parents had called the police and reported her missing, that she was underage and last seen with me. I forgot that my car was parked in front of her parent's home.

Because my mother was supposedly somebody important at the time, the cop didn't fuss over it and suggested I take her home. He would call the parents and let them know they found her. Everything was all right. We were on our way.

On the way over, this born/again Christian acted like she was scared of what her father might do to her. Because she was so attractive and active with incomparable beauty, her born/again Christian father used to sneak into her bedroom in the early hours of the morning, stealthily lift her bed sheet, rub up against her in the night and moisten his pajamas. He had this overpowering, intimidating control over her. She asked if I would accompany her inside when she dropped me off. I consented. I felt sorry for her. Her father said nothing and her mother politely asked me to leave.

Diaspora

Sometimes the stories of our lives intertwine and overlap. The following three stories are interchangeable. They are a direct result of what it means to be bored in life.

What do you do as a young man searching for nothing in a hometown taken over and developed fake? Where I come from everybody says, "There's nothing to do here in Santa." This is an ill-advised offspring of unimaginative minds and class war. For the most part there ain't too many accessible, interesting activities for working class native spics, Institute of Indian Art hoodlums, idle rich white kids in SUVs, and anyone under the age of 21. That is unless you're looking to engage in the most cherished hall-of-fame pastime there exists: consuming drugs, drinking and looking for ass at a bar or house party not necessarily getting it. This town has become the romance for an isolated spirit uprooted psychologically, culturally, and now the memories of it pass my life with suspicion.

There are not too many people from Santa Fe that live in Santa Fe. Santa Fe has been bought, sold, re-bought, whored, auctioned, interned and embalmed. It's a webbed strewn mausoleum for the super rich; a purgatory for the average; and an unkempt graveyard for the newly dignified gay retiree. Growing-up I lived the youth of my life burning out at the age of eighteen. Alienated from myself and who I was, forfeited my identity like my virginity, cheap without something to remember. Higher education taught me who I wasn't. Life taught me to hate. Hope is a spontaneous dust storm I fear to contemplate. Besides, where I come from is a place yet recognized.

Sometimes I cry relentlessly in my study knowing one day I will be forced to renounce my origin. Like many local native people I cannot afford to live here any longer. The wages do not complement the cost of living. And the ridiculous piece of ordinance legislation requiring businesses with twenty-five or more employees to pay a minimum so-called "living" wage of $8.50 an hour that could never be enforced not that any governmental whore representative would actually try and do anything good for the ordinary sheep out there just trying to be all they can be by being the trained monkeys they were meant to be. There aren't too many available good jobs in the small city. No real promising opportunities for spics that grew up here. I'll be all right because I have people to mooch off of, my skin is real pale, and my diction of the English imperialistic language is impeccable and more proficient than any whiteboy. But I also have been that little beaner cleaning up your crumbs and nasty dishes full of leftover shit; that little spic lifting those bags of fertilizer carrying it to your car and smiling for your anorexic white ass as I wished I could shoot you in the face; and that insignificant shit you accidentally step over on your way to the next hole. Survival is a lie. Right now I am planning the best way to sell-out. I must handle it with compassion. The day I truly sell-out is when I'm able to make a living off my writing. The second I exchange my sacredness for a handout in order to feed my anatomical orientation and satisfy my horny inclinations.

The Runner

We weren't learning shit in school anyways. I told him let's go and rip off some tapes. He didn't hesitate. He was always down for something by the time ten in the morning intoxicated him. He was cool. He was my Super Protégé In Criminality (SPIC). He was one of those working local Hispanics in a garage always smeared with grease. A built dude that looked like a short Indian with short straight black hair. He had an antic smile and subsequent snicker making the time on this desecrated earth seem short. He had just obtained this small piece of shit white and navy blue Chevrolet truck. The sale sticker was still being used for the license plate so we felt it was the best opportunity we had to do a runner.

The sun had risen almost to its apex, sweltering the people walking around outside in late spring.

We left campus with no problem. He drives like a fuckin' idiot. He was doing seventy down Cerrillos swerving through cars all the while carrying a conversation with me looking at me more than the windshield hugging a Michelob in his curled right fist. I was smoking weed. We pulled into an empty lot on the rail yards across Baca Street, far enough away from the store to not get trapped there and close enough to make a successful getaway.

The truck was stashed under some honey locust trees providing some shade on the east side of an Allsup's at the intersection of Cerrillos Road and Baca Street over on the west side of the rail yards. We both observed the geo-strategic layout of the area.

I went into the store first. I knew the entrance/exit had those standing beige plastic alarm barriers that detect metal clips attached to merchandise. There were four people in the store, all white dudes, three definite employees there, two I had seen previously, one stocking shelves and one more guy hanging around, talking to one other employee but I couldn't tell if he worked there or not. It didn't matter, he was some kind of ally for them and foe for me. There were no other customers in the place. The store had just opened for business for the day. SPIC and I went our separate ways looking for the music we love. I already knew which tapes I wanted: *A Constipated Monkey* by Kurious and *Hard to Earn* by Gang Starr. The rap tapes were kept in plastic, locked casings that had to be opened by one of the employees upon request and as one opened the case the employee stood right there right next to you while you contemplated whether or not you were going to purchase the item and if you did decide to go ahead and purchase an item you would have to hand it to the employee that unlocked the casing for you so the employee could take it behind the counter to the check-out register five feet away. Rap music seems to be the preference of mostly young people and spics in the city. I asked the dude behind the counter if he could open the plastic casings for me because I wanted to view a few cassettes he had in his possession.

"Dude, could you open the plastic casings for me because I want to view a few cassettes you have in your possession."

The enemy behind the counter by the entrance/exit kinda patronized me with a glare of suspicion in his racist countenance. He was about six feet tall, skinny like Shaggy on Scooby-Doo, with rickety dirthead dirty blonde hair and misplaced freckles counterfeiting his reddish tinted skin. I knew I could take him if he tried to play hero and chase my partner and I out the entrance/exit when I decided to make a run for it. After all, the motherfucker didn't trust my appearance as much as my innate proclivity to steal from the successful rich white man robbing the land of its essential minerals like my inactive being lost spiritual.

Recently I was having dinner with a British woman at an East Indian restaurant in downtown Santa Fe for Christmas Eve seated next to a table of about six Hebrews. The main runt Heeb sitting at the head of the table with his conformist spectacles and spineless back and balding dome against the painted mural wall in a crowded room was talking to some old taller Heeb bitch that looked older than Strom Thurmond's and Ronald Reagan's corpses committing premeditated fellatio.

"The Hispanic population is not into achievement the same way we are," he intimated with an arrogant air of pompous self-righteous superiority. The tone of his clammy voice turned my stomach and all I could do for the rest of the night was drink wine instead of eating because he started saying:

"I'm serious. We strive for a higher standard of living than the Hispanics. They're more family oriented and not into achievement the way we are."

"You said that already," the Heeb bitch answered.

"Oh, yes of course. Well, think of this scenario: you have cousin Jose smoking marijuana out on the porch; uncle Fredrico coming out of prison; sister Maria is pregnant at sixteen and she doesn't know who the father is and then you have some ancient fossil of at least one of the genders sitting in a recliner glued to the television dying of diabetes holding a rosary whispering lamentations in Spanish that isn't spoken by the younger generations because the old clog understood the importance of learning the English language and that is why they don't nourish achievement in the same manner we do."

"Mmm hmm."

And that is why I steal from the enemy owned businesses in town because I feel rectified. The lanky enemy slowly moved his coward ass from behind the counter to the plastic casings along the shelves held in chains taking a small shiny gold-plated key hanging around his neck from a cheap necklace unlocking the padlock linked through the chain links eyeing me with superciliousness. I knew exactly what I wanted and what I was doing. I outsmarted this older asshole as the other whiteboys in the shop were not paying attention or at least I thought they weren't paying attention.

SPIC was surprisingly nervous and indecisive. I got what I wanted and handed it to the shop keep and then slid over to SPIC seeking what he had selected. He had a copy of The Pharcyde's first album, *A Bizzare Ride Into the Pharcyde* which he had to acquire in the same fashion that I had to go through; and I think the other one was The Eagles or someone like that.

"Are you ready?"

He hesitated, then nodded slightly in reluctant approval. I was relatively at ease with the situation. The enemy that assisted me already suspected what I was about to do. I eyed the two audiocassettes I was not about to purchase. He went along with the whole routing because he didn't have any probable cause to accuse me of something I hadn't done yet. SPIC didn't help this dickhead's suspicions.

I was at the cashier register. SPIC forgot to keep in step with me. He slowly approached. The enemy that helped me began to ring me up. As the cashier bent over to grab a plastic bag for my cargo convenience I hustled the two tapes stacked on the counter into my clenched palm and ignited out the front entrance/exit setting off the obnoxious alarm beepers squawking away as I heard some dude toward the back of the shop yell, "He's running!" SPIC hadn't moved yet. Before the guy behind the counter that helped me could leap over and grab SPIC by the sleeve, SPIC stepped off. I was leaping down over the four grayish-white concrete steps onto the parking lot pavement establishing a tremendous head start. The chase began with SPIC taking his leap but not keeping up with me. I was already crossing Baca Street when I looked back and noticed the guy behind the counter that was assisting me was barely exiting the store with some other chulito on his heels yelling and hollering SPIC was starting to cross Baca Street I was halfway across the empty sand lot on the west end of the rail yards almost at the stashed getaway vehicle when I looked back again and saw the enemy gaining on him they all began to cross the empty sandlot on the west end of the rail yards kicking dust the enemy was gaining on him closer and closer almost within arms length they had him I stopped because I felt they were going to get him and a fist fight would ensue all for a value of forty dollars that we liberated from the capitalists that always ran a racist store harassing the local Hispanics and patronizing the patron dumb sounding Hispanics looking for music you couldn't find in a mainstream outlet looking like they had no business in this store I heard the many tales from friends and relatives especially my auntie who is quite the connoisseur of music I was prepared to kick one of the whiteboys in the face or smash one of them over the head with a rock but serendipity intervened and as the enemy behind the counter who helped me retrieve the tapes the enemy that was first to suspect our inherited disposition and first to give chase had just grabbed SPIC's slow running ass on the shoulder strap of his muscle shirt and flipped literally flipped on his back taking a hard dive onto the muddy ground alongside a puddle of muddy water for it had just rained the previous night.

The other stopped giving chase to attend to his friend's misfortune.

SPIC got away.

As we were about to jump into SPIC's truck I looked once more to find the fallen enemy covered with mud dripping from his downcast defeated face. A tiny gray Subaru looking car drove up to the fallen wanna-be cop and his cohort and the one on the ground bravely points toward us and waves the car forward like some Hollywood make believe scene from some stupid propaganda war movie glamorizing war and its natural violence like some wounded soldier holding his leg or hip or buttocks or crotch or shoe waving on the other soldiers that may or may not attempt to nurse the fallen soldier temporarily but the offensive must carry on the violence must continue and so the car came chasing us as we plopped into the cabin of the small truck me on the passenger side SPIC behind the wheel trying to start the engine SPIC couldn't get it started and the gray car pulled up behind us waiting for us to start the truck not stepping out of their car just waiting there like a good patient animal upon the command of its tyrannical master waiting there until finally the passenger in the passenger's side decides to get out of the car and leaps up to the passenger side window almost grabbing my right arm but then SPIC contorts the engine throws it into first gear drums the clutch and the truck hops onto Cerrillos Road heading west toward Second Street. The little gray piece of shit decided to follow.

It was like you was the director of a movie motor vehicle chase scene seeing urban overcrowded traffic passing you by while you speed eighty on a thirty-five forty-five speed limit zone.

SPIC and I took off our shirts me displaying my newly received tattoo of my initials on my left shoulder no bigger than some centimeters acting tough even though the only tattoo I had on my body was on my left shoulder where it couldn't be seen by any of the passers passing the changed red light hearing horns honk in hatred avoiding any accidents accelerating tremendously with these dumb fucks behind us it was exciting feeling big time living smaller than a snail sneaking into dilapidated nursery early morning sleeping corrosive defying arbitrary authority not aware of our anarchist behavior causing disruption looking for a savior in sentimentality and materialistic masturbation addiction to rap acting like the lyrics I heard in Kurious's curios Puerto Rican philosophy of New York talking about life lived regularly like everyone searching for peace.

I was yelling like a high-pitched bitch. Screaming ecstasy with windows rolled down, hair soliloquizing wildness, youth, and celebration making the passer-by passed conspirators of the paved road jealous.

SPIC was smiling laughing dramatically hardly driving or looking where he was going. We almost slammed three cars on our way to getaway.

We didn't know how we were going to get out of this situation. The enemy was pursuing us obsessively. We passed cars moving, coming and going. I was nervous with my heart pounding faster than it takes loneliness to set in after you've moved into a new place.

"How the fuck are we going to get out of this?" I asked SPIC.

"I don't know," SPIC uttered, finally focused and concentrated on some ill-conceived perception developing in his hazy field of vision.

Down Cerrillos we passed the red-light traffic light at the intersection of Baca Street, propelled past the fabric shop, a porno and Mexican movie rental joint owned by some fat dyke, weaving through cars alongside the Indian school hospital riding through the fire station red light a mural painted by a German illegal immigrant artist on the left all the time the enemy keeping up with us it wasn't bad watching the driver's moves building up the adrenaline with wide open eyes holding onto the cracked navy blue tremulous dashboard shuttering wind skating through our greasy hair as we were approaching Fifth Street and the Pantry Restaurant.

Cerrillos is a four-lane road. SPIC was in the right lane. The enemy had been tailgating us then moving into the left lane pulling up to us telling us to pull over, SPIC laughing at them with the window rolled down throwing a finger at them. The whole time I was wondering why these dudes were so furious about the whole incident. It was only forty dollars worth of merchandise. Perhaps it was the fact that these two little local homeboys outsmarted these honkey off-the-bus entrepreneurial transplants and pulled-off a good one with them knowing what we were up to the whole time. Or maybe not. Maybe they were moralists.

The enemy slowed down and pulled behind us on the right lane. There was some traffic on the left lane narrowly behind us.

"Do you think we can make the bitch?" SPIC investigated.

"What?" That probably wasn't too much of a reassuring response.

"Do you think I can flip the bitch?"

"Wha..." SPIC flipped the bitch. I watched in stillness the oncoming traffic shrouding us led by a semi-truck. We skidded scraping tire tracks on the pavement smoke ascending considerably horns honking and lights flashing from the semi-truck nearly pinching the right corner of the rear bumper. SPIC pushed the gas moving forward looking at the whiteboys on the other side of the street trying to do what we did at a turn-off a bit ahead of where we exemplified skill, waiting because the traffic was thick and they couldn't pass with their horns honking, waiting for a space to clear-up. By that time we had already turned off onto a side road like Third Street or something. We lost them in the labyrinth of undisclosed neighborhoods we knew better than them.

The Violent Ménage a Trois

I staggered courageously in the summer still night with a gun pointed at my head, wondering if she was asleep or awake.

Hours ago I was using an oily dirty torn piece of newspaper advertisement for toilet paper. I was outside in the sticks trying to take a shit peeping into the abandoned car I was hoisted up against, checking out the couple having sex inside.

Earlier even than that in the evening I was shot at.

I don't know why I went. This sort of friend agreed at my inquisitive suggestion that we go to her house to gang bang her.

His younger brother used to bang her and I got pretty close to banging her and it seemed that this sort of friend might've banged her.

It's five in the morning. I'm drunk off gravity, probably one of the worst drunks in my life.

Graduated from high school the night before. I haven't slept well in the past couple of weeks.

This other dude's dad is just out of prison or something and is becoming a bit too chummy with his older male friend hanging around for this other dude's supposed graduation party. This other dude is a friend of my sort of friend and I have only recently started to hang out with this sort of friend even though I hardly know him but he seems like a cool fella though I won't trust him any more than I trust anybody else or myself.

The summer nights in Santa Fe are rustic dead calms serenading the apocalypse of our collective unconscious. I crank my head toward outer space to recognize the stars that have fallen before me.

Parties every single night, what a waste, and here we are on Saturday night at this guy's trailer on the Southside of town with his dad who is acting like an idiot. He refuses to shake any of our hands as we enter his home. There are six of us: my sort of friend, this tall skinny zebra from St. Michael's High School, a loser, me, and two other dudes I hardly recognize but I think they just graduated from St. Mike's as well; and three of them; nine of us altogether getting ready to party in the small shabby kitchen of the other dude's trailer.

On the kitchen table there are five different bottles of different kinds of wretched tequila. It's hotter than the zap on your tongue after licking a fluorescent light bulb when it's been turned on for over an hour. With all these different guys in this small space it reeked.

What the fuck are we doing here? I want to leave but everybody else is getting loaded, taking shots and now it's my turn.

My sort of friend leans over me, passing the bottle "Hey, now it's your turn. You gotta take a huge swig like everybody else." Everybody else was not taking large swallows but being the missionary alcoholic that I am I take down the equivalent of one quarter of the entire bottle. That's how it began and continues.

The loser is cracking jokes keeping tensions down. My sort of friend slowly starts to deliberately aggravate the other dude's dad, challenging him like a rogue lion attempting to take over another male lion's untended pride. My sort of friend just likes to start shit. What am I doing here with these idiots? I have no sense of direction in the world. I have no purpose. I'm wasting my time.

Things happen faster rather than sooner and the cable network doesn't show us the programming we require when harassed by outsiders in our territory.

I wasn't watching when it started, but my sort of friend and the other dude's dad pushed their seats back, screeching simultaneously, pointing fingers in each other's face, yelling like talk show guests rampaging around the arena between peacemakers. The other dude got in between them. He was a skinny macaroni, trying to pry them together not letting the riotous atmosphere disappear. The loser is talking shit. The zebra from St. Mike's is laughing his drunk ass off. The other two are talking shit, backing up my sort of friend and the other dude's dad's friend from prison is half incognito but starting to get upset because my sort of friend has just placed his hand on the other dude's dad's shirt sleeve leaving a wrinkle in a hailstorm. Clamor, confusion, furniture starts moving, the trailer starts to teeter-totter, slowly rocking. This is what happens when there are no women around.

The other dude's dad tries wrapping his counteroffensive claws around my sort of friend's exposed neck. My sort of friend pushes him to the floor. One of the other two guys we was with slams one of the almost empty tequila bottles on the edge of the table watching driplets splash the squinting eyes of the accosted, creating chaos. People begin moving out the front door in one testimonial body.

The loser is kicking shit all over the living room area, tearing the screen door off its hinges. The other dude's dad is screaming out of control. The other dude tries to quell his father's revenge, moving us out the house cuz shit's gonna go down.

As we're packing into my sort of friend's Toyota truck, me in the passenger seat, everybody else climbing into the back bed, I look to the right and see the other dude's dad running out the front door onto his poorly built poorly lit porch fondling what looked liked to be a .30 ought pointing it right at the truck. The lanky other dude from behind just in time pushes the barrel of the gun northward. It let's off a discharge of fireworks into the deficient sky. My sort of friend put it in first and we got the fuck out of there hollering and howling, asking if anybody was hit as a second shot molested the calm of the ongoing hour.

It was at the undeveloped land around Capital High School, partying in the shrubs, worshiping a bonfire with wooden pellets providing fuel that I developed the educated idea to go to her house at five in the morning.

After that high drama at that other dude's chante we left and left the other dude heading out to some outdoors gathering. Partying in the shrubs over a bonfire in Santa Fe is a ubiquitous right of passage like drinking a bottle of gasoline. Under the steadfast stewardship of the moon's lonely solitude, a sense of camaraderie envelops the earth and it welcomes temporal guests for the evening through the early morning. Crickets crocheting in the background. Sparks of fire's insult whist past the ends of your hair causing insecurity. The cadre of people form a primitive tribe, dancing to nothing cuz the battery to some shmuck's car just froze and no more juice except the Mexicanized sangria boiling in the begrimed trough stashed behind some former football players that won't allow anybody a cup unless you're a friend of theirs or some broad for them to sexually harass. This is what poor people do in their hometown to have a good time. Everywhere else is off limits to those that don't belong.

There were nothing but guys again or there might've been a chick or two that nobody seemed to be talking to. I was so drunk I fell asleep walking.

I just remember I had to take a shit real bad.

I ventured off into the woods and spotted an abandoned old rusty car decaying in the middle of the boondocks. It was moving from side to side. I noticed through the cracked rear windshield a naked ass bouncing up and down in rapid detail. I looked in closer. I started to pull down my pants and shorts, squatting as far down as I could possibly want to go. When shitting outside you have to be cognizant of the little dried dead weed stems protruding from the ground that scratch your scrotum while you're squeezing your butt cheeks.

I took a deep messy shit.

I took this shit while watching what turned out to be another something of a friend of mine fucking something in this old abandoned car.

When I was done taking a shit I realized I didn't have anything to wipe my soiled ass with. My hole was soggy, mushy and wet. I knew it was because with my extended index finger I reached around to my hole, brushed the rim authoritatively like a Turk warrior, brought my hand back around to where I was facing, lifted the outstretched palm to my face, and sniffed what was on the tip of my index finger soothingly. Then I sniffed again.

I walked-squatted around the car digging out fresh budding leaves of grass and clumping them together attempting to concoct some kind of ass-wiping device. Luck pissed on me. I found shredded papers thrown on the ground next to an overturned can of motor oil oozing lassitude from its container. I leafed through the papers, feeling for the kindest kind of toilet paper substitute I could use. The advertisement page soaked in motor oil won the contest for its proclivity to silkiness. Or maybe it was the shine.

I proceeded to wipe my ass but had to cut it short because the guy in the abandoned old rusty car was finished and started to get out the car as my sort of friend comes out of nowhere.

"What the fuck happened to you?" He was laughing, drunk off his romanticism.

"Bro. We should go to what's her face's and throw a threesome," was my response.

"That's a good idea. Let's go," he said.

That was the last thing we said to each other for the rest of the night.

I don't know how we even got there.

We drove down Rodeo Road in my sort of friend's truck, so drunk I remember thinking I was on acid because the streets had that sheen kinda gleam that only a drug user could understand. The streets writhed and twitched. They swirled seductively, enticing me to throw up at least once before the ride was over. I'm surprised no cop caught us. Rodeo Road is constantly swarming with cops. My sort of friend was swerving all over the goddamn place; he crossed over the median several times onto the oncoming lanes; he hopped onto the sidewalk and crushed some petit bushes just recently planted there by the hardworking tax-paying back breaking schmucks at the City.

We left all the guys we were with, including my sort of friend's younger brother who I guess we were supposed to rendezvous with there in the woods. They needed a ride somewhere.

It must have taken us an hour and a half to get there even though she lived less than fifteen minutes away from where we were partying.

The early morning cold breeze in mid-summer shunned my inconspicuousness. The crickets stopped flirting. The morning was completely silent except for the occasional passing zoom of an automobile probably owned by some deadbeat worker rising up too early to help the machine function properly.

My sort of friend and I couldn't stop laughing.

We descended his truck. The street pavement felt like melting peanut butter. My stomach was taut from throwing-up. I exhaled a comforting serene breath of mischief telling my sort of friend not to laugh. I found the path to the front door.

Five-thirty in the morning and here we are, two drunk dumb fucks pounding on the front door. "Hey!" was all I could trumpet loud enough for the whole block to take notice.

I was determined to get inside in many different endeavors. I knocked rapaciously like a premeditated drug bust for about ten seconds straight. "Hey. Come on out here baby. I want to fuck you." I knocked again and again intermittently rhapsodizing her name, begging for a bite of something I ain't never done before.

My sort of friend was laughing viciously. I thought he was sobbing.

I knocked and pounded and draped myself all over the front door for about a good half hour.

"Come on. Let's just go," was my sort of friend's capitulation.

"Fuck that," was my only retort. "I didn't come all the way over here risking incarceration just to knock on the door and walk away with my dick in my fist."

"Let's get outta here before you wake up the whole neighborhood."

We were walking away in surrender when enlightenment shined on me gracefully.

"Wait," I said. "We can go around to the side and sneak into her bedroom window."

He didn't need persuasion. We manipulated our way to the side of the house only to discover a seven-foot wooden fence barricading our progress. The fence surrounded the right flank of the house bordering Rodeo Road. My sort of friend insisted I be the first to hurdle the fence. How I did it I'll never know because from what I can recall I could barely hold my ankles in my shoes.

Upon pushing myself upright from the artificial turf that covered the ground with a few chunks of grass and dog shit on my lips, my sort of friend finally fell over the fence. We couldn't stop laughing like two little naughty boys that take tremendous pleasure in doing something they both know they probably shouldn't be doing. There were three windows to choose from. I located her window out of the circles that were pirouetting in front of my obsequious vision. Her window was the only one with drapes tracing the inside contours of her looking glass. I knew because I had been in there before prodigalizing more than three hours watching her tease me with fuck me eyes confessing that she was falling in love with me even though I had just met her acquaintance at the time.

Just as I was about to rap upon her pane, "Freeze motherfucker or I'll shoot!" was all I heard.

I knew it wasn't my sort of friend because I was smiling at him just before I heard the warning and I didn't happen to notice any vocal elements emanating from his oral cavity.

We stood still. We stood more still and stared at one another, not sure if we should move or not. The voice came from an invisible. I took it as a joke. I told my sort of friend to stop fucking around and proceeded toward the window.

"Are you sure this is the window?" asked he.

"I said freeze," was what we heard once more. I was almost positively sure it wasn't my sort of friend saying it. The voice reverberated continuously in my head. It sounded loud then soft, loud then soft. Then it sounded as if I could see the airwaves escaping the stereo speaker when you listen to the radio. The voice really sounded like when you turn the dial of the volume on a stereo high than low, low than high real fast repeatedly. The voice sounded like something I made up inside my head.

"Is that you?" I asked my sort of friend.

"I thought it was you," was his fancy repartee.

"Get over here on this side of the fence or I'll blow your fuckin' brains out."

This time I was certain it wasn't anybody but someone else from somewhere I couldn't identify at the moment. I thought it was a pig.

"Are you a cop?" I squeamishly inquired.

"No. Now get over here now," was the response.

"Alright dude, that's cool, that's cool," I kept repeating softly as if to convince an Afrikan war criminal of tact and delicacy. "We're gonna be coming over the fence now. You don't have to shoot."

"I'll shoot if you don't get over here now, right now," he demanded and I knew it was a he because the voice was deep, direct, and rough and psycho and distant and cold.

"Alright, alright, we're coming."

"Now!"

"Alright. I'm coming over the fence right now. Don't do anything." I fell down once again surmounting that tall stupid fence, wondering if my sort of friend would follow or wait till I got shot.

At that moment I couldn't even really be scientifically certain that there was anybody on the other side of the fence. I only climbed over because I knew we had no business there at someone else's house at five-thirty in the morning wanting to violate someone else's daughter. I was hoping either absolution or death rested on the other side.

On all fours, really on my stomach, or was it my knees? No, I hadn't enough dignity to rise to my knees. I was on my stomach flat when I lifted my chin and saw her dad abrasively standing with his arms stretched out in front of him in the early cool morning with nothing but his Fruit-of-the-Looms and a .45 Smith & Wesson. His belly was sagging over the elastic brim of his shorts and his thighs were intoxicatingly coruscating and skinnier than they were supposed to be on such a domineering figure.

I began to laugh.

"What the fuck are you laughing at? Don't you know I could kill you and nobody would ever know what happened to you? Where is the other guy?"

I sobered up magically.

I couldn't be absolutely sure if it was her dad, but I figured it was her dad because I couldn't possibly conceive of any other middle-aged pot belly motherfucker that would be out this early in the morning pointing a gun at my forehead wearing nothing but his briefs. A slight breeze tickled his crotch where there was a little yellow stain made of tiny circles. He asked me what the fuck were we doing at his house at this certain hour.

"What the fuck are you doing at my house this early in the morning?"

My sort of friend finally tumbled over, laughing his anus off until he raised his head in sanctimonious supplication looking at this bald three-quarter naked man, not knowing which one of us to point the gun at. He decided to keep it locked on me.

I had been to her house on several occasions legitimately. I even ate supper with her mother, father, and sister once but I really couldn't discern if this cowboy was really her father or not. This guy putting this gun up to the skin on my forehead was bald, a lot more corpulent, and not as sophisticated as her dad first seemed upon introduction and immediate subsequent impressions. Her pops was some kind of famous golf pro at some rinky-dink dust dive with nine holes for the super-rich to get their kicks jerking-off all day at a gated reclusive spot off-limits to those without a membership or a better way to get in. This ape with the gun just didn't seem like him.

"Answer me goddamn it, what are you doing here?" he demanded.

"It's cool, it's cool. Your daughter told us to come here," I answered without hesitation.

"What?" he responded.

"Swear to God, she told us to come by and she would let us in so we could party. Honest." I wasn't really thinking about what I was saying. I could care less if she got in trouble. I was trying to distract. I cautiously started to crawl away toward the street where we were parked. The barrel was aimed directly at my face. I wasn't nervous but sober. I had to do the talking because my sort of friend was scared out of his lust. He couldn't utter a mumbling. I crawled and crawled until her dad told me to stop moving, then told me to get out of here, then told me to stop once again.

The scumbag was fucking with us. When someone has a gun to your head, you pretty much do everything they tell you to do with the least resistance. I honestly wasn't aware he had a gun pointed at my head until I was safely out of his reach. He turned to go back inside. I noticed the gleam from a stretched Dirty Harry barrel. He clicked the hammer back into place.

The Intersection

He was staring me down from the passenger window of a truck I thought was owned by a cousin of mine. I stared back. He stared. I stared. He started conversing with his hands.

We had just pulled off the road going to Capital High School, turning right onto Airport Road in my piece-of-shit- peeling blue lacquered Oldsmobile that was handed down to me by my older other brother in less than sub-standard condition. My imaginary Smarmy Patron of Indecent Compunction (SPIC) was in the passenger seat laughing as usual giving me encouragement because I was forced to turn the steering wheel with one hand since my right forearm and hand were confined to a cast bending my wrist forward making me look like a fag and feeling inferior like a retard.

Over my left shoulder I concentrated my impressionable focus directly at the gentleman in the parallel motor vehicle passenger's seat giving me the finger and mouthing with his lips some obscenities I couldn't discern. I wasn't looking at the road in front of me. This simpleton didn't have the decency to roll down his window. I took note of the fog building on the inside surface of the glass, a façade of temporal stillness. His silent admonitions heightened with intensity. I continued to defy his aggressiveness with sarcastic facial images mimicking his prejudicial gestures.

"Do you know that guy?" SPIC asked.

"No, do you?"

"No," SPIC concurred.

I glanced at SPIC for a scheduled intermission and delineated the apprehensiveness in his astonished expression. His eyes were open, his mouth adjusted, and his neck slightly twisted a centimeter or three toward each side cautiously, like entering a new relationship.

If there's one thing I can't stand in this world is when someone fucks with you for no reason whatsoever, especially when you don't know the individual. I didn't know this guy. I'd never seen him before. I didn't know why he was starting shit. I got pissed. Immediately I understood that I possessed a policeman's baton underneath my seat that I had stolen from my girlfriend at the time who said she got it from her stepfather who said he got it from some pink farm animal he had a confrontation with and supposedly he detached it from the pink farm animal's armored belt while they were immersed in some sort of homosexual wrestling grapple before the pink farm animal could notice that it was missing.

I quickly peeked one more time at SPIC disregarding any flashes of assurance. Automatically the gas pedal accelerated and I cut off the truck to my left and slammed the brakes making the truck behind me almost cause an accident. I heard his wheels screech. Traffic came to a meditation in the middle of the noon hour. I took off, antagonizing my pursuers. I halted, I paused, I falsified ignition and impetuously launched my car forward spasmodically teasing this asshole to try and keep up. I lost control of my thoughts or I was losing control of consciousness in a zone like sports commentators of the mid to late '80s early '90s used to say Michael Jordan was in when he seemed unstoppable. SPIC had temporarily ceased to exist. I pulled back parallel to the truck, shouting insults inaudibly across Airport Road flicking this punk off. He started to get heated. He was raging at me. Both our windows were still rolled up. I checked the windshield inside rearview mirror suddenly turning the steering wheel all the way right pulling over on to the embankment on the side of the road pulling into an as yet to be developed sandlot in front of Sweeney Elementary School firing out the car not turning it off forgetting to put the car in park SPIC catching it before it rolled away watching the truck drive by with the illicit cretin in the passenger seat now throwing me two fingers and laughing and then pointing at me there on the sideline of racing traffic jumping up and down yelling my ass off telling that bitch to pull over and get down so we can settle this meaninglessness. I hurried back into the car and took off once again.

I don't know what I was thinking or what I was going through. I'm not prone to violence and I'm not a fighter of any discipline so why would I even bother with some loser like this little prick starting shit for no reason in a moving automobile no less. Am I sure he was even referring to me? Of course he is because there's no one else around and I don't know him and SPIC doesn't know him or at least he says he doesn't know him so now I've already committed myself to fighting this idiot that I don't even know nor never encountered plus my right hand is inaccessible because recently I severed two tendons under my skin when I put my right hand through a Plexiglas-protected fire extinguisher casing at Capital High in the presence of the same girlfriend I had stolen the police baton from.

I pass him on the right lane of Airport Road, speed past other motorists and finally park my car behind a black Toyota 4 x 4 at the crowded intersection of Airport Road and Cerrillos Road, one of the most busiest and squalid traffic intersections in town.

One second, one brisk look at SPIC and that's all it took.

War is abhorrence. Under the suppression of the sun, I touch for a gun only to find this police baton. In the grip and tightness of a sweaty palm the baton stiffens and readies itself for defiance of a character unwarranted. SPIC didn't say anything. I shot out the car for the last time with a conflagration in my eyes so burning I could see the smoke billowing out my nostrils like two twin tin smokestacks about to combust. There were several vehicles parked behind me waiting for the light to turn green, the operators of the vehicles unsure of what I was doing. I was definite in my intentions, yet confused on how to proceed. With what hatred it must require to kill or seriously injure someone. A force of force enters you and possesses you and commands you to strike severe action as if it was justice understood. The enemy truck was behind the two vehicles I had passed and not noticed. I was focused for the first time in my life.

"What the fuck motherfucker, you want to talk shit now?" and before these words completely escaped my careless verbal orifice, I unleashed the baton like an antiquated obsolete Roman emperor reciting a decree with pompous authority, complacent vulgarity, and disinclined bravado on the passenger door opening then quickly closing because the cat that was talking shit to me and started the whole thing attempted to get out of the truck and stand his ground when he saw me approaching but when my weapon thrashed and dented the passenger door he backed-off and retreated back to relative safety for the moment.

I felt more alive than ever because the adrenaline victimized every artery, nerve, and pore of my body. I didn't think about my right hand. I didn't think about the guy I didn't know who looked scared like a startled rabbit inside the cabin of the truck. I went berserk. I smashed the mirror on the passenger door sensationally, observing the shards of razor mirror zipping beneath my knees, shattering on the pavement upon contact. I slammed and left an indenture on the hood of the truck. I broke one of his headlights on the front end. I was fucking shit up.

The driver, who presumably was the owner of the vehicle stepped-out and said, "Hey! What the fu…" but then he stopped in the middle of this utterance because I think he might've recognized me cuz I recognized him as soon as he stood outside the truck. He was my cousin, the son of an uncle's son-in-law that I hardly knew nor never saw.

I didn't give a shit. The moment is uprising. I could've killed. People stuck in traffic at the traffic lights started to pay attention. No horns were honking; nobody got out of their car; nobody told me to move my piece of shit when the light turned green. The guy in the passenger seat of my pseudo cousin's truck backed down but glared painstakingly through my vacillating comportment. Unbeknownst to me, people slowly started gathering around the center of action. About thirty to forty little spic and white trash gangsta replicas, or wanna-be gangsta replicas all wearing black and white baggy garments barely hanging on to their malnourished spray paint sniffing under six foot dimensions covered with black baseball caps advertising white cursive lettering of some professional sports team from the West Coast enclosed in on me like a leaking burrito with a torn tortilla led by this black kid that just recently got into town. He militantly breast plummeted up to my face, tilting jitteringly from side to side spitting sparse showers of saliva as he spoke voraciously slowing down only to flex. Huge protruding black veins kept pulsating simultaneously. Sweat crept onto the sweltering obsidian skin each side of the bulging temples.

"Yo motherfucker what da fuck you think yo doing? You fucking with my homie? Creeping up on him out here in the middle of the road swinging yo stick like some GANGSTA! Starting shit what da fuck is wrong wich ya? What set you represent? You wanna die motherfucker?" he asked.

Before I could consider a cordial response the little miscellaneous followers behind him charged in on me screaming and yelling and that punk that I attacked in the truck came forward right behind the black kid and started talking shit. I couldn't make out what he was saying because it hadn't quite registered yet on what I did and how this situation had the potential to escalate out of control in a very bad, unhealthy, retributive type of way for me. It was bizarre, this amalgamated crew that gathered so efficaciously out of nowhere. You can't get a minority to sacrifice one hour of their meaningless life to attend a political meeting that might change their materialistic wish-fulfillment fantastic infatuations of easily ascending the radical technologically stacked and contrived ladder of opportunity for a gerrymandered chance at squashing other minority competitors attempting to master social upward mobility; but I'll be goddamned if they won't declare collective, somewhat chaotically organized presence at a street fight that in the near distance won't achieve anything worth achieving. The black dude was the leader, the dude I went after was white trash, or a coyote perhaps, and a bunch of little spic greasy bastards behind both of them backing them up. Santa Fe really is a diverse town. Black men, much less black women, were rarely ever seen in Santa Fe before this place became a center of cash and homosexuality, I inappropriately thought at this moment. I don't have any problem with a black person being black. I didn't and don't have any friends that are black. I used to play basketball with a few black guys at The City of Santa Fe Fort Marcy Complex Recreation Center Facility, or simply, Fort Marcy. This one Bobby Brown looking chump with a slanted fade, cheap sunglasses, rented sneakers and couldn't play basketball worth a shit was a cocky bitch but harmless. This big older veteran named Initial, who claimed to be from Chicago, used to intimidate all the lanky whiteboys that showed up to play pick-up ball on weekends. He was a cocksucker when I first knew him but turned out to be a half-assed decent individual that indirectly taught me not to trust anybody. These guys or any other black guy that showed up to play would talk a lot of shit and never pass the ball, but they sure weren't better than me nor worse.

Everybody in Santa Fe jocks black people and the black people eat that shit up. Even I in the late '80s and early '90s, around the time rap music was becoming mainstream, got caught-up in the black chic that was pervading media everywhere. I used to wear this Malcolm X t-shirt and this nice black Malcolm X hat with an embroidered rainbow colored X sewn into the center until one day this haggard dirty white bitch that used to work at Fort Marcy part time as an aerobic instructor and wanna-be New Age spiritualist dancer asked me if I knew anything about Malcolm X and I answered no and she lectured that I shouldn't wear symbols or images of certain personalities, especially political ones, especially Malcolm X on my clothing unless I knew what they were about or what they stood for. I never wore the hat again.

My life has been put on pause without my consent many times, notwithstanding counting the forgotten grievances accumulating beneath a worried gaze.

The soul brother threatened to end what potential I might've possessed. He keeps jumping up and down like a pogo stick with his arms stiff hanging down on his sides, clenching his fists and ready to strike. I can smell his odor ten feet away. I never like this fuck. I used to see him around town. I remember when he first arrived in Santa Fe. He was quiet, bashful, and quite respectful toward other human beings. Then about a year later, he became a gangsta. He changed his image and started holding hands with all the spic whores in town that just love to fuck moolies. He started picking on people because he was physiologically stronger and bigger than most of his opponents and peers and took over the Eastside Locos as their leader even though most of the members of the Eastside Locos lived on the Southside of town and not the Eastside. He and SPIC fought once. He beat the shit out of SPIC and SPIC'S friends, including me, stood by and watched. SPIC held his ground except for the bruised face, swollen eyes, cut cheeks, and bleeding nose that wouldn't stop bleeding. This outsider got in my grill, spitting saliva, rapidly repeating what he was saying about the end of my existence and SPIC is the one attempting to play mediator. This planet is confusing.

The crowd kept growing and closing in on me. A low-statured greaseball tried snatching the police baton out of my left hand but I was able to tug it back into my possession. The only true cognizant moment I had during this whole affair came when I decided to slowly but assertively start to walk backward toward my car where the driver's door remained open and I felt if I could only get closer to my car I can throw this club into the car before these pricks take it away from me and use it on me. As I was attempting to move backward the guy that started the whole thing lunged at me and close fisted me on the side of the head. The hit was demure but the momentum moved me back vigorously and just a foot or two away from my vehicle. I languidly attempted to toss the baton into the driver's seat but I didn't make it because I was keeping an eye on the crowd and the dude that just hit me. The baton clanked against the sideboard of the car, fell on the pavement and rolled right into the open palms of the little greaseball that just a minute ago tried to yank it out of my hand.

That's when it was over.

The black dude pushed SPIC aside, skipped up to me, stopped, strenuously pushed right into my breastplate knocking the breath out of me, lifting me off my feet landing on my back smacking my skull on the pavement.

Life, consciousness, and love separated from my eyesight. I felt the ulcer of the world take revenge.

At that necrophilic moment the sheriff of Santa Fe County happened to be cruising by with several of his deputies. This whole incident was taking place right in front of The City of Santa Fe Police Headquarters. He put an end to the demonstration by sending the thirty or so gangstas away in their own direction and walking over to me to see if I was dead.

"Are you okay?" he asked.

"No, I'm not okay. Those guys tried to jump me. Did you see how many there were?" I stated.

"But are you okay? I just want to know if you're okay?"

"No, I'm not. One of those guys has a billy club and hit me over the head with it?" I testified.

"Oh," was his only response. By this time the wanna-be gangstas scrambled and abandoned the area.

I was shaking all over. My breathing felt like I had two pistons violently undulating under my rib cage area. The sheriff started to gather his deputies and turned his back on the scene. Everybody kind of went his or her own way except for me, bewildered and dumbfounded to a point that made me almost want to guffaw. SPIC grabbed me and guided me to the car. I asked him what happened and before I knew it I was twisting the ignition, pressing the pedal and relaxing the gearshift into drive. The traffic light turned green, probably for the fifth time since I exploded out the car.

Inside Burger King I was paranoid. I kept checking over my shoulders, looking for that mob to show up any instant. I can't believe the sheriff just sent us on our way. No arrests were made, nobody was detained, and no questions were asked. He just sent us on our way. And he knew damn well who he was dealing with because these feckless thugs that almost killed me were probably on the sheriff's watch list. He probably arrested some of them at one point or another. Gangs used to be the big issue then as they are now although in a place like Santa Fe, "gangs" or "gang members" or "gang violence" or my personal favorite, "gang-related," are well-contrived euphemisms that mean more than two spics hanging out together. This is how it reads in the law books in Santa. Serious.

These weren't gangstas in my notepad, but punks. But even punks can run amok. I was shitting bricks all afternoon because that was the first time in my life that anybody made me feel like I wasn't in control of the immediate situation. The autumnal sky grew gray clouds. The afternoon turned cool after the hot morning. "We have to fight them, we have to throw down," was all SPIC could say. I told him that I wasn't fighting anyone. Besides, how could I? My right hand was completely incapacitated and even if it wasn't, I wasn't about to take on thirty people with only SPIC as my backup. As far as I knew at this moment they were probably plotting to shoot me. I kept waiting for the drive-by, sitting there at Burger King unable to eat my lunch for my stomach was tight and upset. "Dude, I'm telling you we have to get them. We gotta get them before they get you. That black dude don't mess around. He won't stop until you either stand-up to him and throw down or he gets rid of you." I listened to SPIC and became more anxious than I already was. He was right though. I had to get them, or at least the leader, before he got me. My reputation was at hand. What reputation? My pride was insulted. I didn't even know I had it until my feet were lifted from me. I knew these wanna-be gangstas wouldn't let me get off that easy for what I did to their homeboy and the other guy's truck. Machismo was more important than reason and self-preservation.

Upon my return to school, every member of the student body seemed to have already furnished themselves with the lunch hour extravaganza. Kids I knew came up to me and asked how I was, was I hurt, did he hit me, did I hit back, and so on. Kids that seemed to have had a previous encounter with the black kid, presumably on the receiving end of his onslaught, viewed me with ingenuous admiration and insincere awe. Through the passage of their eyes I relived the agonizing history of their personal encounter with him and didn't understand whether or not I should feel apprehension or encouragement. Other irascible students mocked me and asked me when the funeral would take place.

Before the lunch hour was over a fight broke out between two unevenly matched guys. The tall one took advantage of the smaller one right away. The smaller one didn't seem too positive about being in the middle of a fight. A crowd gathered around automatically, cheering on the stronger of the two. Before the teachers in the hallway could stop it the fight concluded. The taller stronger more aggressive one decked the smaller one flat on the jawbone and knocked him down cold. I thought it was over but the smaller one surprised us all and got back up and started in pursuit of the taller guy who was already walking away in victorious pomp. Right before the smaller one could mount the turned back of the taller one, the taller one pivoted, calculated the oncoming movements of his opponent, dodged to the side when the smaller dude tried to tackle him, grabbed him by the shirt and flung him into the lockers. The smaller dude slammed hard and fell to the floor again. For sure it was over now. Instead of walking away the aggressor decided to take a few steps back, measure the distance, and right when a teacher was climbing through the thick crowd the aggressor stepped up like a football punter and kicked the guy on the floor directly in the face so hard you could hear the skin smacking the leather of the shoe and a bone break in several places. That kid lay unconscious, face down in a gathering stream of blood. The other one got away.

I wasn't comfortable at school. I didn't have anywhere else to go or at least anywhere else I could feel safe for the moment. The principal beckoned me to his office over the omnipresent loudspeakers of the intercom. Entering his sterile office, I didn't know what to expect. I had always been a problem student and visited his office on many occasions. I was familiar with the usual routine of chastisement, atonement, and release. But this meeting felt different. He approached me with gentility and expressed a solemn concern for my well-being. It wasn't the fact that it was his duty to perform such responsibilities, but more so that he was quite familiar with my assailant's history that made me feel his sentiments were genuine. He told me how this kid came from a single mother home, a mother that was attempting to raise four young children under the stench of severe poverty; he had been in and out of juvenile detention centers here in New Mexico and in his previous places of residence; he had been arrested several times for aggravated assault, breaking and entering, grand theft, weapons and drug possession, "gang-related" activities, and he had beaten the living shit out of some kid and condemned him to the intensive care unit for approximately three months. The bombardment of information suffocated me and vaporized any inklings of assurance I might've thought about harboring for the near future. Since it was the school's responsibility to look after the safety of its students, he advised me from venturing outside into the parking lot during breaks between class periods and informed me that I would have to have a police escort follow me home every day until this whole thing blows over. I didn't know how to respond. The last thing I wanted was a cop shadowing my every movement outside of school, much less inside of school because I was rapidly gaining a clientele of marijuana smokers and becoming the top provider of weed in the school. I used to sell dope to kids from the locker room while basketball practice was taking place. I received his commandment with oxymoronic relief.

The principal sent me on my way back to class when the bell for the commencement of seventh period, the final class of the day, rang. My last class for the day was basketball. I was the starting point guard of the varsity basketball team. I had to choose basketball as an elective course in order to practice before actual basketball practice began. Public school is a fuck-off epoch in one's socially controlled life. I couldn't participate in the physical exercises on the court. I was confined to the trainer's domain to soak my wrist in a hot bath, endure electric shocks, and conduct monotonous, rehabilitative techniques to hasten the healing process of my lacerated tendons. I couldn't get the incident out of my mind. When the bell rang I didn't have any idea on where I should go, what I should do, and whom I should turn to for help.

I was walking out the front doors to the gymnasium, hoping that I wouldn't be attacked. Stepping outside into the fresh air, I noticed that no one was around. I was a little late getting out of the trainer's office. Mostly all the other students that had to wait for rides were gone. The school grounds looked abandoned. There were no teachers or other adults around. I felt alone and sacred. I didn't want to go home. I didn't want to leave the premises. I didn't know how to proceed. My police escort was nowhere to be discovered. For the first time in my life I feared for my personal safety.

SPIC suddenly appeared in sweatpants and a torn, raggedy warm-up top, amplified and bolstered. I was rife with immobility and doubt. "Are you ready?" Ready for what? "To fight." What? "I went home and changed clothes to prepare for round two." What? "You should see the crowd of people out there. Everyone in school is out there waiting for you to fight that kid you almost attacked with that club." Are you serious? I can't fight. Look at my hand. "That doesn't matter, you still have your other one. You should see all the people out there. There's like a hundred people gathered out there." Out there referred to the twisting and slithering road that led to the parking lot at Capital High before it was developed into a sub-division entitled Tierra Contenta. "They're all lined-up for about a quarter of a mile. We should have sold tickets." Who else is out there? "Everybody. Almost the whole school, all those little gangstas that were there earlier and about forty more of them. I don't know where they came from, and a whole bunch of cops." Then nothing's gonna happen. Those guys aren't going to jump me with cops around. "No, but they're not planning on jumping you. I talked to the black kid and he says that all they want is for you and that other kid you attacked to fight one on one and see who wins." Then how come you're all dressed-up for battle? "You never know. Never trust a black man."

I couldn't believe what I was hearing. I was in no condition to fight, not that I wanted to fight. My actions earlier that day were committed in a complete state of momentary insanity. I didn't even remember some of the specific occurrences at the altercation. I was completely out of character at the moment and when reality finally returned I was consumed with fear. My police escort finally pulled up and asked me if I was ready to leave. I had no choice. I told SPIC to forget about brutality, I was into survival for now. He was disappointed, but understood. Driving out of the parking lot I could see the throngs of people crowded around the embankments off the main road leading out onto Airport Road. SPIC was right. Tons of people gathered around the area and according to SPIC most of them had been waiting there for at least two hours. The cluster of little wanna-be gangstas started to throw shit at my car while I was driving and one rock dented the rear fender of the passenger's side of the vehicle. I arrived home without a massacre incident and was actually pretty grateful that the police officer escorted me home and protected me. It was one of the few times I experienced something good from the police. I hate to admit it.

I was rebelling against my image that I thought I had to maintain for the benefit of my mother's career. So much for that. The five o'clock evening local news broadcast on channel thirteen announced as its lead headline: IMPORTANT WOMAN'S SON INVOLVED IN GANG FIGHT IN BROAD DAYLIGHT. Fuckin media. Always getting it wrong. It was hardly a gang fight. The news said I halted traffic for about half an hour and that the "gang" fight was brutal. My father was watching the broadcast at the time and couldn't believe what he was witnessing. My mother shortly arrived and both of them cornered me on a staircase as I was trying to flee upstairs to my bedroom. I sat on the steps and listened to them express their disappointment and betrayal. Tears began to scorch my cheeks. My father repeatedly asked what was wrong with me. Was I psycho? Didn't I have respect for the family or for myself? Why was I so prone to getting in trouble lately? What the hell was wrong with me? What was wrong with me? These five words reverberated throughout my con-of-science with impunity. I cried and cried and deserved every tear that tore through my soul. My mother was more compassionate, but tremendously concerned. I realized that they did care and I was not alone.

The only thing that can save me is my writing, my art. I am constantly attempting to lose myself, consequently losing my mind. The room surrounds me, spins dizzy and I feel faint. I try to remember moments in my life that could've existed in someone else's memory.

The next day I purchased a gun. I walked into first period at school, asked some Guera from Eldorado if she knew where I could get a gun, she said yes without hesitation and seemed quite enthused about the prospect of helping me obtain such a counterproductive criminal device. The following weekend I met some cat that offered me a stolen pistol lifted from some stupid cop. I rehearsed it well inside my head.

I would do it like a white man. I would undertake reconnaissance for a breathable fallacy in order to obtain necessary information, not to exceed the hapless position of being identified. I would select him at his weakest. Firstly, I'd find out where he lives. Then, I would take note of any family members, especially his mother and sisters, if any, and young children that he may or may not care about. I would find out their names, their places of work, their most frequented establishments in the city, their friends and associates and the license number on the vehicles they may or may not operate. I would track and record his every move within the city limits. Find out where he stays, where he plays, where he hangs out and who with. After enough information has been reconnoitered, I'd move forward, lay low, and plot his assassination. I'd catch him one night when he's partying, getting drunk, screwing some slut and vulnerable as a little kitten licking milk from a saucer. Since he was a gangsta, I'd figure he'd be getting home on one of these drunken nights late in the early morning when the wind chills in the summer and the stars seem brighter even as they disappear into the dawn's unbearable maroon canvass. I'd be waiting, unseen by some object nearby that would provide cover. As soon as he wallows up to the front door, that's the moment I run behind him, put the cold steel barrel of the cop's gun to his head and splatter his brain matter all over the peek hole. I would get out of the area immediately, disassemble the gun in an out of way open field or mountainous area, bury the parts in different places after I had cleaned my fingerprints even though there wouldn't be any for I would have been using gloves, black gloves since it was nighttime, and then I would drive off to a big city already previously designated and leave the country never to return. All necessary arrangements and precautions would have already been taken care of beforehand.

I don't care to give away all my ideas in full detail just in case I ever do really murder somebody. God knows there are plenty of candidates... and my list keeps growing every day. Besides, I don't desire to give the stupid cops out there a head start. These are only my musings, beggared and derailed, lost in apparition, bemoaned throughout eternity like a wasted life. So much hunger, so little appreciation. Too many tourists preparing the onslaught of slave master relationship and occupation. The only reason I didn't kill that sonofabitch is because I figured sooner or later he would fuck himself over because that was the type of individual he was. Self-destructive. He was not worth the ruining of my life. If I kill him I would surly be caught and sent to prison for a very long time and prison would ruin me. Nobody gets away with murder in Santa Fe. Even as stupid as the cops are here, the criminals are even stupider, except for developers.

Several years later when I was way past myself, I read in the newspaper about him. He and the guy in the passenger seat of that truck I ambushed, the guy who started the commotion that day, both went on a rampaging crime spree that crossed three state lines. They were caught in a neighboring state after they had robbed eight people by gunpoint, taken four of them hostage, raping and severely beating one elderly woman, and trouncing one young lad unconscious. In the primordial morning before the birds whistle and the branches twitch, in a rural area inside a small farmhouse surrounded by a field more hospitable to mice, a family of three wondered if they would witness the end of the year. He had a shotgun and the other a semi-automatic pistol. The S.W.A.T. team had just arrived. The standoff lasted approximately five hours. Shortly after the noon hour, for reasons no one will ever know, he ran out the back door about one hundred yards from the farmhouse while his compatriot hustled interference, knelt down abruptly in the damp weeds with tears strolling down his ebony cheeks looking up to the cloudless sky sticking the wide barrel of the shotgun into his desiccated mouth and pulled the trigger once.

Part II: Birth

Spirit of Madness

"Dying shamans prophesy that a spirit of madness takes over a magician undergoing ecstatic journeys to the underworld to retrieve a soul that has been lost."

5:13 p.m. Wednesday, May 8th:

Last night I was with this chick trying to get a hard-on after three years or so of negligent abstinence, leaving her house around 11:00 p.m. The only reason I went out there was because I second thoughted that I might be able to get a piece of ass if I tried cordially like an Argentine gentleman. She had come by my house earlier. I forgot that the first night I met her the first night I spent with her laid out in her mauve Volkswagen van on Alto Street, I had no choice but to wake up next morning her already awake. We didn't fuck or anything. We held each other all through the mid-spring early morning. I had no choice but to allow her to drop me off at my current residential address even though I suppose I could've walked home since I didn't live too far from where we were parked. I wanted her to know where I lived so she could drop in on me whenever she pleased without calling first. About a week later when I had the house all to myself--a big dark hidden haunted house ancient sinister adobe palace on top of the hill overlooking the inferior minions--she came walking by with her mutt looking for me. She banged on the door. And then she banged some more. The curtains were drawn and I could see her sinuosity. I wanted to open the door but I didn't. I let her knock until her knuckles got sore. She persisted for quite a while to my vagrant surprise. I stood on the opposite side of the front brown solid wooden door standing on the mud floors silent, listening to her arrhythmic rapport.

"Hello?"

She called out soothingly several times and I didn't care. I honestly wasn't sure if I really wanted to open the door or not. I felt paranoid. I am paranoid. I sleep with the centipedes and bathe with dirt molecules. My clothes are used and I can't afford to purchase shampoo sometimes. Nonetheless, she left me beleaguered. I started running around the living room in tiny pirouettes, smiling to myself pulling on my hair. I noticed she stopped knocking. I peeked out the window. She was walking down the driveway up the neighboring driveway so I rushed upstairs up the small saltillo orange-red tile stairs trying to catch a glimpse of her as she headed back toward the dog park. There were trails that led to an open dirt park called Ortiz Park. It used to be a landfill in the old days behind my house for years before the City of Santa Fe decided to convert it into what is known only in local dirthead circles as a dog park. This is a place where if you're someone that lives on the Eastside of town you can bring you stupid little dogs, or obnoxious big dogs, to roam around freely as if they were human or the equivalent of you. They invade our town, then our neighborhood, then our lives. One of my delightful pastime engagements is to take my vicious mutts back there and terrorize these bastards and their little dogs too. The bastards constantly get upset, yell at my dogs and try beating them with sticks or whipping them with their leashes or throw rocks at them but my dogs are too swift and smarter than the dumb asses and then they yell at me and lecture and scold me then I threaten them looking like a mean surly greaser. Then they leave without incident. I'm positive animal control and the stupid police are looking for me but they'll never be able to prosecute since I euthanized my animals last year.

This broad resided just a few streets down on Ephraim Street. I watched her upstairs. Then I went upstairs again and watched her again.

She looked good. I didn't feel like taking my dog out. I think I already took him out earlier but I can't recollect. I decided to chase her.

By the time I got my shit together and got out there to follow her it was a biting early summer wind beating my sensitive skin on my face turning it dry red making me want to go back inside. I pursued and pursued and came up with nothing. I remember going all over those broken beer bottle strewn pieces of multi-colored glass hills passing all sorts of ugly individuals but I didn't see her.

I took the dog back and walked over to her house through what once appeared to be a snippet of civilization. I was already feeling hot physiologically. I went anyways. I toked some weed before I left and almost got lost on my way to her house even though I've lived in this Torreon neighborhood all my pathetic life. The streets remind me of an old Mexican town that I've never actually seen. Pink houses, light blue, lime green, mustard yellow, open porch spaces surrounded by gross chain link fences with some starving dog attached to a chain or rope with threads coming off unable to escape bondage barking at you for the full length of the entrance to the yard. Little brown unwashed children running around laughing as if they were possessed by childish demons causing trouble and fun because it's only fun when you get in trouble. The streets were calm at dusk.

I finally reached her rental unit and met her roommate and some African immigrant her roommate was screwing and hiding from immigration officials. I didn't stay too long. We drank, we sang, we talked, we took our shirts off and hugged each other and kissed each other's skin softly and then I went home. I've been smoking a lot of weed lately. I've also been drinking a lot of alcohol and worrying like every day every hour every second crazy about this chick I fucked several years ago without a condom that I didn't know. It was a one-night stand. It was a stranger. I abstained. Here I am chasing another. Life sucks.

Lately the marijuana just hadn't been doing me right. I'd smoke it and get hot like a fever floating around inside my forehead making me dizzy and tired and nauseous. The guy I used to buy from is a schmuck who sits around his adobe hut all day in the dark watching Fox News.

The early summer late spring chill air was cool patting the nape of my neck. In heaven untamable bassoon horns must sound romantic to the wanderer and the childless. On my way back I felt weak climbing over the hill that leads to my house. No one was there.

I got in, closed the door behind me while flicking on the light switch to my left to see how to stick the key into the keyhole figuring out how to turn it and lock it and secure myself against the cannibals out there. Instinctively I bounce up the small saltillo tile orange red stairs. On the second floor I realize that I still have some weed left over. Up the brown hollow wooden steps leading to my room on the third tier locating my stash pulling it out amongst the gratuitous junk mixing it up crunching the compacted bud crumbling particles of cannabis onto a *High Times* magazine I located. I roll a joint and decide to watch *Schindler's List* in the master bedroom.

I woke up the next morning feeling ill. Tired mostly. I decided to go for a run on the trails behind my house. The sun was relentless by mid-morning. I hadn't run in about five or six years and I smoke too much weed and drink too much liquor. My allergies been kicking up lately. Pollen, dust, pets, mold, air, anything. It is my patriotic duty to pop a pill each day in the name of Pfizer the manufacturer of Benadryl the light yellowish tint dye-free translucent kind. I can't tolerate the old-school pink example. I hate living like this. I'm getting fat. I run, cross-country style, for about a half hour and nearly die barely breathing feeling faint halfheartedly swooning sweating like a fountain upon my return. Immediately I light up half of the joint I didn't finish the night before while watching *Schindler's List*. Turning the movie back on was not a problem. I had left off where Schindler is giving water to the Jews in the railroad boxcars who are dying of thirst under the hot sun baking them suffocating them and Schindler puts his reputation on the line in front of the Nazi pigs just laughing on the sideline when all of an instant I sense a moving rush swiftly swimming up my arteries around my heart to my head making the world feel cold outside and heated inside. My brain submitted. My heart rate increased then decreased and increased again and then decreased again until I couldn't tell whether I felt a pulse anymore. I could feel the blood expanding throughout my upper body then falling back down then rising again then falling back down. I felt hot. A fever was coming on. I know it. I can feel it. I put my hand to my head. It feels like a fever. I feel hot. I freak out anytime I get ill and nobody is around to either escort me to the hospital in case of an emergency, or better yet, to kill me. Where's the thermometer? I don't think we have a thermometer. I won't be able to measure whether or not I have a fever. I put my hand to my head again. What happens if I get sick and nobody is around? It's okay. I've been through this before, remember, back in the college days I got sick plenty of times and took care of myself and nursed myself and consoled myself and convalesced so there's nothing to worry about. I thought of when I was a child playing on the Gonzales Elementary schoolyard playgrounds on the miscellaneous equipment outside of school hours; sliding down the monumental slides climbing back up backwards swinging silly recklessly free leaping from the black plastic chained swing as it swooshed forward thrusting me forcefully. No thermometer. Get a wet rag, a wet rag, that'll do it. I got a rag, soaked it in cold below temperature water for a long time. The ignorant sunlight stepping into the house from the windows blackened slightly and my knees twitched prepared to capitulate. My lungs feel obliterated. Head tickled. I caught myself before I collapsed. I need to lie down.

As I lay on the bed in the master bedroom during mid-morning some of the birds have stopped singing but the summer mist is still soothing undulating below my perspiring lower small of my back before the afternoon heat settles in.

10:00 a.m. Thursday, May 9th:

The neighbor who lives above me should shoot his dogs in the head. They never cease barking, especially in the morning or when a stupid cop's siren comes howling through the neighborhood for no goddamn reason. I'm paralyzed, prostrate, and glum. I can't feel the lower half of my body much less the upper half. Breathe slowly. That's it, calm down. Take in a long deep slow breath through your mouth, release it slowly through the nose. That's it. Breathe. Slower. Breathe. Oh god my heart is speeding. It's going through discombobulated palpitations. I feel sweat. It's cold. It's cold in here. I can feel my facial skin turning pale. What day is it? Thursday. Shit. I don't have anybody to call if something happens to me. I have no friends. No way am I calling paramedics because you can't trust hospital staff and I can't afford it anyways. It's all right. You'll be all right. Just calm down and come down from this high a bit. Let yourself go. This has never happened before. Calm down. Breathe. Take a deep breath. That's it. Enjoy the high. The crucifixion of Christ is mythology utilized for secular power enhancement and nobody cares about the massacre of Rwanda anymore. We put away our memories like dishes after being scrubbed once. This can't be happening to me what I don't know what is happening to me the world must be moving around outside as I'm inside stuck lying down when I had plans to take a bus downtown and see if I could spot strange distant tourist girls to try and seduce and haul home. You can still follow through on your plans if you wait a bit till you come down. I'm not coming down though, the high is increasing and the tight squeezing between my temples is tightening tighter there's flashes before my eyes my vision is hazy, cloudy, I can't move. I can't make a decision. What am I supposed to do?

10:01 a.m. Thursday, May 9th:

To be consumed with your self is a harmless blanched relationship with ghosts. Patronize my flesh. Listless wish commenced for sacred conditioned distribution of commodities not needed in gentrified communities where nobody knows anybody anymore and nobody can trust anybody anymore. I don't desire to care anymore. Reckless excursions have left lesions of multiplying fears embedded in my brain. What's that on the vigas? I shouldn't take shrooms anymore. A couple of weeks ago I purchased an ounce of cheap mushrooms from the same schmuck I used to purchase cheap swanky Mexican weed from weed that was probably stuck in some wetback's ass for several weeks before it hit the northern part of New Mexico. From this second forward I vow never again to drink one single drop of alcohol; to never again inhale soft tetrahydrocannabinol smoke for recreation or re-creation; never again to trip and feel the heaviness of earth laugh flamboyantly taunting my many misunderstandings. I will never do this again.

12:00 noon. Thursday, May 9th:
I'm still lying here.

2:37 p.m. Thursday, May 9th:
I'm still lying here.

4:45 p.m. Thursday, May 9th:
I'm still lying here. Silent

6:00 p.m. Thursday, May 9th:
I'm crying. Life has forsaken me. The decisions I make are so powerful that I can cause tsunamis on the island shores of Indonesia while I'm cooking fried vegetables massaging my thighs methodically. I don't know what to do. I didn't come down from my high. This has never happened to me before. I could try and get up because my legs are sore and numb; my back is aching so much I can sense the ripples in my spine become rubber; my neck is stiff; and I've peed twice in my boxers.

The sun is starting to go down. Nighttime will be here soon and I haven't done all the daily chores. It's just the dog and I and I bet he's starving. I got to feed him. He hasn't been outside all day. I smell shit somewhere in the house.

After a few more minutes I rise from the bed and my head is still spinning. I'm starting to feel artificial. I've lost all direction of time and the gravitational pull of the globe means nothing to me. Your words are lost because they're meaninglessness. Subtle gospel chants on the television channel 23--the evangelical Christian gimmick carnival arousing the desperate masses. How did it get on this channel? Who is this fool and what happened to *Schindler's List*?

"...and God said to Abraham, 'if you don't get busy with that sacrifice you jive turkey, I'm a gonna smite you with self-righteousness'."

"Yes sir," responds the crowd.

"...busy people, crowded streets, you meet someone to find out they have a past that's none of yo' business. And Jesus said, 'let not the apostolic become the apostle, but henceforth the desecration you console inelegant shall reign in fury mercilessly.' And the apostles followed and the rich became greedy and business became money priority before social concern of others that could benefit you more in your busy everyday endeavors that don't have to be underhanded. I'm not a good man!"

"No sir," rang the crowd in perfect unison.

"...and still my brothers and my sisters continue to deface the culture and disgrace the race having more than an afternoon holiday jamboree on all fours. I'm telling you I believe. I believe Jesus is coming and we can rejoice like the rivers when their released from a damn;'

"Yes!" banged like a shotgun.

"But if you listen to the devil..."

"Yes sir."

"I'm telling you. If you listen to the Devil..."

"Amen."

"That Satan..."

"Sing it."

"That Lucifer..."

"Say it."

"...that fiend that tried to tempt the Lord into seeking power here on Earth even though he knew he knew that everything is temporal and perhaps this existence is nothing more than a moment preparing us for the next step..."

"YES!"

"...the next rapture..."

"Hell-e-luuh-ya!"

"...the next level..."

"Praise the mother!"

"...and the foot is still on my neck; and the eyes are still on my back; and the food is still too high-priced for the average consumer to consume. Quit blaming me Satan! That's what you gotta say when that devil sonofabiii--"

I turned the channel off cuz it was aggravating my headache. I don't normally watch those channels. They scare me. I didn't need to be more scared than I was right now. I'm just gonna go feed the dog, eat and go to sleep. I don't feel well.

3:35 a.m. Friday, May 10th:

The eyelids shutter wide open. You know right away that you're not going to be able to go back to sleep. You get up and walk around the brick floor of the room you occupy for now and wonder. I'm tired of asking the big questions. I've lost connection with the outside world for quite a while now. All I do is swarm inside this house like a fish in a cesspool. The outside world looks plastic every time I peek out the windows. I think I'll read a book. What book was I reading? I think I was reading Kafka's *The Trial*. Better not. I don't even know what's going on in my head right now so I don't think I should continue reading that. I'm scared. I'm gonna lie down and close my eyes and try real hard to go back to sleep. Last night I went to bed at 9:43 p.m. and turned and tossed until I started dozing off around 1:59 a.m. but didn't fall asleep until 2:22 a.m.

5:15 a.m. Friday, May 10th:

I'm afraid I'll never be able to fall asleep again. I was once scared before. It was the day of my birth. Inside the womb ensconced in the threatening decidua oncoming quickly for the sake of discovering why I had to be trapped inside this anatomical incorrectness. Powerful like a drunk gorilla, my pubic hairs hide every time I surmise something is happening horrible. Uncontrollable is more like it. I should call Emergency. Not yet. I should rise but I don't want to. I don't want to rise out of bed anymore. The sun should be coming up soon. I can hear the early birds commence the nest.

10:00 a.m. Friday, May 10th:
I turned on the TV then off and just lie there with the window above my head open blowing in some cool wind. I have no appetite. I don't feel like drinking anything. May the days pass forth before I find myself hidden in a judicious premonition. I feel like you feel when you're hung over even though I haven't had a drink in several days. God hates me. Jesus desires to molest me. Allah doesn't acknowledge my naked superiority. King David wasn't real. People are killing people all over the world. There are riots and movements of ideas we can't contain.

10:05 a.m. Friday, May 10th:
I managed to phone my auntie and persuade her to bring me a sandwich from the defunct Noon Whistle, but I was unsuccessful in convincing her that I was sick. I haven't eaten anything since Wednesday night.

10:07 a.m. Friday, May 10th:
When is she going to arrive?

10:10 a.m. Friday, May 10th:
I think she said around noon.

10:40 a.m. Friday, May 10th:
When is she going to arrive? I can't wait this long. I think I'll get out of bed.

10:41 a.m. Friday, May 10th:
Returned to bed.

10:43 a.m. Friday, May 10th:
The dog must be starving. I can't remember the last time I fed him.

11:00 a.m. Friday, May 10th:
What's on the brain dead monitor? Don't turn it on! Where is she?

11:01 a.m. Friday, May 10th:
When is she going to arrive?

11:11 a.m. Friday, May 10th:
I can't ever venture outside these adobe walls any more. The sun is too close to the earth. Two minutes exposed to it and I start feeling sick. The wind irritates my cheeks even when it is not blowing. Everybody that is living right now is stupid. Everybody is pretending to be something they can never be. They live by a label granted to them by their peers they call friends that don't really care about their well-being. I have no friends or anybody I can rely on in this world. I am alone. Nobody cares about me. I don't care about myself. I disregard my health by eating at fast food establishments all the time. I can't afford to buy groceries at Wild Oats or Whole Foods not that I would even if I could because I can't stand the kinds of people that shop there on a frequent basis. They're all a bunch of self-centered, egomaniacal, inarticulate, rude jerks. Anybody that drives a motor vehicle is a jerk. Anybody that smokes cigarettes and blows the smoke in my direction is a jerk.

11:59 a.m. Friday, May 10th:
Anybody that has sex is a mistake; anybody that breast feeds is reluctant; anybody that body builds is homosexual; anybody that is homosexual is fixated; anybody that belongs to a religion is stupid, the

cops are stupid, the bureaucrats are stupid, similar to the dirt that builds up under your fingernails when you haven't clipped them in quite a while and when you do finally clip them the moldy dirt emits a peculiar kind of odor that smells like sweaty toes. Other people's children are all brats because people shouldn't be having children anymore. Why are all these stupid people breeding stupid children who are just going to turn into stupid adults like their stupid parents. Everybody is a slave except for me because right now I'm confined to this bed with the same clothes I had on yesterday and I didn't take a shower today. I didn't take a shower yesterday. I don't plan on taking one tomorrow. I don't like taking showers besides I'm contributing in a positive way to my community and the environment since Santa Fe is still stuck in a seven year drought for the past twenty years and we are constantly bombarded with warnings in every public restroom facility in almost every business in town that conserving water is always in season and that is why when I walk around the city around midnight to early morning by myself draped in all black I turn on all the spigots I can spot protruding from the side of a home only on the Eastside and just let the water waste because that's the type of individual I am.

12:00 noon Friday, May 10th:

Where is she? She said she'd be here around noon and now it's noon and she's not around. Where is she? Where is she supposed to be? She doesn't work that far away. I'm starving. I can't remember the last time I ate.

12:01 p.m. Friday, May 10th:
Where is she?

12:01 p.m. Friday, May 10th:
Where is she?

12:02 p.m. Friday, May 10th:
Fuckin bitch.

12:47 p.m. Friday, May 10th:

Finally. I hear a car. It's pulling up the driveway. I get out of bed and my head spins and I nearly black out. I fall back to the bed and lie there. I try it again. I get out of the sticky sheets and feel exceptionally frail. I look out the window. It is she. Somehow my underwear has managed to come off.

1:33 p.m. Friday, May 10th:

But please auntie stay. "I can't" Why not? "I have to go back to work" Can't you take off? "No" Please? "No" I don't feel good. "What's the matter?" I don't know. I have a fever, here, check and see if I have a fever. "I don't feel anything." But I do I know I do. "It's all in your head." I feel weak. "You'll feel better now that you ate." Will you take me to the hospital? "For what?" I don't feel well. "It's all in your head. I have to go." Can I call you if anything happens? "What's going to happen?" I don't know. "Well, I'm going back home tonight and it's an hour away so I don't think I'll be able to help you if anything happens." Thanx. "Well, just rest and you'll feel better. I'll check on you later on." You promise? "Yes" You sure? "Yes. Now go upstairs and lie down." But I've been in bed for more than twenty-four hours? "Well, read a book or something." I'm unable to. The words on the page won't stand still. "Then go walk the dog." I'm afraid to venture outside. "Then smoke some mota or something. I got to go back to work. I'll see you later." She quickly crumpled-up her sandwich wrapper, downed the remnants of her soda pop as I noticed her jugular pump twice pushing the toxins southbound towards the pit of her stomach, stood up out of the chair she was sitting on, walked over to the trash receptacle and threw the contents away then grabbed her keys in a hurry and was already slamming the driver's door to her automobile before I could ask her if she had any barbiturates.

1:45 p.m. Friday, May 10th:

This is the longest day of my life. The hours don't pass. Why do I even look at the red digital numerals on the face of the clock? There is no time. I think I'll just lie here with my eyes shut.

3:45 p.m. Friday, May 10th:
The heat is a biosphere overshadowing my resting body. There are very few cool breezes left in the atmosphere. My limbs are trembling. The hair bristles at the end of my pigment evolve erect because I am cold all over. I have goose pimples on my triceps on my calves on my neck on my nipples in my soul. I think I'm going to die.

5:00 p.m. Friday, May 10th:
They said it would only take them a few days. I think they're supposed to be returning tonight.

5:11 p.m. Friday, May 10th:
I received a phone call from them. They told me they wouldn't be coming in tonight but that they would make it in tomorrow night.

5:13 p.m. Friday, May 10th:
I can hold out for tonight.

5:21 p.m. Friday, May 10th:
I think.

5:55 p.m. Friday, May 10th:
A lucky surprise. My auntie returns to check up on me and decides to take me out for dinner, help me feed the dog, and even takes me to rent a couple of videos and keep me company for a while. She says she even might stay over tonight. There is a God (as long as I get what I want).

7:00 p.m. Friday, May 10th:
We rented *The Score* with DeNiro, Norton, and Brando; *Pollock* with

Ed Harris as the reckless artist; and some stupid movie called *Pax* or some shit like that with Kevin Spacey as some stupid alien that comes down to Earth and shows the earthlings what living in peace is all about or some stupid morality tale that made me gag.

7:25 p.m. Friday, May 10th:
We bought some steaks, corn on the cob, and potatoes and brought it back to my house. While I was out in that disgusting ritual more commonly referred to as society, in an Albertson's grocery store no less, my feet began to buzz and I could tell people were looking at me as if I was sick and contagious. My auntie said it was all in my head.

We decided to barbecue and my uncle, her brother, decided to join us for dinner since he was getting off work.

The early evening sank the sun as the moon commenced its inarticulate sermon. One star appeared near the crescent and I propositioned a wish:

> *Star Light, Star Bright;*
> *Please make my wish*
> *Come true tonight.*
> *I wish I may, I wish I might*
> *Star Light, Star Bright.*

I can't remember how it goes not that I ever did.

I wish for this feeling to end. I wish to fall asleep tonight. I wish for someone to stay the evening with me. I wish to eat this delicious food. I know this is more than one wish but I have to wish for something because you see I still feel hot even though my auntie and now my uncle say that I don't have a fever and I don't look sick and that it is all in my head but I still feel weird like I never came off my high from puffing that joint yesterday. I think something is happening to me. I feel so scared. I feel so frightened and I don't know why. I can't stand or sit still or calm down. I wish I could kill myself.

7:48 p.m. Friday, May 10th:
I couldn't finish my meal. Hardly ate anything. I haven't eaten since I can't recollect when. I can't sit still.

8:00 p.m. Friday, May 10th:
We decide to watch *Pax*. I think I am really going to be sick. I'm buzzing all over the place and I can't sit or lie still.

9:55 p.m. Friday, May 10th:
The movie is almost over, thank God. Throughout the monotonous torture of the movie I've been trying to come up with something to try and make at least one of them stay or at least watch another movie. I can tell both of them want to leave. Don't go, please don't go.

10:15 p.m. Friday, May 10th:
They left.

10:31 p.m. Friday, May 10th:
I try to watch *The Score* but it turns out that that is another stupid movie that is making me want to throw-up so I turn on the television programming instead but everything on the television anymore makes me want to throw up and fuels an inexplicable fear inside me. The claustrophobia is tormenting so I turn it off and throw my clothes off my body and run around the house stark naked screaming and yelling for someone to help me. I think I'm losing my mind because my body now feels like it is overwrought with adrenaline and the energy can't escape and I can't sweat no more and the dog is barking right in my grill and every girlfriend that I ever had I left because I treated them all like shit because I was afraid like I am now at this minute not knowing why I'm afraid.

12:00 midnight Saturday, May 11th:

I can't fall asleep. I am awake.

1:00 a.m. Saturday, May 11th:

I am really awake.

2:01 a.m. Saturday, May 11th:

I turn to the left; I toss to the right; I position myself back on my back to stare into darkness.

3:33 a.m. Saturday, May 11th:

This must be what the experts refer to as insomnia.

3:34 a.m. Saturday, May 11th:

We were throwing rocks at each other all day. I'd hit him then he'd peg me. Mom would yell at us from inside to cut that shit out. We didn't stray too far from the front yard. We chased each other around the basketball pole, the strewn lumber, and the parked cars that didn't work. Why we decided to throw rocks at each other I do not know. We were just little kids bored out of our minds. He is two years my elder. I think he started it but it was most likely I who was the one that started it because that is the type of individual I am. We made it to the top of the hill on my father's property line. Separated by a row of ten-foot junipers we kept thrusting stones over the brush like artillery aimed at nothing in particular. Primarily we kept to tiny pebbles because the young humanitarian inside both of us didn't desire to injure the other. Since we couldn't see one another it was very difficult to make a connection. Finally, after about twenty minutes, he landed a sharp pink pebble that struck dead center in the middle of my cranium and felt like it pierced right through. Revenge is a motive seldom understood. The object of the arms race is to discover and utilize bigger weapons in order to subdue your enemy and rule forever. I violated the rules of engagement prematurely and cupped inside my hand a rock the size of a golf ball. Without really knowing where he was standing on the opposite end of the juniper shield I catapulted the rock over the brush higher than I expected. I was only five years old at the time so my strength took me by surprise. The rock seemed to travel a lot further than the force I put behind it and subsequently felt when I let it go. It floated into the air like an inebriated hawk ascending the sky and I had no idea where it would land. It landed on his head. I knew this because he let out a scorching cry and our mutual barrage ceased all but thirty minutes. The smart and compassionate thing to do would have been to walk over to the other side of the evergreen fortress and see if he was okay. Instead, I just stood there overtly languishing in my concern but covertly relishing my fatalistic precision. The war zone fell silent. I wasn't quite sure what to do. I spotted an even bigger rock the size of a honeydew melon and began to bend down to see if it was too heavy for me to lift much less throw over the ten foot trees and try and hit him again. I wanted to see if he was still alive.

It felt like the voice of an angel speaking directly to you. For some reason, as I was bending over to lift this petite boulder, I just felt like I should second-guess my modus operandi, stop what I was attempting to do for the moment and look over my shoulder. As I stood proper, twisted my shoulders, turned my neck and tilted my gaze heavenwards I saw only a black space like a television set turned off.

I could hear my brother laughing overindulgently on the other side of the trees as I pulled back my hands from my sobbing face. Apparently he must've been thinking the same thing I was and beat me to it. The rock that slammed my face was even bigger than the one I was about to pick up. It didn't hurt at first, just a slight sting. But when I had my hands about a foot away from my eyes all I saw was red. My hands were soaked in my own blood. I released a scream that sounded more appalling than an Amazonian monkey being butchered by a stone hammer. The blood trickled in slow motion from my fingertips onto the ground. I went into shock and ran, looking for someone to console me. My brother received the worst beating of his life.

4:34 a.m. Saturday, May 11ᵗʰ:

It takes you nearly forty-five minutes to get out of your car parked in the parking lot before you walk through the automatic sliding front doors up to the receptionist and confirm your fake name you gave them over the phone when you made the appointment. You look around the sitting area in front of the receptionist's chest level desk hoping you don't see anyone that could recognize you. The receptionist is unsympathetic to your worried gaze. She doesn't even want to make skin-to-skin contact with you just in case. She confirms your appointment, gives you a number and some papers to fill out while you wait. Name, address, date of birth, occupation, male or female, age, how many sexual partners have you had in the last year, have you performed oral sex, have you performed anal sex, do you have multiple sex partners, have you ever had a sexually transmitted infection before, do you have any of these symptoms on your genitals: rash, blisters, warts, chancre; do you have any of these other symptoms: rash on your hands or feet or both; blisters around the mouth; constant fatigue, constant fever, lethargy, nausea, vomiting, itching in the anus, itching beneath the scrotum, sores in your mouth, redness, hot flashes, loss of appetite, Kaposi sarcoma, pneumonia, loss of hair, blindness, consistent pain during sexual intercourse, a whitish, yellowish, green discharge emanating from the urethra or the vagina, painful urination, pain in the lower abdomen, shortness of breath, yellow skin, jaundice, paranoia; is there any reason you might think you have contracted a sexually transmitted infection; how long has it been since your last sexual contact; are you into bestiality; did you use a condom; are you allergic to penicillin; and so on until you've filled out over three pages of questions that break you down and make you feel more humiliated than you were when you first walked in. It takes about an hour or so before the clinician, not a doctor, can see you depending on whether or not there are other people waiting for the same reason. On Fridays there seems to be more people getting tested than on the weekdays. Only the indigent come to the County. The female clinician, it is almost always a female in

Santa Fe, finally calls your number and you stand up in front of the other waiting degenerates who are pretending not to look at you. The fear is indescribable. It is worse than entering jail for the first time. The clinician escorts you to a private room far in the back of the building. She sits you down and opens a file. The first time I went it was a gorgeous clinician with red hair and big tits that did the initial briefing and I knew that God hated me. The clinician asks you the same kinds of questions and the same number of questions you just answered on paper only it is a lot harder to confess and give honest answers to the embarrassing questions even though you know you should in order to try and receive as accurate a diagnosis as possible. After the interrogation the clinician parades you to a dingy examination room that doesn't have all the required equipment one would find in a doctor's office of private practice. The clinician then leaves you alone to ponder your decision-making process and what you value in life. There are way more important and enjoyable things in life than sex. I'm just not sure what they are. After about thirty minutes another clinician posing as a nurse comes in and tells you to pull your pants down to your ankles. You comply and she immediately squeezes your nuts and tugs and yanks your penis every which way. She then straps on a rubber glove, tells you to bend over and gives you a cavity search. Then she tells you to turn around again. You start to pull up your pants but she asserts that she's not finished yet leave your pants down. You feel more vulnerable with your pants around your ankles than you do completely naked. While you're standing there half-bare feeling the flush from the open window blow past your country bumpkin, you see the clinician pull out a silver instrument about the size of a ball point pen with a hook on the end. She tells you that this might sting a bit, count to ten. This procedure is known as the gonorrhea scrape. I've had a boulder slammed in my face, kicked in the nuts thousands of times, slashed wrist, punctured skin with sharp object countless times in all sorts of places, plenty of bee stings, bit by a centipede that wouldn't let go of my bare foot as I screamed and tried shaking it off while taking a shower, foot squashed by a horse, thrown off a horse, banged head on pavement, cracked skull, lots of tubular things rammed up my rectum, sick to the stomach so many times, hair yanked from their roots, poked in the eyes, broke my nose, beaten to a raisin, kicked in the face, arms twisted and given Indian burns, burnt my flesh over a flame on all different parts of the body, broke my arm, my leg, sprained ankles, sunburn, tattooed, pierced, tonsils removed, appendix removed, branded, upturned nail under the bottom of the foot, ears pulled to opposite ends, alcohol poisoning, went head-on with a linebacker and injured my spine and knocked the breath out of me, hit by a car, landed on face numerous times, shot my foot, injected needles, overdose, frostbite, dog bite, cat clawed, road rash, scratched, bitten by people, teeth pulled, gums drilled, migraines, acute diarrhea. I've even smashed my thumb in a vice until it swelled and turned so purple I thought it was a plum. I have had my share of physical pain and I can say that there is no physical and/or psychological pain as excruciating, tormenting, and merciless than the gonorrhea scrape. You don't want to look. You look up to the ceiling counting to ten as fast as you can but once the hook enters your urethra you feel it scraping against the mucous membrane. You can't even cry. It is truly horrible. All you think about the whole time it is happening is that you will never have unprotected sex again. The ten seconds lasts infinitely. As soon as the scrape is over that is when the real pain begins. The loose skin, or the slit, at the tip of the urethra swells and stings for days. You dread the moment every time you have to piss. You would have been better off contracting gonorrhea. Forget about an orgasm. You can't even walk straight for days. It hurts every time your penis brushes up against the cotton of your underwear. It sucks! It really, really sucks.

After that they just send you over to another clinician who extracts two pints of blood from your system, one for HIV and the other for syphilis, and then they send you on your way weak as a cancer patient and utterly disoriented. Two to four weeks later you return for your results and if you're found positive you become emotionally paralyzed and subject to government monitoring and experimentation and all sorts of therapeutic treatment that's just going to make you feel worse than you already do at the moment. You become a statistic. Your life is over.

5:47 a.m. Saturday, May 11th:

I turn to the right; I toss to the left; I throw myself onto my stomach and plow my left cheek into the pillow staring at the wall.

7:25 a.m. Saturday, May 11th:

I stink.

7:52 a.m. Saturday, May 11th:

I feel hot. I don't think I'll ever be able to fall asleep again. My body smells like a dead bird baking in the sun for days combined with the pungent stench a squashed stink bug gives off.

7:59 a.m. Saturday, May 11th:

I should kill myself.

8:00 a.m. Saturday, May 11th:

I realize I need salvation so I turn the TV on. It's the Christian channel--channel 23.

A cartoon! I love cartoons, even as an adult. I grew up on cartoons. I was molded on cartoons. Cartoons are the only shows on television that make any sense and depict life in a more realistic fashion than the human shows (i.e.- *The Simpsons*). Only this wasn't *The Simpsons*. This was a weird-ass religious cartoon about some bible story. After watching it for a few squints, strictly out of curiosity, I discover it is about David and The Lion. Is it David or Daniel? Personally I've never read the Old Testament tale so I'm not too familiar with the narrative so I figure this cartoon might be able to fill me in on what I'm lacking. All I know about the fable is that David, or Daniel, we'll just refer to him as the Hebrew; the Hebrew slays the lion. That's all I know about the tale. But in this interpretation of the story the Hebrew doesn't slay the lion at all. When the Hebrew is just about to gnash the lion with a sword, the lion stands on his hind legs, speaks in a queer voice, and suggests to the Hebrew that perhaps there is some way for them to work out their differences. The Hebrew puts down his sword, motions his index finger on his left hand to his lips, and begins to ponder the ramifications of his decision. The lion then proceeds to lecture David, or Daniel, on the vicissitudes of violence and shows him through a musical number consisting of a flashback montage of older Old Testament myths (i.e.- Adam and Eve, Noah and the Ark, etc) that we can all get along if we just try. I hate anthropomorphism. Watching this cartoon sober is worse than dissolving acid and watching Terry Gilliam's *Fear and Loathing in Las Vegas*. After a few musical numbers involving the talking and singing and dancing lion, David, or Daniel, Abraham, Moses, Noah, Joseph, Amos and Andy, and Solomon, Jesus suddenly appears wearing a halo and holds hands with the lion as they form a circle of holding hands turning counter-clockwise in the heart of the Bible Belt on top of the geographical United States as the Earth spins round and round and round and round and round. Click!

I'm definitely going to kill myself.

10:31 a.m. Saturday, May 11th:
I need a thaumaturgist.

11:15 a.m. Saturday, May 11th:
Still in bed.

11:17 a.m. Saturday, May 11th:
If I survive today and tonight, I think I'll go to church tomorrow.

11:22 a.m. Saturday, May 11th:
Still in bed.

11:23 a.m. Saturday, May 11th:

The dog is whimpering.

11:59 a.m. Saturday, May 11th:

Still in bed.

12:28 p.m. Saturday, May 11th:

Still in bed. Naked.

1:16 p.m. Saturday, May 11th:

Still in bed. Naked. And the dog is still whimpering.

2:35 p.m. Saturday, May 11th:

I think they're supposed to be returning today. They are the only people I know and can rely on any more considering that I grew up in Santa Fe. I have another brother who lives here but he's always working and hard to get a hold of. If they arrive in town tonight, or if he would come around I could probably get over this whatever is happening to me. What is happening to me? My body is asleep but my brain is vibrant as an electric razor with brand new batteries. I have to get out of this bed. My limbs are stiffening, muscles are taut and aching, my brain hurts as if someone kept jabbing a finger into my temples repeatedly, small bed sores are starting to appear on my hamstrings and buttocks and I'm dehydrated. I gotta do it. I gotta get out of bed. I can't. I must. I can. I can't. What if something happens to me? What is happening to me? Nobody is around. I don't even know who I am anymore. Where am I? I'm in my house. I haven't left this room in a long time. My whole body aches severely. This is what I get for isolating myself for years and abandoning all my friends, even the pseudo ones. I'm alone.

3:42 p.m. Saturday, May 11th:

Married to my paranoia I require words to comprehend the interior sickness shaping the collective unconscious of mayhem and compliance to describe the world and how I feel:

Distribution. War. Inevitability. Depression. Irreverence. Attitude. Painstakingly. Virgin. Altitude. Freeloading. Underground. Samba. Inventiveness. Creativity. Energy. Solar. Cosmos. Occult. Derelict. Insubordination. Fantasy. Phantasm. Indispensable. Marathon. Fortitude. Insanity. Sickness. Psychiatry. Science. Pseudo. Scientology. Forthcoming. Foreclosure. Poverty. Stamina. Heartbreak. Travel. Destination. Lost. Low. Timetable. Presentation. Business. Venture. Capitalist. Puzzle. Together. Divided. Country. Bloodshed. Association. Deviation. Song. Incantation. Chant. Fire. Storm. Dog. Gazelle. Bashful. Rose. Cheek. Christmas. Consumerism. Heat. Water. Poison. Dirty. Filthy. Infestation. Arbitration. Pastoral. Faith. Servitude. Liberty. Achievement. Accolade. Trophy. Wife. Eyes. Bulge. Overweight. Feminist. Percussion. Violence. Shutter. Windfall. Explosion. Death. Blood. Gore. Wipe. Heal. Discover. Unearth. Live. Love. Lust. Languid. Laugh. Litany. Tyranny. Triumph. Music. Prostitution. Success. Flower. Crumble. Mince. Telephone. Reform. Watt. Yakitori. Xerophilous. Chastity. Embarkation. Toxin. Imbecile. Distant. Precise. Endowment. Profit. Strength. Downtrodden. Oppression. Consumption. Infidelity. Peddler. Moonshine. Ballad. Chorus. Tragedy. Freelance. Saber. Mescaline. Denouement. Castration. Fever. Intense. Bucolic. Gemeinschaft. Deterioration. Multiplicity. Forever. Flammable. Vitreous. Examine. Hallucination. Sensual. Limestone. Reggae. Insurmountable. Zamindar. Undervalue. Transpicuous. Fetish. Hullabaloo. Publish. Jaguar. Instrument. Fulminate. Castigate. Community. Intravenous. Bulk. Order. Fascist. Latin. Orifice. Construction. Dossier. Vulgar. Pornography. Fellatio. Entrails. Fauvism. Epaulet. Salsa. Quagmire. Cruelty. Misdemeanor. Teach. Prison. Palliative. Fructify. Pachuco. Shoulder. Loneliness. Sex. Memory. Systemic. Brainwashed. Toothpaste. Prescription. Tongue. Stephanotis. Poltergeist. Fiend. Ritual. Burial. Sorrow. Wistful. Hope. Fury. Apology. Infinitesimal. Barbaric. Cut. Polite. Gentleman. Cymbal.

Flute. Mortal. Spirituality. Phony. False. Start. Murder. Homeless. Fiction. Brazen. Roar. Casualty. Plastic. However. Disturbing. Plot. Conspiracy. Theory. Ruthless. More. Greed. Hoard. Place. Restaurant. Sun. Flu. Polarize. Money. Spell. Curse. Worse. Morose. Farewell. Ligature. Bolero. Glorious. Beautiful. Aggrandizement. Town. Ministry. Guitar. Anelastic. Beaver. Condom. Destruction. Education. Fuck. Gimmick. Hate. Infidel. Judicious. Kimono. Likuta. Mountebank. Necrophiliac. Obstreperous. Patronymic. Quarantine. Rectrix. Segregation. Tantamount. Undulate. Vaudeville. Weird. Xenobiotic. Yammer. Zenith. Zero. Yeast. Xylophone. Whore. Venereal. Unnerve. Tempest. Simple. Rotunda. Quiet. Poor. Over. Never. Mustard. Loquacious. Kind. Jester. Impasse. Hysteria. Gnu. Fame. Empire. Destiny. Career. Breakthrough. Anxiety.

I think I'm going crazy. I have nobody to talk to, no car for transportation, no achievable goals to fantasize about, no drum to pounce, nothing to look forward to, no motivation to utilize my talent, no faith in any idea and the trappings of Western civilization have me walking in solitude inside my imagination condemned to a bus ride on a dirt road living in pauperism no matter how much money I make giving it away just for the fun of it.

4:30 p.m. Saturday, May 11th:
We were meandering down the halls ditching class late in the day. I hadn't seen her or talked to her in over four months. I broke it off toward the end of the summer. She cried and I didn't care. My empathy for women who cry lasts for about one second until I become disgusted. I promised I'd contact her in about a month and we'd see if we could reconcile my idiosyncrasy. She agreed because she had no choice. It had been four months, school had already commenced, the fastidious autumn was upon us, and here we are talking, walking down the hallway together ditching class. The only reason I decided to converse with her was because there was no one else around when I happened to bump into her, she was looking enticing, and I never did get to penetrate her loins. Other males

had been salivating at the sight of her presence. I couldn't stand it. Perhaps it was the desire other men had for her that made me desire her more than I ever did and convinced me to re-establish my ulterior motive.

The hallway was catatonic. Nobody else was in sight. She was not the garrulous type. She was one of those girls who needed to talk to you on the telephone although when the conversation began over the line in about four to five minutes she would become mute and all you could hear over the line was the buzzing sound of electromagnetic radiation confiscating your brain activity after you finished talking to yourself for about two hours straight. She would go for hours without saying anything. It used to annoy me beyond cognition. This was one of those moments. The corridor was so hush I could hear the slight chant of teachers in their classrooms giving fraudulent lectures on math, computer science, keyboarding, Spanish, and political incorrectness.

We strolled about twenty feet without an utterance when I decided to come up with a brilliant inspiration. I was to the left of her, she was to the right of me. I noticed a fire extinguisher Plexiglas box casing a couple of steps ahead of us. Her silence was one of the reasons I broke it off with her. I figured I could get a rise out of her if I quickly lunged in front of her and slammed the Plexiglas box casing making a loud noise to shock and awe her. So I quickly lunged in front of her and slammed the Plexiglas box casing making a loud noise to shock and awe her and she stopped short backing off thinking I was a complete idiot. I achieved my purpose. When I retracted my hand and arm I smiled her way and she was looking at the Plexiglas box casing pointing her finger at it. I wondered what it was that arrested her attention. I focused on the Plexiglas box casing and saw broken pieces of Plexiglas inside the box casing and on the floor, and I also spotted a trail of blood splattered all over the box and the wall, cascading below to the carpet floor. Plexiglas is neither glass nor plastic, it is more like plastic glass. Automatically I turned my right palm upwards and observed a pool of blood draping my forearm and flushing out of my wrist faster than the onslaught of technological advancement. Before I freaked-out and plummeted into shock, time collapsed as my eyes were drawn to what looked like to be a white sparkling fragment of something embedded between the lacerated flesh inside my wrist. It was difficult to analyze what it was considering the fact that I was losing large amounts of blood rapidly as I felt my heart pump hysterically and simultaneously a thread of blood would squirt out of my wrist. The white sparkle looked like a piece of glass stuck in my arteries but later on I found out that it was one half of my main tendon chopped and snapped like a rubber band stretched to its limits. I was somewhat calm. The shock settled in. I thought I was going to die because I thought of all those movies I had seen where someone slashes their wrist and shortly thereafter dies. I reacted. I screamed like a bitch and took off galloping down the hallway. Fortunately for me we were on the far end of the school nearly a quarter mile from the nurse's office. I've never ran so fast in my life squeezing the middle of my forearm trying to substitute for a tourniquet with my left hand yelling and dodging miscellaneous individuals who happened to be in the hallway. As I raced I was periodically banging my head into the lockers walled-up against the interior. I used to love to sag my pants so halfway to the nurse's office my pants dropped to my ankles and my penis was wagging side to side up and down through the pee hole in my boxers. I almost tripped. It was very difficult to run that way but I wasn't even conscious of this at the moment. Before I hit the nurse's office which was adjacent to the principal's office at Capital High School, one of the assistant principals was in the hallway outside the door to the principal's office, saw me charging like a cavalry, commanded me to stop running and when I didn't he tried grabbing my shirt to slow me down and consequently tore it off my torso. Escaping his futility I leaped into the nurse's office and pounded my blood covered arm onto the nurse's assistant's desk begging for someone to help me. Unbeknownst to me the lady sitting at the desk was neither the school nurse nor the nurse's assistant. She was some novice secretary who just started the day before. She screamed louder than I did at the moment, slapped both her hands to her cheeks, and ran out of the office faster than I came in.

I knew for sure now I was going to die.

A crowd started to gather around the office and after about five minutes or so, continuously losing more blood, the nurse's assistant came in (the school nurse was on vacation), briefly assessed the melodrama, used my torn shirt to soak the blood that was making a mess of all the papers stacked on the desk, and left the office. The shock felt like when you receive mild electric shock therapy for muscle contusions and you can feel the electrodes pulsating throughout your nerves causing internal tremors. It is almost like when you hit your funny bone near your elbow unexpectedly and you get that fuzzy feeling, but since the adrenaline and endorphins take over during shock you only feel a minute sensation of internal quivering all over your body.

The nurse's assistant returned, ripped open a Kotex package and taped the tampon around the floodgate that was now my wrist. She applied a tourniquet near my elbow and instructed me to keep the arm elevated until I got to the hospital. This other assistant principal immediately grabbed her car keys and raced me over to St. Victim's Hospital. When we arrived I had to wait almost an hour before emergency services could see me. What was even weirder was when I entered the waiting room for emergency services my mother was already there but was unaware of what I was doing there with my right arm wrapped-up in improvised dressing. Apparently my father was having problems with the gout and needed some assistance and medication. She approached me, asked me what the hell was going on. I told her what had happened through sharp breaths and a trembling voice. She said I was a fuckin' idiot.

Finally, the doctor was ready to see me. A nurse at the hospital shoved me over to a gurney with brown stains on it. The doctor came in, stuck a needle into my skin and the pain subsided. Morphine is the friend of the destitute. Before all my sensation departed he stuck his fingers into the open wound and I could feel him twiddling my tendons and tissue. It was moderately erotic. I was released the same day. I didn't die but I did happen to ruin my basketball career. It took roughly two months of strenuous and painful therapy to commence the healing process. I made it back just before our first game for the basketball season. I should've never played that year. The doctor and everybody else for that matter informed me that my hand would never be the same. My right hand has lost most of its motor skills, acts up every time rain or cold weather is on its way, and the fingertip of the thumb on my right hand is completely numb. I can't type the way I used to with both hands and my future is dead. I was forced to become southpaw and learn everything over again. Tying my shoes has become problematic to say the least. I can't even masturbate properly any more.

5:00 p.m. Saturday, May 11th:

I received a phone call from them and they told me that they wouldn't be back into town tonight, they might have to stay another night because things were not running smooth over there. Needless to say I was disconcerted.

5:10 p.m. Saturday, May 11th:

For ten minutes straight I couldn't sit down, I didn't feel like eating, the dog couldn't stop barking and salivating and jogging around in semi-circles; thunderclouds began to converge above, the gray sky acknowledged my intestinal foreboding, I couldn't stop pacing, I couldn't stop pacing, I crawled up and down the red orange saltillo tile stairs seven times creating patterns and childish games to keep me preoccupied; I started to hear feckless voices emanating from rooms I hadn't explored ever since I found myself alone in this big house; the utility room, the concrete fall-out shelter, the mouse infested garage, the second bedroom on the third tier which hadn't been used in ten years, the downstairs bathroom, the second floor portal and backyard, the den, the walk-in closet in the master bedroom, the master-bedroom where I was stationed, the room the place that I hardly left over the course of three and a half days as the rain began to drizzle and the thunder rebounded near the roof and I couldn't stop pacing, I couldn't stop pacing, so I walked and hopped and skipped and danced up and down the red-orange saltillo tile steps chasing the dog around the second floor red brick corridor letting him out in the backyard out the portal running in my bare feet because I hadn't properly dressed in over three and a half days; my body was weak, my joints creaked, I still felt exceptionally hot and I broke out into a cold sweat, shivering tremendously. Suicide was slowly turning into something plausible and favorable.

5:17 p.m. Saturday, May 11th:
This is the second longest day of my life.

5:18 p.m. Saturday, May 11th:
I am surely abandoned.

5:19 p.m. Saturday, May 11th:
No one can help me, not even myself.

5:23 p.m. Saturday, May 11th:
I don't know why or what is happening to me.

5:22p.m. Saturday, May 11th:
I'm scared.

5:30 p.m. Saturday, May 11th:
I decided to watch *Pollock* starring Ed Harris as the hunger artist.

7:54 p.m. Saturday, May 11th:
Tom Wait's melancholy melody is too much for me to handle.

7:57 p.m. Saturday, May 11th:
Let's rewind the credits and play it again.

8:00 p.m. Saturday, May 11th:
He became prolific when he became sober; but he never could escape the lure of the bottleneck. Death is more enticing than weariness.

8:07 p.m. Saturday, May 11th:
I haven't had a drink in over two weeks; I haven't had a toke in almost three and a half days; I haven't committed any heavy drugs in a long time; my palms are sweaty, my heart is inconsistent, my breathing is unpredictable, my worrying is out of control I worry about the status of my sexual health I worry about my vow of poverty I worry that I'll never be able to ladle a beautiful woman again I worry that I have no distant future nor immediate future I worry that I won't make it through this ordeal I worry about my parents' health I worry about nuclear disarmament I worry about economic failure I worry about the diminishing lack of artistic integrity in every conceivable form or genre I worry about becoming homeless I worry about becoming possessed by the devil I worry about contracting cancer, HIV, herpes, muscular dystrophy, diabetes I worry about the red shit on my face I worry about my mental stability I worry that I'll never get involved in political culture as extensive as I want to in order to contribute to the self-destructive debate about methods of organization to circumvent right-wing domination and stop the onslaught of mainstream intransigence; I worry I won't be able to die in time.

8:33 p.m. Saturday, May 11th:
I am silent now.

8:41 p.m. Saturday, May 11th:
I think I'll try to go to bed.

8:45 p.m. Saturday, May 11ᵗʰ:
No one is coming to rescue me.

8:47 p.m. Saturday, May 11ᵗʰ:
Maybe I should masturbate. I should just kill myself.

10:11 p.m. Saturday, May 11ᵗʰ:
I toss in the center, I turn over, I toss to the left, I toss to the right, I turn over onward forward backward inward outward introversively pervertedly loosening the top blanket losing the sheets pulling off my drenched underwear maniacally scratching my head watching the dandruff filter onto the pillow in the dark turning over on my belly burying my face into the pillow deep pounding my fists on the mattress sobbing wildly chewing on the pillow case sobbing erratically trying to stop even though I can't stop sobbing, although I appreciate the suggestion from Chrissie Hynde.

10:13 p.m. Saturday, May 11ᵗʰ:
10:14 p.m. Saturday, May 11ᵗʰ:
10:15 p.m. Saturday, May 11ᵗʰ:
10:16 p.m. Saturday, May 11ᵗʰ:
10:17 p.m. Saturday, May 11ᵗʰ:
10:18 p.m. Saturday, May 11ᵗʰ:
10:17 p.m. Saturday, May 11ᵗʰ:
10:15 p.m. Saturday, May 11ᵗʰ:
10:16 p.m. Saturday, May 11ᵗʰ:
10:19 p.m. Saturday, May 11ᵗʰ:
10:20 p.m. Saturday, May 11ᵗʰ:
10:21 p.m. Saturday, May 11ᵗʰ:
It takes an hour for a minute to pass. It takes a second for a lifetime to fade. It takes a minute for a decade to succumb. It takes an hour for a minute to pass.

10:42 p.m. Saturday, May 11th:
10:41 p.m. Saturday, May 11th:
Headlights reflect off the adobe walls in the master bedroom. The cackle of the gravel outside over the driveway signals someone is here. The car door pops open and closes shut. Footsteps tread and step up to the front door the key goes in, twists, unlocks, the hinges squeak, the screen door slams, the hinges squeak, the front door thuds, the key enters and twists the door is locked. The refrigerator door opens; the refrigerator door closes. Lights reflect through the doorway of the master bedroom. Shoes clapping on the orange red saltillo tile floors outside of unison. I can smell the booze from thirty feet away.

My brother enters the master bedroom, drunk, says hello, asks if he can crash here in the other bedroom, asks what I am up to, going insane I respond, cool he says, exits the master bedroom but before he can take his leave I call him back and say, "Thank you".

11:01 p.m. Saturday, May 11th:
I feel a lot better now that my brother is here and wants to stay the night. I'll finally be able to go to sleep and kill this insomnia.

11:17 p.m. Saturday, May 11th:
I turn and toss, toss and turn.

11:35 p.m. Saturday, May 11th:
I toss and turn, turn and toss.

11:56 p.m. Saturday, May 11th:
I turn.

12:28 a.m. Sunday, May 12th:
I toss.

1:52 a.m. Sunday, May 12th:

I am wide awake.

2:44 a.m. Sunday, May 12th:

The rain is pouring down thick; the thunder hasn't ceased; my stomach is growling sick; I don't feel hungry; I'm dehydrated; I feel like I have a fever; I've yet to come down from my high from the last joint I hit; I have a headache; I have cramps in every muscle, in every joint; I haven't traveled more than ten feet at a time every hour for the last two days; I'm going crazy; I think this is what anxiety feels like; I'm anxious to do something but I can't focus long enough to make a decision and follow through on it; I can't formulate a complete thought; I can't formulate a complete sentence; I'm incapable of conversing with myself; It is cold then hot then cold then hot then hot then cold again and then it stays hot. The crickets are mating; the storm is calming; I'm feeling hopeless; I'm wide awake; I have no energy to do anything; I have no motivation to try and overcome this madness; I want to wake my brother up and talk way into the early morning with him about nothing in particular; I am so afraid; I have no control over my thoughts any longer.

3:33 a.m. Sunday, May 12th:

I became an alcoholic at the age of twenty-three. Almost half of the continent of Africa is dying of AIDS. I became addicted to weed at thirteen. Plutonium-283 is now being manufactured once again in the United States. I became addicted to cocaine at eighteen. Global warming is real. The summers are getting hotter and hotter and the winters are getting drier and drier every year ever since 1990. I sacrificed my virginity at fifteen to the neighborhood whore. There are over thirty-nine wars taking place right now in the early 21st Century. I stopped believing in God at twenty. Little kids in Africa are some of the greatest trained murderers in the world. More and more species are becoming extinct every year. I have diseases I can't even pronounce the names of and the doctors don't know what causes them, what they are, where they come form, or how to cure them. Hundreds, if not thousands, of Iraqis are dying each month when I write this. The right nostril of my nose is closed and I can't breathe out of it. Hundreds, if not thousands, of Palestinians are terrorized, harassed, and murdered frequently for no goddamn relevant reason. Tens of thousands of children die every day from curable diseases. I'm going blind. A woman is raped every two to three minutes. I've been to jail three times. More than half the prison population in the Unites States is black or brown, indigent, and/or minor drug offenders. I ran away from home at eleven. Millions of homeless people have nowhere to go in the wealthiest country on earth. I've beaten the shit out of three kids in my life, nearly to death. Only when white kids shoot each other up in school does gun violence become a national concern. The roof of my house leaks. The world is overpopulated. I developed hemorrhoids at seventeen. Weaker men are still being gangbanged in prison. I've been beaten by police twice. The police can arrest, detain, or enter your home anytime they feel like it in the so-called greatest democracy this world has never experienced. I throw up at least twice a month. The food we digest in one of the most developed places on Earth is indigestible, poisonous, and synthetic. I hate my neighbors. Development is first priority in Santa Fe and as a result has destroyed the ambience that initially attracted the people who developed it. I go through about seventy-one different moods in one day. Everybody is on drugs. I seek out physical pain just to calm down. You shouldn't breathe oxygen anymore. My hair started falling out at twenty-two. Los Alamos National Laboratory is only forty minutes from Santa Fe. I'm overweight. McDonald's is still on the Fortune 500. People worship money. Christians are taking over every aspect of our lives big time. I'm obsessed with my own dysfunctional penis. At least one hundred new cars hit the overcrowded streets of Santa Fe each day. There should be another nuclear holocaust. When is the Earth going to go? I contemplate suicide by the hour. Symbols such as flags and anthems have no validity. Private property is not private. Public education is mass incarceration. Adults are bullies. Bullets are abundant. Weapons are manufactured in the northern White regions of the world and distributed amongst the southern Brown regions of the world instead of food, infrastructure, and medicine. The dead resurrect each night from the graveyard behind my house and perform matrimonial séances to invoke the spirits resting beneath the blades of grass drying up. Artificial turf is more water-friendly than humans interacting with nature. Nature is a whore that has used up all her lubrication. Immigrants crossing the Rio Grande border should consolidate guns and human resources and shoot back at those crackers hunting them down screaming "this is our land" after they erased the Native except for the descendents now operating mellifluous casinos robbing poorer brown people. Divide and conquer did not end with the British Empire. Pharaoh Sanders is a better saxophonist than Cannonball. Louis Armstrong bent over too many times for the white man. In these times the slime ball lives in luxurious mansions in the foothills; the chump is proud to wear a uniform; the simpleton does what he is told to do without thinking about it independently; there are no more teachers left, only babysitters; the scumbag drives a Mercedes Benz, a Jaguar, a Beemer, a Hummer, a Volvo, an Audi, a Cadillac, a Land Rover, a Range Rover, an SUV, a Lincoln Continental. My balls burn and itch. Women are not interested in me because I don't have a fat wallet, a fat bank account, a fat paycheck, and a fat ass. Materialistic preoccupation is confused for marketable spirituality. The lakes are drying up. The dams have usurped our way of convenience. The forest is disappearing. Water is unclean and unsafe to drink, to bathe in, to wash, to distill, to taste, to paint, to mix, to cup, to gather, to carry, to sanctify. This keyboard is filthy. High culture is the lowest form of human potentiality. Only impoverished artists create the best art. Once an artist succeeds, the artist can no longer produce anything worth deliberation. Cat-call scientific repercussion supernatural elements hidden above stargazing awestricken crowds personifying mediocrity enameled inconspicuously strange way of making sweatshop garments indefinitely for the price of satisfaction with atrophy hog-tied to barbwire wrapped around the neck of rich wealthy people regardless of race orientation even though there is no blood left in the arteries shaken from bone meal deposited into the soil of our apotheosis displayed in front of the people who are no more important than a golden penny bathing under illumination waiting in line like everybody else for service for my servitude exposed jeopardy perilous infatuation with micro-organisms taking shelter in a chewed carcass awkward consecration tepid stammer plenipotentiary makeup five cent roster announcing special event calendar entertainment beguiled forlorn wreckage paradigmatic hysteria effeminate prelude to a three-legged waltz shamanic chants reverberating throughout my head speaking the Gospel in Arabic cursing my enemies within untouchable Pollyanna turned around venomous whitewash national security state of affairs of husbandry infidelity secret code password nocturnal engagement with devils dancing lugubriously like a snail's carcass twisted in circles and pentagrams and the Star of David burning the flesh of negligence the Cross of Jesus melting like candle was sodomized infant telling dirty jokes in closet reformations gerrymandering political dissent obnoxious liberals not knowing what to do except make money and exploit the idea of free living excessively tiresome jogging walking on jagged broken beer bottles escape from prison computer Internet fiend junkie whore callous malfunction hungry cavity contrasted with highball investments making sinister profits in the name of dominance sugar-coated rum shop billiard flexed forearm fantastic comic strip tease adolescent know-it-all ignorant decadence empire decadence Wildean philosophical decadence unabashed decadence unapologetic decadence crustaceous decadence literary decadence musical decadence Spanish decadence English decadence car salesman cheap hooker lipstick brush over abundance of food top shelf ignominious blasphemous prayer meditative flicker switch spark spook scare careless accident killing machine manufacturer tall tale pigment Grimm brother child pornography Michael Jackson exoneration Martha Stewart vacation Tolkien misinterpretation multi-million dollar pathology sociopathic Samaritan pat on the back timing patronizing confidence shallow remembrance of times

when the times were not like the times we're living in if you can call it living
in times of times that time could not time accordingly to time awareness
enlightenment avant-garde hoard selfish greedy mundane proclivity to
feast on the sullied brethren of religious monstrosity sexual organ playtime
timeout in corner contemplating murder for the seventh time in less time
than I have time to decipher time freestyle macabre H.P Lovecraft Aryan
heretic Wittgenstein dreamer Heidegger nonsense waste of time downtime
poultry virus infecting Asian philanthropist Carnegie steel exploitation
asbestos   inhalation   downtrodden   foot   massage   fetish   hardcore
pornography on the dish makes a lovely dish for your lovely wife draped in
an apron house dust magnificent deceit playful puppy broken neck floppy
disk attrition atrocious malfeasance timetable chart presentation business
irresponsibility the Sundance Film Festival is a creation of celluloid
disproportion we now have a Nazi Pope that used to be a Nazi Ronald
Reagan is finally dead and we should all be celebrating mourning is for the
guilty mass murderer serial killer Midwest incubation O.J. Simpson did it
but who cares leave the dead where you found them detective cocksucker
incompetent jester juggling retractable blades in sequential time fashion
supermodel anorexic bucolic beluga ontological benediction for the grace
of the sacrifice converted into monetary refinement banking malpractice
credit card extortion mafia hit man snitch overturned sentence bargain
principal compromise everything for the sake of social upward mobility
enchantment land of discarded gravediggers burial ceremony taken for a
ride in a hearse that cost five thousand ducats to rent Mr. Police Officer
you are not a pig I'm sorry you are a duroc decimal system outdated file
cabinet paper trail magnanimous tattle-tale virtuous reward nurse skirt cop
a feel less than average fat tub of shit undulating red carpet tug of war
sabotage corporation sabotage government handout sabotage individual
relationships sabotage expensive restaurants with stink bombs exploding
on the Plaza scaring tourists not enough more sabotage of wealthy
landowners sabotage of wealthy entrepreneurs sabotage the galleries
spray paint graffiti little whiteboys and blame it on the beaners on the

Southside residential trailer apartments trapped density no justice now not ever ringleader master subjugator fan belt requirement disillusionment rudimentary horizontal visualizations random copulation fragment discovered by paleontologist hunter ornithologist physics instructor collapsed from too many trigonometric intoxications spirits gathering probably mirage landfill mismanagement everybody seems to be sucking dick lately everybody seems to be kissing ass lately everybody seems to be doing what they are told to be doing lately without questioning anything everybody seems to be selling out lately everybody seems gory lately everybody seems to be whoring lately everybody seems to be going to hell lately everybody seems to refrain from thinking lately everybody seems to ride the mainstream lately everybody seems inebriated lately everybody seems small lately everybody seems horny lately everybody seems stupid lately everybody seems repetitious lately everybody seems repetitious lately everybody seems incapable lately everybody seems bloodthirsty lately everybody seems vengeful lately everybody seems controlled lately everybody seems fake lately everybody seems like a robot pushing buttons laboring relentless losing time becoming self-centered living in the world amongst seven billion two-legged organisms by themselves everybody seems lonely lately everybody seems sad lately happiness does not exist argumentative reluctance sheep herder tortured inmate swept off the streets of Afghanistan Middle Eastern defilement desecration of Koran the Bible should be used for toilet paper as well fallen child calling for help nobody hears crying wolf is pleasure French tickler lambskin edible glow-in-the-dark mechanism juice blender smoothie coffee mocha latte whipped cream lance corporal beheading there should be more of you electric eel sting ray occupation zoo trapped exhibit jolly holiday excursion gas price grotesque theatre vanishing way of life force laser guided missile air comptroller lackadaisical warehouse Wal-Mart heir missing spoiled-rotten silver spoon chimpanzee experiment PETA rhetoric celebrity harangue Rush Limbaugh needs a butt fuck cramp intestinal excruciating sensation sensual bridal gown torn seamstress laundress librarian old bag tormenting aging wrinkled reflection Harriet Beecher Stowe log cabin mythology Joseph Campbell indoctrination occult supernova particle article written by obese Paul Bunion looking fag religious leaders should be assassinated political leaders should be tarred and feathered history should be re-written the environment should be destroyed animals should be belittled plants should be uprooted water should be contaminated air should be polluted musical instruments should be recycled and incinerated White people should rule forever and Brown people should continue to submit without consequence the world map should be withdrawn the world is flat there is no such thing as gravity cells are figments of scientific imagination drill for more oil everywhere give more money to the rich a woman is a bitch is a bitch I guess work for less stress over the end of existence nuclear weapons should be deployed commit genocide against the unemployed distribute healthcare amongst the wealthy and the healthy spit on the sick and step on the poor believe in everything you are told and then some and more superstitious reverie late night catacomb secrecy ostensible ramshackle teardrop shambles crumble pyrotechnic mania lawsuit collaboration stunt performer unorthodox Woodstock was a joke the sixties is broken nostalgia wipe your nose then shave your ass cut your lower lip pluck your pubic hairs three at a time the time is running out it is time to put our children to sleep permanently to embrace anarchy as something that is not viable to shove your dick into the mouth of George Stephanopalous burn the museums commit atrocities against humanity burn books hide the bread rotate priorities fabricate truths eat earthworms bathe in grease harvest technological apologies renounce capitalism shoot the saintly designate the unholy feast endlessly frolic innocently fornicate unobtrusively mandate border patrol indefatigabilities eradicate academic credentials astound the commercially available community burn the libraries devise more IEDs create chaos perpetuate jingoistic theories fulminate decency lie to your brother disrespect your mother disregard your sister disobey your father betray your friends acquiesce to your boss talk no more close your eyes the Armageddon and Apocalypse fantasy chess pieces used to manipulate the masses into believing life has meaning deconstruct your lobotomy support militaristic authority revere your temporary survival keep to yourself communicate with invisibility embrace self-destruction champion appropriation of property advocate state controlled industry lose everything methodically chastise spirituality propose new ideas that don't make sense accumulate material blessings to overwhelm those with nothing live alone die alone smile alone sing alone bathe alone breathe alone dance alone travel alone eat alone work alone dream alone plan alone build alone topple alone think alone see alone taste alone feel alone talk alone hear alone smell alone because now you are alienated working for something you will never possess nor have the time to enjoy you live in a plastic world divested of everything natural more and more people are populating where you are filled with animosity towards your love is just a sound you hear sometimes when you're tired of being alone there are more external forces that have control over your existence than you are willing to admit take a look around you and witness the viciousness of the homo sapien as she and he continue to devour everything that was once sacred the pillars of egomaniacal architecture have begun to fall there is no one to call to help your charity is another tool of psychological imperialism college recruiters are no different than army recruiters you live in a world of fear fear is everywhere fear dominates the airwaves the lessons the steeples the channels the grocery store the shopping centers the traffic signals the commotion fear is the order of confusion you cannot escape fear is not the enemy fear is yourself lost in sphere floating in outer space death is not a substantial escape route fear will overcome fear will prevail fear is why you continue to live fear motivates you fear antagonizes you fear uplifts you fear is your strength your God your Jesus your Messiah your condition fear is your condition fear is your condition fear is your friend fear will set you free fear is your sanctuary fear is your asylum rise-up with the rest and proclaim fear as the Almighty you've been searching for all your life because fear will accept you while the rest of humanity rejects and forsakes you there is no alternative left fear is the energy every non-believer talks about when they are discussing cosmic spirituality fear is the church pew fear is the hate you see around you every day when you step outside your window fear is the friendly smiling in your face and finding new innovative ways to destroy you fear is your addiction fear is your habitat fear will dominate you fear does dominate you fear is you misunderstanding and your rebellious behavior that makes you believe you are unique fear is that freak you see in yourself fear is destroying your health there is no way avert the fear that grows incrementally every second inside of you fear is your hunger pain fear is your emotional pain fear is your pain fear is your pain fear is the hate you see all around you every day when people yell and scream and tease and fight and argue and scold fear is life and living in fear is doing what you are told fear will never grow old fear has been around for centuries before you were born and there is nothing you can do about it except accept fear as your master you are a puppet you are a machine you are a tool you are a cog you are robot you are nothing fear is your master and you will obey you will obey you will be true and loyal and defend fear no matter what fear is the essential the substance the broker the medium the mediator the terminator fear the politician telling you what you think you might want to hear fear appeals to your desire fear is the disciple now come along and hold hands with fear as fear walks along before you unveiling the answers inside of you you've been looking for forever fear will not let you down fear is the father the son and the holy prophet that tells you what you think you might be thinking about what you might want to hear fear is here fear is here there is no need to be afraid everything fear has to offer has already been paid for fear will save fear will maintain fear will guide you towards your early grave now say thank you say a prayer and join fear for the final moments of this jovial occasion fear is the ultimate persuasion there is no where to go you are under control hide under you bed for the moment and realize fear is not your opponent only the dead can overcome fear only the dead know what this is all about you will only have freedom when you are free from death and free from fear come near come over hear participate in the requiem of the dead.

This is all in your head.

5:23 a.m. Sunday, May 12th:
I should really masturbate.

5:55 a.m. Sunday, May 12th:
I don't think I'll ever be able to fall asleep again.

8:00 a.m. Sunday, May 12th:
I wish my brother would wake up. I'd at least have someone to talk to. My body is exhausted. Time is lost to me. I've wasted so much time in my life. I'll never be able to live life the way I envisioned it at one point in my life.

10:11 a.m. Sunday, May 12th:
I have no motivation to get out of bed.

12:00 noon Sunday, May 12th:
I am so hungry and yet I don't feel hungry.

12:07 p.m. Sunday, May 12th:
It's hot in here. Or is it just me?

12:52 p.m. Sunday, May 12th:
I can hear my brother descending the steps that lead to my room where he slept. I have no desire to get up.

1:09 p.m. Sunday, May 12th:
I have no desire to live any more.

1:38 p.m. Sunday, May 12th:
My brother finally convinces me to get out of bed and suggests that

I take a shower 'cause I'm starting to really stink. I can't smell a thing. The only reason I get up is because he says he'll buy me something to eat. I need to eat. I also need to drink something. I'm so dehydrated my lips feel like used sandpaper. My hair is coarse and oily. My breath reeks every time I open my mouth to inhale air. I feel so weak and energetic at the same time. I'm still hot. The breaths are coming in shorter now. It's hard to breath as I stand and walk. I can't sweat any more. My feet ache every time I step. Arthritis has infected my hands. I'm starting to shake noticeably. The fever never left me and I never came down from the high. My brain and body are going through minor withdrawals. For ten years straight I abused alcohol and drugs at a very vulnerable age. For the last three months I've been drinking and smoking every day all day. It starts with a miniature of Stoli before 11:00 a.m. By 3:00 p.m. my father and I have downed at least three of them sometimes five. In addition, we've also consumed one half of a six-pack of beer each. By 5:00 p.m. we've finished off a bottle of wine. Throughout the course of our beverage intoxication we've been smoking weed the equivalent of about half of a quarter ounce of cheap shit. We're forced to purchase weed every other day. By 6:00 p.m. both my father and I are passing out when my brother shows up and asks me if I want to go out. I never refuse. All night from about 7:00 p.m. to 2:00 a.m. I induce more booze and more drugs. Why, I do not know. In the evening I switch to cocktails and we start sniffing cocaine all the while still smoking weed. Since I start snorting it is essential that I smoke cigarettes as well. The only reason my body can take it is because I'm young, but this is exactly the same reason why I'm aging faster than I should be. This has been the daily routine for the last three months consecutively every day without a break. Maybe there was one or two or a few more days that I stayed sober but I do not recall them because they didn't' feel like I was really sober anyways. It's taking a massive toll on my body and brain. I can't think properly any more. I've stopped reading and writing. My stomach is protruding and swelling, making me look like a whale walking upright. My skin is pale all the time with a slight yellow tinge. Every morning I wake up hung over and sick. When I defecate my feces comes out real hard, in small pieces like I'm constantly constipated, and very dark almost as if there is blood in my stool. My hemorrhoids are bleeding more often. I can't sit down properly sometimes. I know I've done considerable damage to my liver and I'm not even twenty-five yet. My lungs feel tight. I cough spasmodically the first instance I awake. I'm spitting phlegm out all the time. Sometimes there are slight traces of blood in it. I always feel lethargic. I know I've done considerable damage to my brain

3:34 p.m. Sunday, May 12th:

Out in the city I can't recognize my whereabouts or myself. I've lived here all my life and I don't know where I am. The streets look unfamiliar and hazy. The sun is too bright. My eyes hurt. I want to go back home inside where I know I'm not safe.

4:23 p.m. Sunday, May 12th:

I bought a meatball sandwich from Subway and immediately threw it away after my brother dropped me off and said goodbye and told me to take it easy. I begged him to stay with me but he said he had to work. I wish I had someone to stay with me right now. I don't feel good. I'm terrified. I know I won't make it through the evening.

6:00 p.m. Sunday, May 12th:

I received a phone call from them. They told me they were halfway home and they should be arriving in town around 11:00 p.m. I am relieved for the moment. Saddened that suicide is not an option any more.

7:00 p.m. Sunday, May 12th:

After locking everything up and drawing the shades and double-checking everything and checking them again I feed the dog and watch him eat. After he finishes I move upstairs up the red to orange to orange to red tile saltillo floors up to the master bedroom stripping down to my underwear curling up under the sheets lying on my side staring at the radio clock turning on the radio to 99.5 Magic F.M. The Dee-lie-la national syndicate broadcast is on. I fuckin' hate this bitch and her stupid show. Nothing but a bunch of degenerate Midwestern and Southern hillbillies calling in voicing their self-inflicted social problems to her and she does nothing but acts like a flunky psychiatrist and mother figure putting down these hopeless nobodies. And after she's finished playing Dr. Laura Schlesinger and Dr. Phil in one, she infects the airwaves with her Christian proselytizing and patriotic banter. The conservatives have truly taken over. But I turn it to this station because the music is soothing and boring and perhaps it might help me relax a little and maybe even fall asleep.

8:00 p.m. Sunday, May 12th:

You have those moments where you haven't slept in quite a while and then when you attempt it again you slowly start to doze off even though it doesn't feel like you want to sleep but you doze off to that intersection where sleep and consciousness converge and just as you feel like you're catching some Zs and pictures start to formulate inside your head all of a sudden your eyelids blink wide open and you know you're not going to be able to fall back asleep again.

8:05 p.m. Sunday, May 12th:

I jump out of bed flinging the sheets from my cover and pace up and down the room down and up pacing the room up and down up and down and up then down and pacing to the left pacing southbound pacing to the east pacing down and up the floor looking over at the bed wishing I could fall asleep don't worry they are arriving soon and they said they would immediately come over here and check up on you after you told them how you felt and how you've been feeling this entire weekend shaking and dry heaving and cold and hot very hot and sweating and dehydrating and hungry and hypertensive and hyperesthetic and hyperglycemic and hypercholesterolemic and hyperparasitic and hyperphagic and hypnogogic and hypertensive and hyper and hypochondriacal and hypnotized and hyper very hyper super hyper really hyper very hyper I can't stop moving I must move if I stop moving I die I pace I'm pacing I pace up and down pace down and up pace to the right of me pace to the left pace up pace west pace down pace east pace north pace south pace pace pace pace pace pace prance prance pace pacing pace over there pace here now over there now here now here pace nowhere pace pace pace hyper hyper hyper pace hyper pace pacing pace up and down and north and down and down and down déjà vu. Pace pace pace.

8:15 p.m. Sunday, May 12th:

I jump out of bed flinging the sheets from my cover and pace up and down the room down and up pacing the room up and down up and down and up then down and pacing to the left pacing southbound pacing to the east pacing down and up the floor looking over at the bed wishing I could fall asleep don't worry they are arriving soon and they said they would immediately come over here and check up on you after you told them how you felt and how you've been feeling this entire weekend.

8:22 p.m. Sunday, May 12th:

Don't worry. Don't worry. Don't worry. Don't worry. Don't worry.

8:55 p.m. Sunday, May 12th:

I jump out of bed flinging the sheets from my cover and pace up and down the room down and up pacing the room up and down up and down and up then down and pacing to the left pacing southbound pacing to the east pacing down and up the floor looking over at the bed wishing I could fall asleep don't worry they are arriving soon and they said they would immediately come over here and check up on you after you told them how you felt and how you've been feeling this entire weekend has sucked. This entire weekend has sucked. This entire weekend has been the shittiest fuckin' weekend of my life!

9:00 p.m. Sunday, May 12th:
Don't worry. Don't worry. Don't worry. Don't worry. Don't worry.

9:20 p.m. Sunday, May 12th:
Here I am pacing the halls squeezing one hand in the other squeezing real tight cutting off circulation squeezing eyes wide open pacing rapidly hyperventilating trying to catch my breath stopping squeezing my sweaty palms hyperventilating nervous as a raccoon foraging nervous and hyperventilating stopping short pacing fast trying to catch my breath squeezing my soaked palms hyperventilating nervous fast losing control losing consciousness nervous as an amateur pianist at her first recital hyperventilating pacing awkward blanking out squeezing my wrists cutting off circulation maybe I should masturbate maybe I should kill myself maybe I should read a book maybe I ought to lie down again maybe I should go outside maybe I should jump from the second story maybe I ought to pet the dog maybe I should call emergency I should call emergency I need to call somebody I need to talk to somebody I'm nervous hyperventilating I should call emergency I'm squeezing my palms rigorously pacing intentionally I should lie in bed and listen to silence I'm scared of what I don't know what is happening to me why is this happening to me what am I afraid of there is nothing to be afraid of maybe I should call somebody maybe I should call the suicide hotline maybe I should kill myself maybe I should smoke some weed I should kill myself kill myself kill myself kill kill kill kill kill kill myself maybe I should call emergency I should call emergency I need to talk to somebody I should call emergency I need to call emergency don't worry they'll be here soon a couple of more hours no less than a couple of hours an hour and forty minutes to be correct I still have sense of time I'm not going insane I still have control over my faculties I'm calming down I'll lie down and wait and lie down and wait and lie down not worrying.

9:30 p.m. Sunday, May 12th:
Ten minutes have passed.

9:40 p.m. Sunday, May 12th:
Another ten minutes.

9:50 p.m. Sunday, May 12th:
Ten more minutes.

9:51 p.m. Sunday, May 12th:
9:52 p.m. Sunday, May 12th:
9:53 p.m. Sunday, May 12th:
9:54 p.m. Sunday, May 12th:
9:53 p.m. Sunday, May 12th:
9:52 p.m. Sunday, May 12th:
What?

9:53 p.m. Sunday, May 12th:
9:54 p.m. Sunday, May 12th:
9:55 p.m. Sunday, May 12th:
9:56 p.m. Sunday, May 12th:
9:57 p.m. Sunday, May 12th:
Hurry the fuck up!

9:58 p.m. Sunday, May 12th:
9:59 p.m. Sunday, May 12th:
9:58 p.m. Sunday, May 12th:
Jesus Fuck!

9:58 p.m. Sunday, May 12th:
9:59 p.m. Sunday, May 12th:
10:00 p.m. Sunday, May 12th:
Finally!

10:10 p.m. Sunday, May 12th:
Ten minutes.

10:20 p.m. Sunday, May 12th:
If I can make it through ten minutes I'll make it.

10:30 p.m. Sunday, May 12th:
Yes!

10:40 p.m. Sunday, May 12th:
Yes! They'll be here soon.

10:50 p.m. Sunday, May 12th:
They'll be driving up soon. Look for the reflection of the headlights off the walls.

10:51 p.m. Sunday, May 12th:
10:52 p.m. Sunday, May 12th:
10:53 p.m. Sunday, May 12th:
10:54 p.m. Sunday, May 12th:
10:54 p.m. Sunday, May 12th:
10:54 p.m. Sunday, May 12th:
10:54 p.m. Sunday, May 12th:
10:54 p.m. Sunday, May 12th:
10:54 p.m. Sunday, May 12th:
10:54 p.m. Sunday, May 12th:
10:54 p.m. Sunday, May 12th:
10:54 p.m. Sunday, May 12th:
Jesus-fuckin-Christ the fuckin clock won't move! Oh God what is happening to me? Hurry up! Hurry up!! Hurry-the-fuck-up!!!

10:54 p.m. Sunday, May 12th:
10:54 p.m. Sunday, May 12th:
10:54 p.m. Sunday, May 12th:
Fuck Me!

10:54 p.m. Sunday, May 12th:
10:55 p.m. Sunday, May 12th:
It's about time.

10:56 p.m. Sunday, May 12th:
10:57 p.m. Sunday, May 12th:
10:58 p.m. Sunday, May 12th:
10:59 p.m. Sunday, May 12th:
11:00 p.m. Sunday, May 12th:
Yes, yes, yes, yes yes! Thank you, thank you, thank you, thank you. They should be here any second. Just lie here and wait you'll be all right you're not alone you're not alone. There is a God. There is a God. There is hope. There is hope in this world. Calm down. You'll be all right. Breathe. Deep Breath. Sit up. Lie back down. Listen to the music. Listen to Lionel Richie's voice. Gosh, this makes me sick. Turn the radio off. Don't look at the clock anymore. Stare at the walls and keep a look out for the headlight reflection. There is a God. You're not alone.

11:05 p.m. Sunday, May 12th:
They'll be here any minute.

11:10 p.m. Sunday, May 12th:
They'll be here.

11:15 p.m. Sunday, May 12th:
Give them a few minutes. They said eleven. It's past eleven. Maybe give them a half hour to an hour you never know it takes some time when

you travel especially by car they'll be here don't worry don't sweat it you'll be all right just give them some time maybe and hour or a half hour they got to be arriving in a half hour to an hour or an hour maybe an hour and hour should suffice you always got to give someone a grace period of an hour when they say they'll be there at a certain hour an hour is good and hour's good an hour an hour an hour an hour an hour it shouldn't take more than an hour.

11:20 p.m. Sunday, May 12th:
Don't look at the clock.

11:25 p.m. Sunday, May 12th:
Don't.

11:26 p.m. Sunday, May 12th:
I don't want to look at the clock.

11:27 p.m. Sunday, May 12th:
It feels like an hour has passed what do you think do you think it's been an hour?

11:28 p.m. Sunday, May 12th:
Don't look. Not yet.

11:29 p.m. Sunday, May 12th:
I think it's been an hour. They should be here any minute now.

11:29 p.m. Sunday, May 12th:
Jesus Fuck Me! What the fuck is going on? They said they'd be here at eleven and they're not here what the hell I'm lying here all fucked up in the head shivering and feeling hot and high and awake and scared and frightened and terrified and hot and my brain won't stop what the fuck

is wrong with them they said they'd be here at eleven and it's past eleven I don't think I can last much longer I'm not going to make it what should I do maybe I should call emergency I should just fuckin' do it I should do it nobody gives a shit obviously they don't give a shit if they truly gave a shit they would be here by now instead of leaving me alone here my brother abandoned me my aunt abandoned me my uncle abandoned me I'm all alone and I don't know what is happening to me I should just do it I should do it I should kill myself no one cares no one gives a shit I can't take this anymore what the fuck is happening to me I can't stand it any longer I don't think I can make it when are they coming who knows when they'll be here maybe I should call emergency nobody is coming nobody cares I should just kill myself there is no God.

11:30 p.m. Sunday, May 12th:
Calm down.

11:40 p.m. Sunday, May 12th:
Ten minutes.

11:50 p.m. Sunday, May 12th:
Another ten minutes. Just chill.

12:00 midnight Monday, May 13th:
FUCK!

12:01 a.m. Monday, May 13th:
I can't take it any more I can't take it any more. I'm hurting all over the place and I can't lie or sit or stand still I don't know what is happening to me I'm very very very very nervous and hyperventilating I can't stand or sit or lie down still. I couldn't take it any longer. I broke down. I had to do it. I ran over to the telephone, picked up the receiver, was about to dial 911 and order an ambulance when at the last second I dialed my brother's

phone number instead. He should be out of work by now. He was there for me last night I'm positive he'll help me out now until they arrive. It'll only take an hour or so.

12:03 a.m. Monday, May 13th:
No answer.

12:03 a.m. Monday, May 13th:
I hung up and picked up and dialed again.

12:04 a.m. Monday, May 13th:
Will you come over? "No" Why not? "Because I'm in bed dude, I'm not going way the fuck over there. For what?" Because I need somebody right now I need somebody here you're my brother. "Just chill out, you'll be okay." I'm not okay I'm telling you I feel like I'm losing my mind I don't feel right I don't feel right. "Just calm down. Smoke some weed or something." No. I can't. I need you to come over here, please. "It's late man. I'm already in my pajamas and asleep. Besides, my girlfriend is staying the night and I can't leave her here alone." Well bring her with you. "No" Please? "No. Just lie down and go to sleep or something." I can't. "Watch TV and you'll go to sleep." It doesn't work. "Read a book then." I can't. "Well then, smoke some weed or something I have to go back to sleep. I work early tomorrow and you woke me up." Please bro, I don't know what is happening to me. Just come over for a little while I'm telling you I'm not going to make it I feel sick. "Well, throw up." I can't. I don't feel well. Just come over until they get here and then you can leave. "I already said no." Please? "No" I'm not going to make it. If you don't come over here I'm going to call an ambulance to come and pick me up and check myself into the psychiatric ward at St. Victim's Hospital. "You're not going to do that." Yes I am. That's how I feel right now. I don't know what's happening to me. "Look. Don't worry so much. They'll be there soon. What time did they say they'd be there at?" Eleven. "What time is it now?" I don't know. "Let me check. It's

midnight." They said they'd be here at eleven. "Well, they're probably just running late or something." I don't think I can wait any longer I'm going to have to call an ambulance. "No. Look. Just give them another hour or so. I'm sure they'll be right there." But what if they're not? "Don't worry." But what if they don't make it? "They will." But what if something happened to them on the road and they don't make it back tonight I'm telling you I won't make it I won't. "Don't panic. Just calm down, do your breathing exercises and chill out. If they don't make it there in an hour or so…" An hour? "Yes an hour or so. If they don't make it there by then than call me and we'll see what's up." An hour? "Yes." I don't think I can wait any longer. "Yes you can." Can't you just come over here now? "No. Now go back to sleep and call me in an hour. I need to get some sleep." Please? "I said no. Now quit bothering me. Just chill out man. I'll talk to you later. Don't worry so much. It's all in your head."

12:05 a.m. Monday, May 13th:
It is so silent, like the sound of fog.

12:07 a.m. Monday, May 13th:
I'm not going to make it. I should call an ambulance.

12:11 a.m. Monday, May 13th:
The phone is ringing.

1:00 a.m. Monday, May 13th:
I talked to my other older older brother long distance from Las Vegas, Nevada on his dime for about an hour. He asked me if they had gotten home yet I said no he said he had something to tell them and he wanted to thank them for everything I said they were not here yet and asked him if he would stay on the line for as long as possible possibly until they came home I needed someone to talk to he asked me what was wrong was I okay I said no I need someone to talk to a familiar voice would he do it?

He obliged me and assured me he would stay on the line for as long as his brand new phone card would allow. I thanked him. I will never forget what he did for me.

1:01 a.m. Monday, May 13th:

His phone card gave out in less than an hour. We exchanged goodbyes when the automatic feminine voice appeared over the receiver and informed us that there was only fifty-nine seconds remaining on the card. That last minute of conversation was all I had left.

1:02 a.m. Monday, May 13th:

I'll be all right.

1:03 a.m. Monday, May 13th:

I can make it.

1:04 a.m. Monday, May 13th:

I can't do this.

1:05 a.m. Monday, May 13th:

Where the hell are they?

1:05 a.m. Monday, May 13th:

Breath.

1:06 a.m. Monday, May 13th:

Close your eyes, turn off all the lights and sound and try to sit here unmoved.

1:07 a.m. Monday, May 13th:

They're not coming. I know they're not coming. What am I supposed to do?

1:07 a.m. Monday, May 13th:

Oh Jesus I can't do this I can't take it any longer I'm losing my mind that's it that's it fuck it I gotta get up I gotta walk around walk around walk around come on do some exercises or something walk around pace pace pace pace jump up and down down and up and down and down run in place break a sweat occupy your mind occupy your mind think think think think watch a movie they'll be here soon I can't try not to think about anything what am I supposed to do I can't pace breathe stop stand motionless jump run go outside I can't I'm afraid it's okay they'll be here soon terrified certain this it is it is not is it what happening don't pick number what the phone cable chord phone talk think phone hungry the pain pace pace pace walk walk walk think think I can't think I can't think I can't pace they'll be here soon should I no you could can't what who where why is this no can't happening he didn't no want to no come here why no one knows I don't know I can't tell this is too much I'm mind losing something they'll be here happening do time what soon the time clock don't look can can't pace pace pace pace squeeze tighter circulation hyperventilating breathe get a hyperventilating paper hyperventilating we hyperventilating don't hyperventilating have hyperventilating a hyperventilating paper ventilating they'll hyperventilating be hyperventilating here hyperventilating soon hyperventilating get hyperventilating a paper hyperventilating sack I can't hyper breathe ventilating breathe breathe pace jump pace walk pace talk pace squeeze tighter pace tighter pace pull your hair punch your face pace walk talk backwards forwards sideways pace pace pace nervous touch nervous sit pace scared anxious terrified what pace think sit pace stand pace move hyperventilating touch squeeze insanity insanity insanity insanity insanity insanity you must call no I can't you have to call no I can't talk the phone no love phone no brother no can't walk outside no afraid nervous vomit spit heave breathe hyperventilating something what is no happening no something don't can't won't when hyperventilating squeeze something wrong phone spit pace pace pace pace pace pace pace pace pace pace pacing still wet cold hot so hot real hot hyperventilating temperature temperament ache pain pace walk still wet cold hot pace pace squeeze tight temperature tighter hyperventilating I can't take it I can't take it I can't take it any longer I haven't slept I can't eat I won't live kill kill kill kill yourself yourself yourself die die call the no I can't hospital no I won't ambulance they'll be here soon I can't I can my mind what is my mind happening they'll be here soon to mind us them they where did they or no can't they time now look they'll be here soon pick phone no outside inside outside inside dog bark loud loud bark dog no insane sanity sick stop move stand move walk move one foot two move loud move outside bark cold hot cold bark pull your hair punch your face pinch your cheeks walk backwards talk backwards something sometime they'll be here soon no yes no yes yes yes yes call now no call something no somehow no yes hospital when I can't I can't I can't I can't I can't I can't take it any longer they'll be here soon no more I can't cope I can't cope they'll be here soon I can't cope there is no hope they'll be here soon left for me stay still pace move pace move pace still now call now call now I'm afraid they'll be here soon I'm afraid of them they'll be here soon I'm afraid of myself they'll be here soon I'm afraid of what I'll do to myself they'll be here soon what is happening to me why is this happening to me I'm afraid I'm nervous I'm scared I'm anxious I can't stop being anxious don't don't don't call yet don't call yet don't don't don't just lie stand move pace pace pace pace pace pace pace pull your hair punch your teeth pinch your cheeks move pace pace squeeze your wrist they're not coming they'll be here soon pace sit shit what can't could they'll be they're not soon coming no not coming not coming no they'll be here not soon coming no pace pace pace stop. Stand. Still.

1:08 a.m. Monday, May 13ᵗʰ:
Wait.

1:09 a.m. Monday, May 13ᵗʰ:
Nothing.

1:10 a.m. Monday, May 13th:
Nothing.

1:11 a.m. Monday, May 13th:
1:11. Make a wish. I wish for…

THAT'SITICAN'TTAKETHISANYMOREIDON'TKNOWWHATISHA
PPENINGTOMEIWON'TMAKEITICAN'TTAKEITPICKUPTHEPHONEAN
DDIALPICKUPTHEPHONENOWANDDIAL 9-1-…

Light reflects off the adobe walls.

Afterthought

The first two weeks were difficult. My palms were sweating constantly. I couldn't sleep well, and I was very afraid to be left alone. Initial detoxification took one month. I'd go through about twelve or thirteen mood-swings daily. My body ached all over. I hadn't dreamt in a long time. I was doing it cold turkey and alone without external assistance from anyone.

One night I was trying to sleep and woke up just after midnight sweating profusely and shaking all over. I meandered around my house for about an hour. I wanted to go to sleep. Since I had no vehicle, I called her, dragged her out of bed and demanded that she drive me to Walgreens to purchase some over-the-counter sleeping pills.

When I got back home I popped twice the recommended dosage and plopped back on my bed.

An hour later I still couldn't fall asleep so I went to my medicine cabinet, found some liquid Nyquil that had probably been sitting there since they invented the stuff, and swallowed what was left in the container (approximately half the bottle).

In about twenty minutes it started to take effect. Mixed with the cheap sleeping pills my limbs went numb, my lips began to fizzle, my eyesight became fuzzy, my fingertips went cold, my body temperature rose, my hearing experienced a slight but irritating ever-present ringing, and my stomach transformed into a contortionist.

I thought I was going to die. I barely was able to fall out of my bed and crawl to my phone and press the seven digits to bother her once again. I could hardly speak so it must've been challenging for her to comprehend what I was trying to tell her. I informed her of what I did before I collapsed. Luckily the phone didn't disconnect so she was able to figure out what was going on more or less. I regained consciousness by the time I heard her car drive up.

At the hospital urgent care made me wait two hours. In the emergency sector it took another forty-five minutes till the doctor saw me even though it wasn't busy since it was early in the week. As Danny Hoch knows very well jails and especially hospitals are two of the worst places you could end up. Personally, I'd rather spend an evening in jail than a hospital. Some thoughtless half-pint schmuck cold-hearted Jew jerk of a doctor from Oregon--many of the emergency doctors are contracted out of Oregon since St. Victim's is a second-rate sorry-ass operated hospital--who had saddlebags under his eyes, reeked of stale cigarettes, and was going bald attended me. He was a total prick and classic asshole who hardly observed me, asked about three irrelevant questions, scribbled some meaningless shit on his clipboard, and exited the examination room faster than young girls today can spot a man with money.

Eventually I was able to calm myself down. The Jew jerk finally came back after an hour, diagnosed me with bronchitis, gave me a prescription for penicillin and was about to leave when I asked him if there was anything he could give me for the anxiety. He said I didn't have anxiety. I said I did. He insisted I was wrong since I was not the licensed M.D. and he was.

He started to turn his back on me but I grabbed him by the arm, told him I was recording the conversation (I was fortunate enough to convince him this was true since I happened to have a recorder in the pocket of my jacket that I use to memorize my poems) and threatened to turn him in to the proper authorities if he didn't help me out. Without any resistance or counterattack he wrote me out a prescription for Xanax.

I filled the prescription (for Xanax, not for penicillin) and received a generic form of the anti-depressant. For a few days I was hesitant to take it. Prescription drugs, especially anti-psychotics, are very powerful drugs and get you addicted faster than any street drug. But the anxiety wouldn't go away and the insomnia and panic attacks were ruining my health, my aura, and my life.

It might have been because I was watching *The Others* starring Nicole Kidman that made me feel sick and forced me to take the generic version of Xanax. Generic drugs are not as potent as the official kind. I popped one tiny pill, .25 mgs., and in half an hour it kicked in. At first it felt like nothing was happening. Then the world seemed beautiful. I could still feel the anxiety but the world seemed beautiful. I literally felt like I was floating. Most of my body was numb. I forgot everything I ever remembered. I couldn't think properly. I wasn't aware of my identity any more and I didn't seem to mind. The world seemed quite lovely. There was no tension in my nerves but I didn't calm down exclusively. Yet, there were no problems I was facing; no problems I ever had; and there would be no problems for me anymore. There was no fear. It felt wonderful.

The drug wore off a little more than twenty-four hours later. When I woke-up the next morning I was still high, very high. I got out of bed, put my feet on the floor, and stumbled my way around the house. When I gazed in the mirror after taking my morning piss, I didn't recognize the gentleman smiling back at me. I never stopped smiling throughout the duration of the inducement. When the drug finally wore off I felt weak, heavy, and had a worse drug hangover than any four-day cocaine or acid bender I've ever been on. The effects didn't wear off for a week.

Recently a companion of mine from Europe pointed out to me how everybody in this country is either on anti-depressants, visits a psychiatrist regularly, or has a substance abuse problem. The Divided States of Americalm is one nation under dope. There are nothing but doped-up zombies roaming the avenues of this toxic land. The pharmaceutical industry and the medical association are primarily in the business of hypnotizing and brutalizing the citizenry. There are no insane people in Americalm; it is the Americalm way of life that is insane. I refuse to become one of their experimentations. Eventually I had to convince myself that I wasn't losing my mind, and in order for me to reclaim my mental faculties I had to fight myself and push myself to the extremities of determination to do it without the prescription drug I wanted more of.

Enlightenment

On any given weekend night, or any other night in Santa Fake, you can hang around downtown at any bar or gallery or any high-class snooty joint or household on the Eastside and discover the marvelous imperialist transplant bastards celebrating their triumphant way of life by snorting and smoking and injecting a heap of cocaine. Cocaine is the primary drug of choice in the Oldest Capitol. Everybody does it: police, judges, city sewers, state workers, Los Alamos Lab employees, scientists, researchers, nuclear physicists, nuclear engineers, bar tenders, cops, gallery owners, artists, musicians, leftist activists, right-wing dingbats, downtown business owners, cult members, nuns, Las Campanas slaves, Texans, stupid tourists, new age hippies, carpetbaggers, insecure queers, butch dykes, cops, old people, young people, cowboys, crackers, spics, wops, kikes, gooks, cops, coons, yatta-heys, Hindis, priests, parishioners, commissioners, doctors, nurses, transvestites, poor, rich, middle-class, golf enthusiasts, cops, security guards, chefs, waiters, dish washers, hotel managers, financial investors, realtors, developers, construction workers, newspaper reporters, casino fiends, cops, prisoners, prison guards, yogis, gurus, Buddhists, Catholics, Archbishops, Christians, Jews, Moslems, Voodoo priestesses, actors, farmers, directors, strippers, governors, cops, senators, congressmen and congresswomen, convenience store clerks, adolescents, children, students (in abundance at prep school), freaks, Zionists, homeless, cops, tribal police, municipal police officers, county sheriffs, state pigs, and especially cops. I know because I've done it with all these types and plenty more. Cocaine is the categorical equalizer in Santa Fake.

Rich spoiled white kids in Santa love cocaine. They buy it as if the richest families in your country are going to stop importing it any time soon. I remember this one chick who did coke so much she needed to acquire a prosthetic tan nose. The last time I partied with her before she lost her facility to breathe and acquired a replacement we were at some crackhead's house on the Eastside South of Capitol neighborhood and she was unable to snort with the rest of her identical affiliates in the front living room with the windows open and the music shattering living it up at four in the morning yelling over-boisterously mega obnoxious disdainfully neurotic disturbing the peace no police in the vicinity she just sitting there amongst her effete kind wishing she could snort but incapable of doing so because she has to tilt her head back and hold the bridge of her nose covering half of it and the nostrils with wads of tissue paper. Her nose wouldn't and couldn't stop bleeding. Every time she'd lean forward the blood would come rushing out and she'd have to tilt her head back to keep it inside. She snorted anyway. She kept blowing her nose every three and three-quarter minutes. Only blood would come out. Every time she would attempt to talk she sounded stuffy. Her eyes were wickedly bloodshot. She was sweating like a fat person after climbing two steps of stairs. Her friends kept making fun of her. That was the first time I got the idea that perhaps using cocaine was not such a wise decision.

The only reason I never got addicted to cocaine is because I never purchased it. People everywhere in Santa Fe, whether acquaintances or strangers, are more than eager to chalk up a line or share a snort with you. Matter-of-fact people at parties are far stingier with their weed than the powder. I had a seven-year engagement with the crap and I ain't never going back.

Two nights till millennium. I'm gonna party for 48 hours straight. 11:00 p.m. We start snorting. I'd been drinking all day. Smoking ganja too. My life is one big fuck-up. There is no tomorrow today.

Downtown. The Bar Hop: Catamount, El Paseo, Evangelo's, Swig, The Bull Ring, etc. It starts off slow. In the car. We snort on the hour. Every half hour after the third line. CD case. Three lines. Easy. Lips are tingling. Tongue is numb. Gums are salty and sweet. Eyeball pupils dilated. Eyelids don't blink. Inside. Can't stand still. Talking loud. Smiling ever present. I want more. Someone says "let's do another line." Okay. Bathroom. Toilet. Top porcelain. Driver's license. Cut. Chomp. Smash. Separate. One for you. One for me. Dollar bill. Roll it. Next. Later. Snort. Sniff. Sniffle. Back of throat. Drip. Slowly. Randomly. Feels like chalk. Unroll dollar bill. Put in pocket. Look in Mirror. Smile.

You're on coke. Everybody else is coked. Girls love coke. I hate coke. Why do it? It's there. I feel unstoppable. Like an arrogant black Superman. Millennium. Two days away. Less. Party. Some more. Drink. No buzz. Hi. Shake hands. Falsetto tone. Don't care. Go away. Hey. Stay. Pretty. Not interested. Later. Midnight.

Let's do another line. Okay. Bathroom. Toilet. Top porcelain. Driver's license. Cut. Chomp. Smash. Separate. One for you. One for me. Dollar bill. Roll it. Next. Later. Snort. Sniff. Sniffle, sniffle. Back of throat. Drip. Drip. Slowly. Hurts. Unroll bill. Tuck in pocket. Look in Mirror. Smile. Teeth pierce. Jaws tight. Swollen nostrils. Sinuses stuffed. Hi. How are ya? What's up? Who? When? How? So what? Party. Fresh. Up. Dance. By myself. Laughing. Smiling. Laughing. At nothing. Drink. No buzz. Shot. No good. Stare. Silent. Laughing. Silent.

One in the morning. Go home. Bro's house. Me, him, roommate. Roommate says "let's do another line." Okay. Coffee table. Credit card. Cut. Chomp. Smash. Separate. One for you. One for me. One for him. Dollar bill. Same dollar bill. Roll it. Next. Snort. Sniff. Sniffle, sniffle. Back of throat. Drip, drip. Slowly. Hurts. Unroll dollar. Pocket. Teeth pulse. Jaws tight. Swollen nostrils. Sinuses stuffed. Go numb. Temporarily. Wears off. Fast. No affect. TV screen. Movie. *Goodfellas*. Chillin. Sort of.

Half-hour later. "Let's do another line." Okay. Same process.

Half-hour later. "Let's do another line." Okay. Same process.

Half-hour later. Bro goes to bed. Tired. Get rest. Gotta work. I don't. Neither does roommate. "Let's do another line." Okay. Joe Pesci. Funny. Same coffee table. Same credit card. Cut. Chomp. Smash. Last of stash. Separate. One for you. One for me. Same dollar bill. Roll it. Next. Snort. Sniff. Sniffle, sniffle. Back of throat. Drip, drip. Faster drip. Hurts. Chalky. Unroll. Pocket. Teeth liquefy. Jaws loosen. Swollen nostrils. Sinuses stuffed. Headache. Temples pulsate. Movie. Moving slow. Not chillin. Tired. Sort of.

No coke left. Tired. Want to sleep. Can't. Gotta party. Two nights straight. Non-stop. I say: "let's do another line." Roommate: "okay." Shit. Roommate pulls out brand new stash. Bigger stash. Little more than eight ball. Mostly rocks. Must break rocks first. Repeat same process. Shit. Let's do another line. Okay. Repeat. Let's do another line. Okay. Repeat. Let's do another line. Okay, okay, line, yes, another, yes, okay, repeat.

By the end of the night well into the early morning all the way to eleven the next morning we snorted about twenty thick-ass lines of cocaine more or less. He kept pulling them out and I wasn't cognizant of him doing so any more. When the movie got to the part when Ray Liotta is all jacked-up on coke, beginning the anticlimactic denouement, I could empathize with the way Martin Scorsese portrayed the feeling: paranoia, extreme neurosis, unctuous irritability, hypertension, pale gray skin, sunken face, and glossy eyes shinier than the cover of a brand new edition of *Vanity Fair*. Cocaine isn't any kind of fun. More than anything else it is a worthless high.

My brother's roommate finally ran out of his second stash. We turned off the television set, the lights, left the radio on some smooth jazz station and tried to get some rest. It is so difficult to sleep when you're coked-up. You lie there eyes wide open awake as a sparrow at five in the morning usually lying on one of your sides curled in the fetal position unable to turn over or move. A buzzing tingling feeling usurps your anatomy. The thoughts inside your head move ultra fast speedily in short indefinite phrases. You feel cold and hot at the same time.

If the sun had been up for many hours I couldn't tell. The blinds in the living room were shut. I sill thought it was the night before. My sense of time died around two in the morning. My thoughts kept racing around the circumference of the top of my skull. I closed my eyes and sensed I had caught some unconsciousness but my conjecture is highly improbable. The smooth jazz station was bothering me because every other song was Prince's *1999* so I changed the channel and the hard rock station was playing Prince's *1999* so I turned the tuner and the alternative rock station was playing Prince's *1999* so I twisted the dial and the Christian station was playing Prince's *1999* only instead of where Prince says in the chorus "I'm gonna party like it's 1999" the Christian version dubbed a lame sounding duplicate that said "I'm gonna pray like it's 1999" so I unplugged the stereo.

Lucky for me the cocaine you get in Santa is crap. It is cut so much you're not even snorting authentic cocaine. Most of what you're putting in your system is either baby laxative or aspirin. This is why your nose burns and drips like urine from the tip of your prick right after you've taken a piss. The dishonest, shady practice of the cocaine dealers in Santa is probably the only reason I didn't die.

It is 3 p.m., Friday, December 31st, 1999. For four hours I lie on my brother's uncomfortable couch listening to my teeth grind. I heard him get up and get ready for work. Any chance of getting some rest was gone. I was so thirsty I swallowed a gallon of water in five minutes. I couldn't urinate or defecate. I was starving but couldn't eat. My body was paralyzed, my mind alert. My brother came in the living room and asked how I was doing. "Alive" I muttered. He gawked and began packing a bowl of some real bright green sticky skunky kind bud. He said I could stay at his place for as long as I wanted or needed to. I declined. I wanted to go home and collapse but I knew I had to stay awake because it was the end of the millennium, year 2000, and I was gonna party like it was 1999. I didn't take all that bullshit about Y2K seriously. I was ready to greet the void. Funny enough I didn't feel all that bad when I got off the couch, walked around his apartment a bit, ingurgitated the water, and sat back down. I was relatively calm and a bit tired. I didn't have a hangover or experience any side effects whatsoever. The high from the cocaine, booze, and marijuana wore off and sobriety once again fooled me. I was ready to continue the intoxication.

The stench of the chronic made me squeamish, gagging as I put the mouthpiece of the glass pipe to my lips sucking a gargantuan portion of deprecation.

In the car discomfort and uncertainty made it a long ride. The fresh air struck my lungs, entered my bloodstream, invaded my thought process and discovered no asylum. I was so inundated with a variety of chemicals I felt like a broke college student volunteering for a university scientific experiment.

Passenger seat. Up and down. Rock from side to side. I could feel the blood drain from my head. My skin went white. Slowly I heard a drum murmur under my left breastplate. My brother said he had to stop at our parent's house on the way. We pull into Murder King to obtain a Coca-Cola for my mother. Waiting at the drive-up window the car is puttering. The drum under my left breastplate went from a murmur to a soft rattle. I couldn't breathe well. I rolled down the window. The window was already down. The carbon monoxide pollution from the overcrowded St. Francis Drive traffic made me ill. I rolled the window back up. I couldn't breathe right. I rolled it back down. The drum started a slow but authoritative snap. The beat of the drum kept time with the puttering of the automobile. My eyes began to scurry back into my sockets. My brother might've asked what was wrong and I think I told him "nothing." I opened the door to get out and run somewhere into some distance but the clerk at the window handed my brother the beverage. My brother shifted the gear and we were gone. I was freezing even though he had the heat turned all the way up. The drum now kept rhythm with the bounce of the car as we drove. We were almost at our destination. I mistook the drumbeat under my left breastplate for the puttering of the vehicle or the puttering of the motor vehicle for the beating of my heart. I thought I could feel my heart the way it would sound when it beat. I felt nothing was wrong with me and I was just panicking a little. Pulling into the driveway of my parent's manor the drum rhythm now felt like a bass kick instead of a snare snap. My breathing pattern caused my chest to heave erratically. I suddenly became weak and almost passed out in the driveway. I didn't say anything to my brother. The only thing on my mind was taking a shower, changing clothes, and what downtown drinking establishment I should hit-up first. Tonight was going to be more eventful, exciting, and dangerous than the previous night. The year 2000, the biggest party night of all time. I had to do something really stupid. I knew for certain now that I definitely could feel my heart pushing up against the underside of my left breastplate and tap and shove into it then retract and pounce up against it and bounce off of it and charge into the breastplate and ricochet off of it. The pace quickened. My brother dropped off the beverage, asked me if I was coming. I told him no I think I'll stay for a while. I was freaking out. I felt I needed to be around someone just in case something happens at sometime. He left and told me to call him later just before midnight. It was already approaching five in the premature evening. Both my mother and father were downstairs in the living room when we walked in. I knew I couldn't say anything about what I knew now for certain about what was going on inside my body. I casually walked through the kitchen unruggled, said hello, and headed straight for the loaf of bread and the refrigerator to grab some water before I embarked for the shower. Bread and water have always worked in the past to absorb the chemical imbalance and resuscitate my vitality enough to barely keep going. This time I couldn't eat the bread. I couldn't even place it on my tongue. The water was going down coarsely. My throat kept pushing it back up. I had to spit it out with the few chunks of bread I was able to force down my mouth. The beat of my heart was a fist punching the inner lining of my chest. It started to hurt. I started to tremble. I had to lie down. I was able to lie on the couch in the living room for about three seconds. My bowels started to move, my intestines cramped-up, my nerves started to vibrate, my nostrils closed-up, chilled sweat soaked the back of my neck, the inner stellar of my crotch, the bottoms of my feet, and the palms of my hands. I couldn't stop my teeth from grinding and chattering. They sounded like a miniature jackhammer used by someone that doesn't know what they're doing and a collection of pulled teeth inside a plastic container utilized by an Anglo musician as a maraca.

I went upstairs. There was no going out tonight. Of all the cocaine I'd ever done this had never happened before. My heart kept pounding and pounding and pounding and pounding kind of like when you first see someone you really want to experience and the nervousness prevents you from making eye contact or doing anything sane. The feeling some people refer to as love at first sight. It happened to me once: it was the first day, or it might've been the second day of my creative poetry class at Highlands University my senior year. I always like the first couple of days of class at college to see what attractive girls you might have a chance at bothering. She walked in late. She was a redhead. There is not enough paper in the world to describe what redheads do to me. She was a redhead, complexionless skin, dark brown eyes, a figure like an airbrushed Playboy model, and an aura as saintly and beatific as a Frida Kahlo self portrait. As soon as she apprehended my attention I fidgeted in my seat; my palms produced enough humidity to make the tropics seem dry; a tight, suffocating passion encircled my body like an uncompromising gluttonous boa constrictor; I became so hot I asked the instructor if we could open the windows though it was the middle of winter; my breathing became rapid; and my heart, oh, my heart, my heart pounded against my chest like a closed, clenched fist slammin' a desktop in frustration. My heart, my heart from the inside hammered away at my chest like a Mexican construction worker roofing a house. My heart, my discordant heart palpitated like Gene Krupa improvising. My heart, my persecuted heart quickly banged against the interior of my chest with a velocity only a gymnast knows as she conducts a triple back flip springing from the pommel horse on her way to the matt. My heart declared peace and waged war. The physical force that oppressed my being then was happening again only this time it didn't feel as ecstatic. I couldn't control my breathing. My heart pounded and pounded and pounded and pounded so much that a fierce pain punctuated through the bone structure and muscle tissue. I knew then that I was overdosing. I suspected that my heart was about to explode. The THC from the potent weed must have stimulated the large amounts of cocaine that evidently remained dormant.

Upstairs. Run. Overdose. Gotta do something. Call hospital. No way. Rather die. Overdose. Too much. Why? Gotta tell someone. Who? Not dad. No way. He'll let me die. Mom. Gotta tell mom. She'll understand. She'll empathize. Maybe something like this has happened to her before. Overdose. I'm afraid. I don't want to die. It's the millennium. I don't know what to do. I'm gonna die, I'm gonna die. God my heart hurts. It hurts real bad. It feels tight. The pounding is getting heavier and faster and the pounding the pounding it hurts gotta tell mom tell mom.

Mom, what she says, I gotta tell you something, yeah, I hope you don't get too upset, what is it? Last night I did a lot of cocaine all through the night till about eleven this morning and I rested or tried to rest for about three or four hours and I came down or at least I thought I came down but when I got up around three this afternoon I smoked some weed some really strong kind bud and then about ten minutes later on the way over here I started feeling this beating in my heart not like a regular beating but an abnormal one and it started to slowly increase and started to pound against my chest from the inside and it just kept increasing and increasing and pounding and my breathing as you can tell my breathing is short and fast and short and fast and the pounding in my heart it hurts it hurts really bad maybe we should call an ambulance and take me to the hospital I think I overdosed on coke last night and I'm scared I tried eating some bread and drinking water but it doesn't work it usually works but it's not working this time what should I do should we call an ambulance cuz my heart really hurts I have to clutch it and massage it just to make it feel more at ease but then it picks-up again right away the pounding it's pounding real bad the pounding, pounding, pounding, pounding. Let's call an ambulance. I need to go to the hospital.

She said no to the hospital idea. If I really felt like I needed to go she would do it but she figured I just did more than I can handle and that the best thing for me to do would be to calm down, lie down, try and eat some bread, drink plenty of water, rest, wait and see if my condition worsens. I tried arguing with her but she warned me that if I go to the hospital the doctors will ask all kinds of intrusive questions, call the police, and I would have to go to jail as soon as I recovered. Needless to not say this was the clincher. I'd rather die than go back to jail. Fuck it. I'd live with my bad decisions or die with the comfort of knowing I almost witnessed the twenty-first century.

Surprisingly she was quite understanding and sympathetic to my malady. As I lay dying like Faulkner she covered me with a soft blanket, fixed me some calming tea, and scrambled some eggs served with a tortilla. For about two hours straight my heart did not cease the puissant knocking. Now and then I'd look down at my naked chest through the collar of my shirt and could see my heart pushing-up a lump of skin every time it would pulse. My heart was trying to burst through my body. It was about to explode. I was debilitated. The party was over before it began.

It took approximately seven hours for the hard pounding of my heart to slow down to its regular pulse. While I was lying on the couch in the living room of my parent's abode, I was forced to watch on television the millennium celebrations across the globe. The major networks showed three-minute clips on how everyone in every part of the world were coming together in a peaceful manner and enjoying the festivities without any disturbance. Leading up to the millennium there were plenty of fear mongers predicting numerous terrorist acts of violence and the Y2K debacle. Supposedly nothing of that sort happened. There are no real terrorist threats, notwithstanding the armies of the world, and Y2K was nothing but a capitalist scheme all along. Reporters from various sources and agencies claimed that this was a New Year's Eve unlike any other. People were calling for world peace and displaying how the human being can live in harmony. The pictures showed people holding hands and singing in Paris, Rome, Tokyo, Beijing, Belgrade, Dublin, London, New York City, Calcutta, Johannesburg, Rio de Janeiro, Moscow, Sidney, and other major metropolitan areas of the world. The reports stated that even in troubled spots from Eastern Europe to The Middle East people were kissing and hugging one another. The owners of the world tried to paint a perfect scenario, but it resembled more of a maudlin debauchery. People couldn't understand, or didn't want to perceive that the beginning of the 21st Century was not the end but the beginning of the end. The destruction of the 20th Century will seem like petty vandalism compared to the devastation of the 21st. Human beings never have and never will be peaceful. We are all manifested organisms of physical smut that ambulates on this planet like a pack of filthy sewer rats vying for the remnants of meat on a diseased decomposing carcass. Hardly into the 21st Century and it is turning out to be a death march more gruesome than the Bataan or anything you think you might've seen in Vietnam. I didn't buy that shit for one second. Seeing through the façade the reporters and reports seemed more concerned with what big city had the best fireworks display and extravaganza. Fireworks are petite bombs, missiles, and sticks of dynamite that represent the violent nature of those that celebrate with them. As my heart slowed down almost to a complete stop and as my lungs pinched inside and filled with oxygen in a cumbersome manner, as feeling came back to my limbs and as blood began to flow through my veins I realized that true peace and harmony takes much more than a midnight frolic. We can dance and sing and drink cheap champagne all we want to, but until everybody has enough to eat of a supply of organic whole foods and everybody owns a home and clean water and adequate quality health care and sanitation and clothes and autonomy without foreign economic interference unless it's in the form of cooperation for financial aid or fair trade, and until everybody, nobody excluded, has opportunities for education, fulfilling work without exploitation, sanctified inalienable rights, protected from corruption and exonerated from fear and time to enjoy what life may or may not offer--something much more than a so-called good time--then the world will continue to suffer and the top primate inhabitant is only falling and failing. Share the wealth and someday we may share the world.

For seven consecutive days after the 21st Century was ushered in my heart felt like a pulled calf muscle in the middle of sleep. It took nearly half a year for the arrhythmic palpitations to calm down. Even to this day, many years later, my heart does not function the same. Every then and now it acts up and sends distress signals to my brain that in turn sends signals to the rest of my nerves to panic. I, like humanity, did not learn my lesson. I vowed never again to snort cocaine after that incident. It only took three weeks until I was out with my brother and his roommate and the Santa Fe cokehead crowd downtown and I acquiesced when the inevitable supplication "you want to do a line" arose. Cocaine is a waste and so is war. Troubled times seem endless. Hope is a yearning wanting to be listened to. My abused heart remains a growing pain.

Robert Cray at The Lensic

I didn't want to go. She kept begging. I didn't want to go because I didn't want her to think it was a date. Lately she had been bothering me a lot at work. Never engage in a sexual interlude with anyone you work with. That and uttering "I love you" in the middle of sex are about the worst mistakes a man can make. She kept begging. I told her it probably wasn't a good idea considering that she was still married. Although she was a neglected wife I would not allow myself to betray my moral values to that degree of an extent. She said she paid sixty-five dollars for each ticket. I told her that if she didn't find anybody to accompany her to the concert I would escort her at the last minute. She didn't find anyone.

I'd heard of Robert Cray but I never actually listened to his music. I was starting to get into The Blues so I figured this would be a worthy introduction despite the fact I was going with a white chick. Not just a white chick but the epitome of a white chick: a British woman. An older British woman.

Lately I had been whoring myself out to older white women. This can be a very lucrative endeavor in Santa Fe for a young virulent Latin spic. There is more than a robust share of wealthy older lonely desperate white women residing in the subterranean foothills of this Southwestern different city willing to pay for a young brown man's superior sex organ. The only drawback is the lack of self-respect. I wasn't overflowing with a surplus of self-respect so I was more than obliged to slash two wrists with one knife. Since she purchased the tickets for a hefty price I decided not to charge her for my impeccable services. The moral value thing.

I have to admit, she looked good. She said she was forty-one. I think I was twenty something at the time. It turned out she was closer to fifty. Never believe anything a woman says. She'd kept herself in shape by teaching aerobics most of her life back in the old bloody country across the pond where the sun never shines and the food tastes like shit. Her body was tighter than most twenty-year olds; her legs were built and solid and smooth and long; her face had some wrinkles but she applied enough beauty cosmetics to cover the baggage. But still, she had an enchantment in her eye similar to innocence; her ass was remarkable; and her tits were still firm, graspable, succulent, and periodically enticing. She claimed her husband hadn't touched her in three years and I couldn't comprehend why. She was hornier than a triceratops. When asked what would it take for some sex after the concert I acknowledged that it would be an honor to fuck her; however, since the Republicans were in office and dominating everything and wrecking the economy for the average slave out there, I took it easy on her and told her five hundred for the night. She accepted and paid me half up front.

When I met her at the overrated restaurant *Rio Trauma* she was wearing a skin-tight bright red one-piece summer dress that showed more cleavage than Elvira and a pair of hot red come-on high heels. She was by far the most attractive older white woman I ever screwed out of money. The other older white bitches I whored myself out to looked more like a combination of Jean Stapleton and/or Nancy Reagan wearing an abundance of cheap silver bracelets on each forearm, turquoise necklaces, broom skirts with all kinds of incongruous neon and dark native designs, overpriced concha belts and panty hose stuffed into pink cowboy boots. Making love to them was like trying to extract ketchup out of a glass bottle by turning it upside down and hitting it from the bottom. I would usually have to take three showers immediately after as opposed to my customary two. Plus, I charged double for those over fifty-five.

This Brit was an exception. All the pansy whiteboys with their wives and children couldn't keep their eyes off her at the restaurant. Since she was a Brit we decided to eat our dinner at the bar. The food made me shit twice before dinner was over but the drinks were half-ass decent enough to merit a moderate buzz. We drank two glasses of chardonnay, a martini, and a shot of Stoli each by the time we left.

World Famous Evangelo's is positioned across from The Lensic. We stopped in there for some more libation. The Lensic used to be a movie house when I was coming of age. A lot of real locals used to frequent The Lensic back in the day when you didn't have to spend over thirty dollars for a night out to the movies. Now, The Lensic has been renovated, transformed into a mediocre performing arts center with some of it's WPA funded Arabic architectural motif still somewhat intact, and caters to and attracts more of a high-end snobbish clientele that wouldn't recognize good art or intellectual exhilaration if it was beaten into them. They remind me of graduates from St. John's College.

Needless to say we were trashed by the time we entered the front doors after the rest of the sheep filtered in. The Brit was astonishing. She was more alive and exuberant than any older white individual I had ever encountered. Before we entered the theatre she was already dancing. Our seats were on the mezzanine all the way to the back. I didn't mind. I came here to listen, not to see, and to take care of business. Some runt schmuck was the front man for the warm-up band. The music wasn't too bad although blues music does not sound the same when it emanates from a white man's fingers and not a black man's soul.

Oddly, the house was full and filled with a bunch of mostly middle-aged geriatric dirty crackers from God knows where that stayed put in their seats even though the music was somewhat lively. There was no cautioning The Brit. She refused to sit down. The nosebleed seats we occupied were practically vacant. I said fuck it and stood-up with her. We danced up and down the staircase at the top of the mezzanine annoying the few people that had no choice but to envy our zest and drunkenness. The Brit stumbled quite often and if it wasn't for me holding her up she definitely would've fallen all the way to the balcony. Positioned as far back as high society would allow scum like us to infiltrate their venue, the ushers could care less what we were up to or how we were behaving. The Brit mounted me in our dark back seats. To my bewilderment I discovered she wasn't wearing any panties. I unzipped my jeans and put it in her. I channeled two paroxysms from her licentiousness and splashed inside of her after about ten minutes or so. One lady peeked back during this performance but before she could cop an ogle at what we were doing I tackled the Brit to the floor foot space beneath the chairs and finished the job on the dusty sticky surface. When we stood back on our feet her hair was out of synchronicity, her dress was wrinkled, her makeup was smeared all over her cheekbones and chin, and one of her shoes was missing.

I told her that the seats we had sucked. She agreed. I asked her what happened to her other shoe. She said she didn't know and decided to take off the one she still had and threw it somewhere in the back row. She didn't care and I didn't care. We started booing the guy on stage and calling for Robert Cray. There was no way the band or anyone else in the auditorium could hear us. The couple sitting closest to us thought they heard something and peeked back and frowned. The effeminate of the duo was the voyeur that earlier tried spying our romantic lust wonder. The Brit asked what she was looking at and squeezed my crotch violently. The lady was appalled. I was happy for the third time in my life. It wasn't a business arrangement anymore.

Right before intermission I told the Brit we should make our way down to the bottom closer to the stage for Robert Cray. She said yeah, hell yeah with a riotous flair and curled upper lip like someone doing an impression of Billy Idol. While crowds of the audience began to filter into the lobby, the Brit and I ordered double shots of Stoli for both of us. We downed those and ordered two more. I wasn't thinking about anything anymore, I was just enjoying her company. When you're with a woman that let's go and doesn't give a shit what people might think about what she's doing with this greaser that looks like an adopted child from a Latin American mail order catalogue, that is when the instance for enjoyment of life supercedes the moment. Most of the people that patronize The Lensic are really there to keep up with the Jones's and try to impress each other with their ignorant rhetoric, tawdry clothes, and chintzy jewelry. The Brit and I were oblivious to the downtown crowd.

When the lights in the lobby blinked on and off several times everybody reacted like the good machines they've been trained to be, finished-off their drinks and hurried back to their seats. The Brit and I hung loose and took down one more drink before we went in to try my scheme. Most of the people had been seated. The lights in the auditorium shut off. We walked down the left aisle and located two empty seats in the fifth row from the stage on the end. Perfect.

Robert Cray came on stage. The Brit and I leaped out of our chairs yelling and woo-wooing because neither one of us could whistle. We kept clapping fanatically while the rest of the audience barely brought their hands together and remained seated. I looked over my right shoulder and saw nothing but white. White skin, white hair, white eyes, and cold-blooded gloom glaring at me voicelessly telling me to sit down and behave. These people were dead. It was a fuckin' rock/blues concert for Christ sake. I wished there were some black people that attended this shindig and from the looks of Robert Cray's observance of the audience he seemed to have felt the same even if all of his band members were white. But I know why black musicians do this. They do this for two reasons: (1) if they're good enough they can make the white musicians look like they know how to play the blues and the music will not suffer; or (2) some supercilious black musicians want to stand out and receive all the attention and flattery alone. What did I care? I was there to show the Brit a hell of a time. I sat down but she didn't. She kept jumping and cheering and clapping and moving out of rhythm to the music that hadn't begun playing yet. I had to yank her down by the skirt. I told her not to get too crazy down here unlike up there because more people can see us and we don't want to bring aggressive attention our way since we were supposedly not supposed to be sitting in these seats. She agreed and as soon as Robert Cray broke into his first song the Brit lunged out of her chair and stepped into the aisle doing turns and struts that made no sense. She kept wiggling her hips as though she were riding a dick instead of dancing. I attempted to get her to sit down once again but there was no stopping her. I said fuck it and danced with her for a little bit with maybe only one or two people out of three hundred encouraging us or joining in. The other people that were dancing remained confined to where they were sitting and avoided the aisle or the front of the stage or the sides. I'd been to many concerts here before and have witnessed people dancing in the aisle or the sides or the front of the stage. Matter of fact, I've seen these walking aisles transformed into a filled-in hopping dance party. This was especially true when members of The Buena Vista Social Club and The Afro-Cuban All Stars played The Lensic not too long ago. White people, mostly white people, crowded the auditorium and danced and moved all over the place violating every city fire code and nobody disturbed them or tried to put an end to the jubilee. I probably made a mistake by telling The Brit about this because now she was perambulating all over the place with excessive amounts of booze on her breath and sweat silhouetting down her armpits and cum dripping down her thighs trying to persuade people to get out of their chairs and have some fun. She tried pulling this one guy onto the dance floor even though he politely refused probably because his wife or girlfriend was sitting right next to him giving The Brit dirty looks. I had to grab The Brit and make her sit down.

As the second song started I could tell through peripheral vision that an usher was headed our way with a couple holding his trail. We just lost the seats. The usher asked The Brit for her ticket stub. She ignored him. He then asked me for mine and I told him that we threw them away we didn't know we needed them. He said that we needed our stubs to be seated in the appropriate place because the seats we were sitting in belonged to the couple he was guiding. I told him that wasn't true these were our seats.

He showed me a ticket that the couple had in its possession that proved I had miscalculated. I rose out of my chair but The Brit refused to leave. She started arguing with the usher. I had to bear hug her and drag her out of that area before we were thrown out.

On our way up the aisle people kept looking at us and wishing we were gone. The usher finished seating the couple and followed us. Before we reached the twin doors leading to the lobby I pulled The Brit over to the side behind the seats in the last row where the losers like single middle-aged men stand against the wall watching the performance or skimpy laden young girls from the rear of the first floor. I recognized a distant cousin of mine and began chattering up a whirlwind with him in order to pretend like I was ignoring the usher. He asked me a second time for my ticket stub. "We threw them away stupid" shot out The Brit's mouth and the usher decided not to bother with it anymore.

We stayed put in the back and grooved phlegmatically as Robert Cray was approaching his third song of the first set. I started to bitch and complain about these dead zombie fucks that belonged in a graveyard and not a blues concert. I redundantly asked The Brit what the hell these kinds of people were doing here anyway. None of them were dancing, standing, moving, grooving, shaking, cheering or clapping when the songs were over or doing anything that would have convinced me they were enjoying themselves. There were a couple of dirthead women standing up where they sat and shaking their skinny ass but not long enough to warrant an applaud. When Robert Cray finished the second jam The Brit and I couldn't stop hooping and hollering and clapping. Hardly anybody else was clapping. The crowd was so cold I could see steam evaporating from the sweat that dripped all over my face and neck. In unfashionable vigor I yelled from the back "We love you Robert!" and he kind of gasped and said he loves us too and The Brit and I jeered and wailed. As the count to the third song could be heard, a short, stumpy spic with a pasted badge on his white T-shirt and a gut protruding underneath it came up to me and told me that I would have to keep it down. I told him this was a concert not a play. He asked me for our stubs. I kind of ignored him. He remained there standing in front of me unsure of himself and how to deal with a sarcastic, loudmouth highly intelligent scumbag with an elderly Brit who were enjoying themselves much more than they should have been since the rest of the audience was filled with cold dead gringos that were probably too embarrassed to get up and start dancing. After all, this was a blues concert composed, played and sung by a black man.

The dumb spic so-called security guard finally gave in and said, "all right, you can stay here," because he had to reassure himself he was still a man since he was a runt. He left and The Brit and I continued our celebration of the freedom of the human spirit.

Not ten seconds had passed when I whispered into The Brit's ears to follow me. She said why and I repeated for her to just follow me and stay close by. Before she could give another response I was already making my way down the aisle toward the stage taking elongated exaggerated steps like I was working out doing leg lunges twirling to the left twirling to the right crisscrossing feet doing 180s, 360s, 720s and leaping then falling to my knees leaning back in supplication extending my arms pantomiming adoration and hopping back to my feet reaching behind me every now and then to grab The Brit's arm and pull her closer closing the space between us. Nobody was cheering me on or laughing or smiling and nobody in the audience thought it was cute. Nobody followed our movements. The Brit couldn't keep up with me, but she was still ambitiously enthusiastic. I took her down the left aisle in front of the stage spinning her around moving behind her grinding my crotch into her ass. Robert Cray began to strum harder on the guitar and sing louder and raspier and bluesier with an unabashed preponderance of soul. After dancing in the front for a whim I saw that the security guard that bothered me a minute ago was now with another security guard, a fatter security guard and headed our direction down the left aisle we had traversed. I instantaneously pushed The Brit from behind. We headed up the right aisle turning some of the same tricks we did down the left but mostly skipping and jogging back to the back in back of the last row hoping to escape and hide in the shadow of the least illuminated segment of the house.

The fat fuck reached out and tapped me on the shoulder. "You can't be doing that," he said to me in a burly rootless English language conveying the wrong idea trying to sound authoritative. I asked him why not and he said because and I said because why and he answered that no one was allowed to dance but I informed him that this was a concert and that's what people do at a concert they dance and he said not this one and that if I or her did it again he would throw us out. As he turned his back on me I thanked him and he turned back towards me and got in my face and put his finger in my grill and said that maybe he ought to just remove me now so I laughed in his stupid demeanor and coyly retorted that wasn't necessary I would be a good little brown boy so all these zombies could feel justified in paying for the overpriced tickets for a show where you weren't allowed to have any kind of fun or enjoy yourself. I think I lose a lot of people when I start formulating long sentences that flow and make me sound more clever and intelligent than I really am. He didn't appreciate my archilochian rejoinder. Two minutes later I was headed down the left aisle again twisting and turning and bopping my head to the rhythm and stomping my feet and swaying and swooshing and hopping and heaving with The Brit in pursuit. Some redneck yuppie looking priss with a Ralph Lauren shirt in one of the end seats in the middle rows somewhere tried to trip me and when I turned to see what the puke looked like he was sitting there with a nasty smirk on his face like George W. Bush has on when he's giving his condolences to families of soldiers that died for his billionaire crusade. He gave me the thumbs down sign and I gave him the bird sign. He was about to get up off his lazy ass but The Brit came strutting by kicking his leg out of the way. We continued with our jocund ballet.

Back at the back of the rows of seats on the floor of the auditorium I was drenched. The Brit was leaning with her hands on her knees breathing hard. My distant cousin was still lingering back there laughing at the both of us giving me a pat on the back and making fun of me with his words but since the noise was so loud I could only see his lips moving. The third song hadn't ended yet when out of the side doors six to seven short fat slimy dumb spics surrounded me with my back against the wall. The fat fuck that warned me earlier was the leader with the little runt as his head lieutenant. The fat fuck said that that was it I was out of here. I took no notice of him and continued cheering Robert Cray from the back. I saw my cousin eerily walk away. He admonished me again and added that I had to leave. Part of not acknowledging these stupid whores was because I was too drunk to pay attention to what was happening around me. The other reason for ignoring them was out of psychological warfare. I knew I was outnumbered and that there was no way I was going to out muscle these underpaid goons. I knew I was about to be thrown out, or "chucked-out" as The Brit tells me. The Brit tried asking them why and negotiating with them but they were already past that point. You could tell they had received orders from higher-up amongst the puffy clouded ones and so now they had a job to do for minimal pay and very little pride. Don't try telling them that.

I bided my time by remaining silent, surrounded like a prison style gangbang. I'd been through situations like this before only with cops instead of rent-a-wanna-be-pigs. It was Fiesta time and I was partying with some boys of mine that I hardly knew but we were cool and got along. We stuck together most of the night hopping form bar to bar in the downtown area. At around one in the morning all five of us piled into a 5.0 convertible Mustang that belonged to a good friend of mine. The good friend was the driver. All of us were lit and one dude had about two ounces of kind bud on him. We were crossing the intersection of West Alameda and Guadalupe heading west on West Alameda when I spotted a squad car to the left of us waiting at the traffic light. Why he was waiting there I don't know since it was his right of way because he had flashing yellow lights and we had the flashing red lights. I warned my friend but it was too late. My friend gunned the gas pedal, popped the clutch, and skidded out of the intersection never coming to a complete stop. There were no other cars around. The squad car flashed its lights, reared its siren without hesitation, and gave chase. Everybody in the car panicked, except for me, and started throwing their half-filled containers of beer out of the cabin of the Mustang. My friend pulled off the main street into a side street with no street lamps and no traffic passing by. I told him not to do it to stay on the main drag but I don't think he was paying attention to me. He was pretty shook-up. Everybody else in the automobile was shook up as well for they were trying to hide the rest of the containers they couldn't throw out under the seat or in the side panel. It was pathetic. When you're caught you're caught. The squad car had us pulled over with our engine off for about two minutes when another car pulled in. Then another car pulled in. Then another. In four to five minutes two more patrol cars showed-up, one a sheriff's car another one an unmarked vehicle. A total of twelve cops convened on the spot to handle five drunken unarmed delinquents. One stupid pig started harassing us right away. This tall dark pimpled scarred face overbuilt torso with scrawny legs pig walked around the car taunting the driver and me in the passenger seat calling us a bunch of fags and little pussies and that he and his boys should beat the fuck out of us since nobody would be able to witness it since we were trapped on a side hidden road. We were located behind the defunct Noon Whistle across the street from Vanessie's. The pig that looked like he used too many bad steroids got all up in my shit and asked me if I was scared. I looked back at his ugly countenance and coolly replied no I wasn't scared but he should be. He asked me if I wanted to go to jail and I told him that that wasn't really up to me now was it and he screamed at me to shut up. He walked away back to his partners. They argued amongst each other about what to do with us. Obviously no one was in charge of these homicidal lowlifes. They finally pulled my friend, the driver and owner of the vehicle, out of the car and put him through the roadside sobriety test. We watched from the car even though the big muscle steroid user kept yowling at us to turn around but we watched anyway, at least I did, and my friend did pretty good considering how much booze I had seen him intoxicate himself with through the night. I would even say he passed the test but the cops didn't think so and handcuffed him and threw him into the back of one of the rollers. One of the younger ones, on instruction from some fat hillbilly cat, imposed a Breathalyzer test on my boy by force feeding the mouthpiece into his oral cavity and then tinkering with the machine. The overgrown pock-marked faggot of a cop came back to the passenger side, swung open the door, and commanded me to get out now with no fast movements. I bounded out of the car and stood him right in the face. He looked like a Salvadoran death squad commander. He also stunk real bad like burnt slices of hickory-smoked bacon. We exchanged some outmatched worthless drivel for a passing, he trying to intimidate me and me making him feel bad about being a cop. Not long into our brief tit-for-tat I recognized how I really insulted him and held him powerless with my amateurish theatrical routine of legalese, acting like I know what I'm talking about. He bowed his head in disgrace, turned his head from one side to the other, turned back to face me, smiled, and bulldozed me throwing me ten feet across the street slamming my back and banging my head into a concrete stucco wall. His rollicking chums rushed over to see what was happening. They continued laughing like starving hyenas. My head was bleeding. The hillbilly that gave the orders to the younger officer for the Breathalyzer test pulled the pockmarked juicer away to the side. I couldn't hear what they were saying but after they were through the asshole that just attacked me walked by, gave me a horrible grimace, pointed his smelly finger and crooked attitude in my face, and warned me that this was not over yet. And then he walked away. Cops are not human. You can't talk to them like human beings or try to reason with them.

Anyways, none of the police officers asked me if I was okay even though they saw blood on my hands from touching the place on my skull where it cracked. When one of my friends who were standing on the side of the car came over to attend me the hillbilly bastard pushed him out of the way and told the rest of the uniformed gang flashing it's colors to surround me like the Roman soldiers did in *Gladiator* when the emperor would enter the gladiatorial arena. All of them were spics notwithstanding the hillbilly. "Looks like you had it coming," taunted the hillbilly while the army of little men laughed. "Next time you talk to a police officer you better show some more respect."

"Fuck you," I grumbled in an innocuous way with downcast defeated eyes sitting on the road rubbing the back of my head.

"What did you say to me boy?" The hillbilly ordered his spic underlings to lift me by the arms and stand me on my feet. He told his spic whores to quiet down. The street was silent. I could hear the heat hum off the pavement. The hillbilly stood opposite me about two feet away trying to stare me down. I stared back and didn't back down. A cop is going to arrest you if a pig wants to arrest you. The calm scattered when he abruptly escalated into my face yelling and screaming and hollering like a drill sergeant breaking in new recruits. Little bristles of brittle spittle spanked my chin and then my lips and then the bridge of my nose and then the space between my eyes and then inside my eyes and finally all over my forehead. He was a short broad shouldered cracker with a well-groomed recently dyed dirty blonde mustache. He had to tiptoe to make it appear he was taller than me. I couldn't stop laughing. I thought his tactics were juvenile and silly. When he finally stopped I asked him if he was done. He did it again and this time I had to turn my face completely away. I knew what he was trying to do. He was just hoping to provoke me enough for me to lose my cool and composure and touch him on his body whether it was a fist, a slap, a straight-arm, or even a tiny tap on the breastplate with the fingertip. Then the dirty pig could wipe his ass and justify an arrest for assaulting an officer and then he can take you in, book you, and while he's processing you he can add a few more charges like resisting arrest and other meaningless linguistic shit like that and then they can haul you to court and the judge will favor the police because judges like to juggle slimy sperm cells of police officers in their coffee-stained constipated mouths convicting you for seven to ten years for assaulting an officer. I on the other hand couldn't do anything about the killer cop almost killing me.

During the standoff I somehow designated the hillbilly the affectionate pet name Cornhusker. I think I told him after he was through spitting all over me a second time in less than one minute that he looked like a Cornhusker to me. With tears starting to filter out my eyes accompanying frustrated powerless breaths I hysterically protested back to him that he had no right to get in my face and threaten my life with his spic goons surrounding me like some B-rated circle jerk. "Yeah. Spic! You, you motherfuckin spics! All of you, doing the dirty white man's dirty work backing up this Cornhusker fuck leading you all like stupid puppies on a lead making you sit and talk and play and turn over and bend over when Cornhusker says it's okay to do so. And you Cornhusker, how long have you been here, what, maybe, three years two at the most. What the fuck do you know about this city you worthless piece of Cornhusking shit. Where you from? No wait. Let me guess. Uhhmm. Let me see, Nebraska right, you're from Nebraska. That's why you're called Cornhusker you fuckin' redneck son-of-a-bitch."

I was too hurt to even care about what I was saying. I wanted to somehow maybe by some miracle grapple with one of the pigs, one of the weaker ones and somehow remove his pistol from his belt, unclick the safety and shoot all of them in their despicable faces. But I knew and know that that is what they want. I remained somewhat calm as I let go a tumultuous lecture to the spic police officers that the spic officers are rarely ever promoted to officers in the department; how white police officers can shoot Hispanic people with impunity while if a spic pig even thinks of using his gun he'll receive paid leave and psychological evaluation for an indeterminate amount of time; and other political elocution and issues I really knew nothing about. I could see it was falling on dumb and deaf ears. For a moment I almost thought I saw one of the spic partners absorbing and comprehending what I had been saying but it turned out he was just trying to figure out what elocution meant. I went on and on and on walking in circles inside the simulated circle jerk pointing my fingers at each and every one of the dirty spic partners bad dogging them for defending and pledging their life to a system that terrorizes and murders their own brothers and sisters and looks upon Hispanics and all brown people and the poor as second-class slaves with nothing else they should be doing but going to church, dropping out of high school, going to prison where more than three-quarters of the prison population in Amerika is brown, working as an Extraction Specialist with the Parks & Recreation Department at the city governmental level (the more commonly referred to title is "garbage man"), getting each other pregnant at a very young age, selling-out to the police department and becoming a pig, selling-out to local politics and becoming a two-faced double-talking corrupt political whore, or the worst of all, selling-out to everything and joining the military. Like *South Park: The Movie* put it better than any military analyst has for the past one-hundred years in the U.S. military: operation put the darkies in front.

I plopped on the ground from brain over usage. Eventually the pigs dispersed and left me sitting alone on the pavement possessed by my own sorrow. In the middle of my tirade the pigs had dismissed the rest of the passengers. Because of the uniformed towers blocking my view and hindering my movement I wasn't aware that I was alone with these murderous knaves. I could've been killed, tortured, beaten, or arrested and taken somewhere never to be unearthed. My passive non-violent resistance saved my ass, but failed to empower me.

Here I was again in a similar situation with more spic goons encircling me in the same fashion. I was trapped. I knew I wasn't walking out of The Lensic tonight. I pretended to avoid their questioning and paid no attention to their presence for about an extra five minutes longer than I expected. I knew I had to force their hand. The big fat fuck on a power trip leading the posse chided me once more that it was time for me to go. A silence hushed over the exorbitantly loud music blasting. He and I peered aggressively into each other's eyes for what seemed about ten minutes but was more like one. That was it. I couldn't take it anymore. I leaned forward into his left ear and projected loud enough for him to hear: "why you wanna do the white man's dirty work?"

"That's it," he said and lurched for my shoulder and arm but before he could grip it I flung it away from his constraint like in the movies and told him that I'll go let me get my jacket and we're out of here. I leaned over to The Brit and confided to her to get her things we're on our way out. I turned to the left toward the double doors ready to leave but then made a quick audible to the right because I adopted an impulsive idea to run to the front of the stage and make a scene having the guards catch up with me near the front and perhaps forcing Robert Cray to pause the concert and I would cry for help for anybody in particular Robert Cray to stop the abuse and wail that all I wanted to do was dance and have a good time and appreciate his music because he really sounded extraordinary that night. We weren't bothering anybody.

Before I could carry out my improvised plan two of the other dudes tackled me and lifted me and pulverized me out the double doors ramming me face first into the wood enumerating a profound thump as the doors flayed and I was yelling at the top of my lungs and screaming and psychopathically laughing and The Brit was slapping the fat ass with her leather purse cheering me on and concurring every word I was saying about how these little pinche spic bitches were nothing but whores for the white man and that I guess the token spic at this wake wasn't allowed to have a good time and that the spic is always keeping down other spics in order to prove to his white master how good of a diligent terrorist and torturer and killer he can be for the filthy beast just like the black and brown Latin soldiers in the U.S. Armed Forces murdering and terrorizing other brown people in the brown part of the world so greedily excessively wealthy white men back in North Amerika and Europe can continue to attend their quaint charades and performances put on by token monkeys on a box smiling for the cameras and dancing for the dead.

Living Briefly in Paradox

It feels like you're suffocating. They were elevating my legs high up in the air as the beer cascaded down my throat almost making me choke. I had my hands on the keg to keep balance and my eyelids squeezed shut tight in order to prevent the suds from stinging my eyes. The rest of the party members were cheering me on and laughing and having a great time. It was my father and uncle holding my legs, keeping me aloft a lot longer than I wanted to be. When they released me I upchucked some of the beer and drained it from my nose. The environment around me felt and looked like when you first dismount from a merry-go-round. These are what party people call "inverts" or keg stands or something like that. I call it stupidity.

I was ripped. I was so drunk Charles Bukowski would've been envious. It was my older other brother's 21st birthday so we celebrated like a bunch of stupid locals not knowing any other way to direct such powerful energy. We procured two full kegs of beer filled with Heineken from Owl's Liquor and decided to hold the event at my parents' house.

Only the family and one other friend of my older other brother's was at the party. We didn't desire to waste the beer. The purchase cost my father more than one hundred bucks and he was worried we would never be able to tap the second keg much less finish the first. Two hours had already gone by and between the few of us there we had barely made it through about a quarter of the first keg. Something unorthodox had to be done. It was my idea. I asked my folks if I could call some friends over, friends I knew who loved to drink beer, especially when it's free, and they obliged. In about ten minutes four of my compadres showed up with sober thoughts and dry livers. In another hour we finished the first keg. That is when the "inverted" method was recommended.

An hour later and the second keg swished the remnants of liquid leftover at the bottom of the well. Between about nine of us we finished off two full kegs in four hours. My body was bloated and my brain was hemorrhaging. I decided to go for a drive.

I told the four dudes who showed up at my bro's party to come with me. Before anybody else at the function could pay attention to what we were up to the Socio Politically Impotent Chicanos (SPIC) and a very intoxicated myself loaded-up into my shit-stained light brown 1979 Ford LTD boat. I was the captain, SPIC in the passenger seat was the navigator, and the other three spics crunched into the back seat. SPIC in the passenger seat suggested that he drive since he was more practiced at driving drunk. I declined the offer with an impolite repudiation.

Nighttime had succumbed. The gauge on the panel was on empty. We made it to Cerrillos Rd. perambulating in the steel horse through Baca Street. I could've filled-up at the Allsup's gas station at the intersection but I decided against it since there were no young people hanging around gathered in a crowd. Usually when you see a group of cars and young Chicano people commingling at an Allsup's, or Taco Bell, or Wal-Mart, that meant that there might be a party or social gathering of sorts ready to take place or already in progress. We used to come together on The Plaza on Friday nights to find out where the parties were and to find out what other kinds of young people were actually residing in Santa Fe. Young people from all sectors of society spontaneously participated. Rich white kids, white trash, well-to-do Hispano kids, poor wretched spics, Indians, newcomers, lifers, Santa Fe High sell-outs, St. Mike's sissies, Capital High hoods, Westsiders, Eastsiders, Southsiders, kids from up North, kids from 'Burque, and young homeless people who lived underneath the park benches on the downtown Plaza. This used to be one of the highlights for many youngsters in the city that's supposedly different.

Back in the ancient colonial times The Plaza was the center of the town. The Plaza was the place where community members could come and socialize and enjoy the day or the late afternoon or the docile evenings. When I was growing up The Plaza on Friday Nights was probably the only place in town where all kinds of different young people could come together to get to know one another, to communicate, to network, to hook-up, to have a good time and stay out of trouble while doing it. Then the tourists started staying. Then the cops started to monitor us. Then the downtown business owners started complaining. Then we were kicked off The Plaza. So now here I am and four other drunk Santa Fesinos cruising down Cerrillos Road headed toward downtown. I couldn't remember being behind the steering wheel. The street looked like a thin dark gray creek and we were lost in the concrete jungle. The music in the car was louder than an air raid siren. The stereo in the LTD only played AM channels so I had to travel with a six battery D requirement Boom Box devised sometime around the early 1980s that I stole from my moms.

We were approaching the intersection of Cerrillos Rd. and St. Francis Drive, one of the worst, terrible, heavily trafficked intersections in the state. Before you reach the intersection there is a Taco Bell located about a small block away. All the occupants in the car, including me, were focusing our attentions at the corporate shithole while the accelerator somehow started accelerating. My head was still turned all the way to the right trying to spot cars or young girls hanging around the parking lot even though we had just passed it by. I thought I might've heard SPIC in the passenger seat say "car," but I wasn't too sure. I slowly turned my gaze from over his shoulder to his funny face and smiled bizarrely. SPIC in the passenger seat sort of halfheartedly chortled and pointed at the front windshield. "Car" I thought I delineated from the movements of his lips but I could never be too certain. The Boom Box was working well for the first time in its technologically archaic mode of existence. "Car" escaped from his vocal chords but it might've sounded like he said far, or star, or bar.

"What?" I wistfully inquired. "Watch out for that car!" he yelled and braced himself stretching his forearms curling his fingers around the butting end of the sun cracked dashboard pushing himself as far back into the cushioned passenger seat as far as possible with eyeballs bulging from the sockets of his nervous disposition. I gave him a comforting drunken expression and slowly started to turn my eyes back to the road in front of me and discerned the effulgent red brake lights on the back of a parked black Toyota 4 x 4 pickup truck charging into the front end of my beloved boat. We were probably doing sixty in a twenty-five mile per hour zone. The rear end bumper of the truck was no less than approximately five to ten feet when I stomped on the brakes and prepared myself for what looked like to be unequivocal death. The car skidded and screeched and bounced and rocked forth and back and came within inches of the tailgate. I almost sobered up. While I was breathing rapaciously the owner of the truck descended his cabin, walked to the rear, inspected his machine's body armor, hardly looked at me, and walked back to the inside of the truck. SPIC in the passenger seat was talking shit to him. I was too surprised to surmise the proximity of extinction.

At another Allsup's further down Cerrillos Road at the intersection of Cerrillos and Guadalupe Street before it turns into Don Diego Street heading south, SPIC in the passenger seat decided he should take over driving responsibilities. I had no objections, but I did have another great idea. While we were at the filling station pumping gas another local deadbeat pulled into the station. He was a guy I knew from way back in the day when I used to frequent The Monica Roybal Center. We grew up in the same neighborhood but he was a couple of years older so I never got to see him that often. He wasn't that interesting of a character. He had a truck similar to the one I almost just crashed into. That's the only reason I conjured another brilliant plot.

Despite what my father believed I was never the one to follow unless I was part of a conspiracy I could profit from individually. Of all the stupid things I once did in an early lifetime, only two things are true: (1) it was almost always my hair-brained notion to seek out trouble and her ensuing delightful intricacies, and (2) I was always sober. Except this time around I was totally wasted, at least until I almost killed all of us. This guy who drove into the gas station was a pseudo-crazy dude who liked getting into trouble about as much as I did. I proposed to him and the rest of the motley assembly that we make life interesting and engage in half-ass insurrection by invading the Eastside neighborhoods and taking out our justified grievances on the gringos' car windows, house windows, walls and front lawns. The conceit of vandalizing appealed to them but they all wanted to do it on the Westside in their own neighborhoods. I never understood this about the spic. He'll rebel and destroy his own neighborhood, like the blacks did in South Central Los Angeles in the early1990s, but mention one iota of fucking with the white man on purpose and he shrinks and panics to a squirm. We are so controlled by fear the possibility of unity is a mythological fable waiting to be written.

We agreed to do it on the condition of compromise: we would break windows and shoot at houses on the Eastside and spray paint on the Westside. I didn't have too much of a problem with this. Recently I had lifted the gun from my daddy's desk drawer and always maintained a loaded .357 Magnum underneath the driver's seat of my 1979 Ford LTD banana boat. Why I packed a heater I will never fathom. Santa Fe was not the type of small city you needed to pack a gun in. That is, not until the Amerikans swarmed in and took over and brought all of their big city shit with them that they were trying to avoid when they moved here in the first place. One thing you must understand is that the neighborhoods on the Eastside used to be occupied by strong Chicano/Hispanic families that went back generations long before the imperial stars and hype were planted on this soil. These Eastside neighborhoods are some of the oldest and vintage neighborhoods in the city, therefore, the most expensive. They should've been fought for a long time ago. For all the rhetoric about integration spoken throughout the 1960s, the gringo came here shortly after, all through the late 1970s throughout the 1980s well into the 1990s till the present day in the early 21ˢᵗ Century, and economically forced the backward Hispanics out of their homes and off the land. Today you wouldn't even think there were any Hispanics, or brown people in what is promoted as Santa Fe and Santa Fe Style and Santa Fe Living and Santa Fe Trend if it wasn't for the burgeoning Mexican/Central American immigrant population taking over at least half of the city down in Little Mexico. But since the local native Chicanos hate the new immigrants from the south, the Chicano got exactly what he deserved. When you're willing to destroy your own neighborhood instead of the enemy's, you get what you deserve.

The crazy dude and the friend he was with followed me to a spot where I parked my car and where we could retreat if we encountered any unpredictable problems. I had done this before on many vengeful occasions. I had a map in my head and a time limit so we could vacate the vicinity before the stupid cops showed-up. We would trounce the South of Capitol neighborhood, head up Old Santa Fe Trail and reach the foothills area near and around St. John's College, swing back down East Alameda, make our way down Canyon Road, cross over to Palace Avenue, and complete our sojourn with trashing one of the more obnoxious downtown businesses. And if we had time, just for the fun of it, we'd drive up the ski basin road just a bit passed Ten Thousand Waves, flip a bitch, and speed down the swiveling incline and fire shots from our cannons at houses without looking. We piled into the bed of the crazy guy's truck. On our way to our first target we pulled over at various places, many construction sites, and collected rocks with size dimension and weight capacity ample enough to throw and aesthetic quality enough to devastate. The first target was the South of Capitol neighborhood.

The crazy dude drove up and down Galisteo and Don Gaspar criss-crossing the side streets like Booth while we in the back shattering car windows setting off alarms costing the newcomer Amerikan a small amount of petty repair he could afford but costing him or her a juncture of convenience they so dutifully worship and would hate to sacrifice. We must have wrecked at least twenty different cars. I had instructed the fellas to single-out luxury cars like Mercedes Benzes, BMWs, Jaguars, Audis, Volvos, Land Rovers, Range Rovers and any kind of SUV. For the most part we stuck to the format. But since South of Capitol is not necessarily a high-end neighborhood, we had to lower our standards and stick with Volvos, Subarus, Hondas, and Volkswagens, and more than an enough supply of SUVs. Once and a while we came across a used Mercedes and ripped the ornament from the hood and fell upon it like a pack of sexually deprived grown men on an underage girl walking home late at night. Sometimes the crazy guy driving the truck would have to bring the vehicle to a complete stop in case we missed a mark. It was pretty difficult to nail a window sailing at 45 m.p.h in the middle of the night. We missed most of our opportunities, but the ones we connected released a tirade of adrenaline surging throughout our frigid skeletons enough to make us want to do it again. If we had to stop we would climb down from the bed, the guy who threw the rock would pick up the weapon, walk up to the car and bash one of the side windows. The rest of us would help him by clobbering and denting the body of the car with baseball bats, rod iron bars, and a police's hardwood black shellacked nightstick baton I had stolen from an ex-girlfriend who got it from her stepfather who supposedly stole it off a police officer during a scuffle. We danced in anarchy's voluptuous ecstasy circling the demolition out of step like a frightened Greek tragedian chorus until a light illuminated in one of the houses above. After we finished off South of Capitol we made our way into the southeast foothills of the Sangre de Cristo Mountains well into the Arroyo Hondo area near El Gancho. I had a rich lawyer cousin who lived out there so I made sure we hit his house first. Several times we had to reload our rocks and the crazy guy had a couple of fifths of whiskey so we reloaded on that too. It was a bit more difficult to attack automobiles in this neck of the forest. The houses built there were part of the "gated community" trend infecting Santa at the time so it became very difficult to always have to mount six foot walls and bombard cars from the inside then make a quick getaway. Primarily we stuck to spray-painting the closed-off walls with pornographic representations of

U.S. public officials and high-profile religious personalities. Shooting the mailboxes and street signs with my .357, the crazy guy's twelve gauge shotgun, and two of the other guys had a .38 caliber respectively and a pinche .22, added authenticity to the fact that there was a war going on.

We sped through the unpaved dirt roads wild as wolves running through the wilderness nocturnal almost flipping the truck. With wind emasculating our hair we triumphed in the back of the pickup raising both fists into the night sky infatuating the moon sending forth unfettered shrills for the ensnared stars to come and join in our temporal emancipation. We savored every friendly punch in the shoulder and every smack on the back and every pass of the bottle like an indigenous tribe waiting around for prophecy and the inevitable. We surrendered ourselves to the hindsight of danger, the relinquishment of apathy. We finally understood what it meant to be animated. For that moment there was no law, no government or legal repercussions we would have to face. I knew what we were doing and the gentlemen entrusted me with their delusions of safety.

I honestly doubt that there was not one of us who understood that our way was dying. We all knew we had no future in Santa Fe. We witnessed how our older siblings were leaving town, heading for Rio Rancho, 'Burque, or Phoenix. There was an ironically juxtaposed exodus taking place. All of us in that pickup truck grasped the conspicuous truth that we didn't come to this side of town. Hardly any of us spent any time on The Plaza anymore. Several of the guys in the truck even unobtrusively commented that they had never been to this part of town before and how beautiful it all was. I could tell by their swift reconciliation of mood that they wondered in utter silence why this was so. Right at that instance, etching the downtrodden confused looks on their collective countenances inside my consciousness, I absolutely harbored no reservation whatsoever that we were doing the right thing.

Cruising down East Alameda we took it easy after I informed my newly dignified posse that there were still some Chicano families that lived here. I seemed to be the only one who knew which houses were still occupied by Chicanos so we were able to avoid them. Heading into Canyon Road I told the crazy dude to pull over. The boys seemed a bit drained so I decided to teach them a lesson about terrorism. I asked the crazy driver to meet us at the end of Canyon Road, or the beginning, depending on which way you're traveling it. He demanded to know why but I said I would apprise him later. He reluctantly nodded in approval and drove to the bottom of the street where it connects with Paseo de Peralta. Nestled into the foothills of the Sangre de Cristos where the top of Canyon Road ends and Upper Canyon Road begins, the night feels cool, serene, anesthetized, and obsolete. One can summon thoughts unknown and séance with spirits that never experienced a human body, hear an antediluvian drum that doesn't beat for the physically obsessed. Standing unmoved at that spot shortly after midnight, we knelt on the pavement and bestowed a prayer to the shadow of the mountain that would shroud our discontent and mask our aversion to submit. The sky covered us with a stingy breeze to humble our exponential arrogance. Subsequent to ritual preparation I briefed the apprehensive guerillas on the purpose of our next uprising. We were going to stroll down Canyon Road under moonbeam auspices and pick as many flowers as possible to construct into a bouquet. At first the boys were dumbstruck. Then they broke out into hysteria and started calling me a pussy and some kind of a fag. I ignored their imbecility and began the decline. The boys slowly began to trickle in pursuit since they had nowhere else to go and no one to take them there even if they did. As we drifted down the gallery strip like the Santa Fe River used to, I educated the young men on how the gringo was going to get a lot more upset about our picking flowers from this street than vandalizing all of their automobiles or disrupting their neighborhoods. It failed to dawn on them abruptly. I went on about how the gringo gallery owner here goes through many pains and ordeals to hire some Mexican to plant their rose gardens and tend them and make sure they have something to brag about to their other inconsiderate gringo companions while they're lunching at Casa Sena or SantaCafe. By our plucking the blossoms, we're disturbing the

Amerikan invader tenfold psychologically since he's, or she in this case, is a self-aggrandized little bastard. You must keep in mind gentleman that the Amerikan thinks he owns everything. Not only here, but everywhere. Look what they're doing to our Arab brothers and sisters. "I ain't no fuckin' Arab," one of the dumb spics declared. All of you here have Arab blood moving through your body whether you want to admit it or not. Spain was conquered by the Moors and ruled for 700 years. In school you heard of this era described as The Dark Ages. Well we're living in the real dark ages now. You ain't no fuckin' Amerikan. You're an illegal alien. The Amerikans came to Santa Fe to take it over and own it, not to share it. This gentle, seemingly insignificant act is going to have the gringo hot and bothered and up in arms wanting to roll some heads but having not the slightest clue who could possibly be responsible for such a benevolent crime considering that the local spic here is too uncivilized and savage to pluck flowers from a stem. This is the equivalent of a ghost stealing your sleep in the middle of the night. They will have no problem blaming kids like us for the vandalism, but this alone will have far reaching implications and a crushing impact. By the time we wake hung over from all this rowdiness, he'll be weeping alongside his sexually suppressed wife unsure about how he's going to make that extra million this year. The world he created is a ghetto, shit in it.

Between five of us we picked nearly all the flowers that had blossomed during that time of year. All that was left were rows of green bushes with stems and leaves lazily blowing in the gust like a bent inconsiderate wrist waving off somebody else's misfortune. As the boys bunched red roses, white roses, yellow roses, pink roses, snapdragons, trumpet vines, daisies, sunflowers, and other splendid species I couldn't identify because I'm a dumb, uninformed spic, I interrogated them about how they thought the these kinds of people were able to grow such lush gardens on this side of town even though we were supposed to be in the midst of an unscrupulous seven-year drought and every citizen within the city limits was supposed to be conserving water. I explained to them how these gringos spent thousands of dollars on plants and plant supplements every year. They knew I knew what I was talking about since I used to work at a local nursery in town near my neighborhood but quit shortly after I was hired because I didn't like the way they exploited the Mexican workers and I wasn't getting paid enough to clean up toxic chemicals and the entire operation was being run illegally and the owner was a redneck millionaire who owned many more businesses so I decided I didn't want any complicity in such malfeasance. They listened with acute curiosity. I encouraged them to take it all and to give the unique bouquet they concocted to their mothers, grandmothers, girlfriends, sweethearts, and/ or sisters or nieces. This land belongs to no one, not even our ancestors much less the bloodstained Amerikan that is unhealthily obsessed with privatization. I recommended that next time they wanted to take their girlfriends out on a date, instead of cavorting them over to an expensive restaurant downtown where the clientele and the staff didn't want you around and where you would have to save a year's worth of slave wages just to pay for the meal; instead of taking them to some sleazy bar, guide them up and down Canyon Road and pick a bouquet of flowers for her and guarantee she'll fall in love with you interminably. Even though you might have to endure some nasty thorns and some dabs of blood exiting your fingers, the punishment befits the recompense. Peace unto you my brothers from another mother. May the hawk recognize us from above as she hunts for bankruptcy, and may the rattlesnake beware the footprint.

Before we hopped back into the truck, the guy with the .38 pulled out his quete and let off six rounds into one of the galleries igniting a small fire inside the building. This unplanned act screwed up the rest of the evening's events. While he was parked at the end of the street in darkness, the crazy dude confided to me that he had seen several cops patrolling the area. We both figured that they were probably looking for us. We had been busy now for almost three hours and it was only a matter of time until we were busted. I advised the boys that perhaps we should cut our losses and call it a night. None of them wanted to stop. The crazy driver concurred my counsel and it took a bit of time but the crew eventually conceded.

The crazy dude dropped my four boys and I off at my stashed vehicle and told me that he would never forget this night, it was the most fun he had ever had. He still had about three-quarters left of one of the bottles of whiskey and bequeathed it to us as a parting gift. I thanked him and he drove off into a realm of life I'd never encounter him in again.

The boys were restless. They couldn't stop bragging and telling fibs about how many windows they'd abolished or how many caps they'd popped. They thanked me for the adventure but I remained silent and acknowledged their gratitude with an air of satisfactory humility. Even though we hadn't spent much time on this Earth getting to know one another, we all felt like brothers for the time being. I decided to drive each one of them home. Three of them lived in the Bellamah section and the other one lived way out on Highway 14 next to the prison. We had a few cans of beer lying around in my car that I guessed we purchased from Allsup's earlier after I almost killed all of us, so we opened them and shared. One of the homeboys pulled out a joint he had been saving in case we had made it to a party. Since we didn't he felt that now was as good as any time to spark up a leno. The night could only get better. Cruising down Siringo Road after crossing St. Francis Drive at three in the morning we felt like the only people who mattered in the world. We were all smoking the joint, even the two guys that never really smoked. We were passing the brews around and the bottle of whiskey taking shots, and we were all reciting Nas' *One Love* on the Boom Box even if we didn't know the words to the song. Nothing in the world could ruin our enjoyment.

Approaching the intersection of Siringo Road and Yucca Street I spotted a city police car with its lights turned off trying to hide in the dim where the street lamps are unable to cover. It was camouflaged within the indiscernible confines of the College of Santa Fe campus exit. By the time I reached the traffic lights at the intersection it was too late to turn off onto a side street. I had a green light. Anything I might've done outside of continuing on by would've aroused his suspicion. I became serious enough to tell the guys in the car who were generating exquisite amounts of raucous to calm down until we see what's up with this pig. I knew for damn sure I wasn't speeding and all the activity and excitement from tonight had sobered me up so I know I wasn't swerving yet at that moment I did have a whiskey bottle to my lips downing my second shot. I wasn't tanked, just paranoid. Once I passed the intersection where he was parked he instantly clicked his headlights on, pulled up behind me and gave a quiet chase. He followed me for about a quarter of a mile without flashing his obscene red white and blue lights or spotlight. He didn't do anything to give me an indication that he was going to pull me over. The street was clear. He stayed roughly three car lengths behind me. I wasn't breaking any laws except for the fact that the car was packed with underage minors manipulating open containers of alcohol, the cabin was filled to the sealer with marijuana smoke, good shit too, nobody had their seatbelts on, I had no insurance nor a license, I was driving while intoxicated, and let me see…oh yeah, we had three stolen fully loaded lethal weapons, two of them unregistered. The boys started to panic a little and so did I but I didn't showcase it. I had to think fast. I had to do something. Turning off to a side street was out of the question. I couldn't speed up or slow down. Pulling over would've been about the dumbest thing I could think of. I had to think of something better. About halfway across Governor Miles Park, or National Guard Park, the pig flashed his lights real quick and then turned them off just as fast. Was he pulling me over or what the fuck was he doing? He didn't flash them again or say anything on his intercom and shine his spotlight so I couldn't tell if he was pulling me over or not. I had to think fast and do something because I knew we were busted and headed for jail if he pulled me over, come up to the driver's window, and I was forced to roll it down. One of the homeboys suggested that we do just that and when he comes over to the window we would take out our guns and shoot him down like a deer in the center of the road. I didn't think that this was such a bright idea so I said no let me handle it and I did. I came up with a brilliant impromptu. I decided to pull the fucker over.

I'm probably the only cat in Santa Fe, no, the only cat in New Mexico, no, no, the only cat in the Divided States, no, the whole fuckin' world, I'm probably the only citizen in the entire universe to ever pull over a police officer for a crime he has committed. His crime was fucking with me and my homies and the good time we were having. At the intersection of Siringo Road and Camino Carlos Rey I turned to the right and turned to the right again into the parking lot of Miles Park, or National Guard Park, adjacent to the basketball goals. I mercilessly maneuvered the gearshift into park, pounced out of the car and marched up to the driver side of his patrol car as he pulled into the parking lot after me. Normally if you do this in any situation a cop thinks he has the right to kill you and more often than not he will gun you down for exiting your car without him prompting you to, at least it's like that in Albuquerque. This cop couldn't gather his composure and I was already yelling at him like he was a worthless child before he could get out of the car. I kept berating him and bitching and complaining how cops had been harassing me a lot lately and I was tired of their shit I was going to file lawsuits why was he harassing me he was following me and harassing me and fucking with me because he wouldn't just pull me over he was harassing me I kept repeating this word harass and brutalizing and abuse of power and probable cause (before the Patriot Act days) and other legal defense catch phrases I know stupid cops love to hear. I wouldn't allow him to sneak a word in. He seemed unsure of himself and how to handle me. He was a cookie cutter dumb fuckin' rookie. I broke him down and scared the shit out of him more than he could've been aware of just how scared he had me at the moment. Because my mother was supposed to be somebody important in town I suppose I got away with it. He didn't write me a citation or even bother to look into my automobile. All he did was tell me that the parks close at ten o'clock and he was wondering why I pulled over into this park. I retorted that I wasn't pulling over into the parking lot of the park I was pulling him over to find out why he was harassing me. He repeated that the parks close at ten o'clock. I hollered at him and lectured him a little more making him feel like a turtle retracting it's brevity of bravery back into the protection of the shell. I scolded him and let him know that I was on my way home he could follow me home if he wanted to that way he could deal with my mother. He said that wouldn't be necessary and wished me a safe journey. What a chump. I lost more respect for police officers that night than I never really had for them in the first place. My adrenaline took over and I taxied the three idiots that lived in the area, the three idiots that wanted to go out shooting (as they put it), home in a hurry.

The other guy and I, the one that lived out on Highway 14, decided not to go home. We drove back over to the Westside of town. It was slightly past four in the morning. Our minds were awakened once again by the near miss and the booze and weed left in our possession. By the time we pulled into the parking lot at DeVargas Mall I was stewed again and so was he. Before I could express my inklings he was already out of the car running up to several parked vehicles sitting there in the vacant parking lot and busting the windows with my stolen police baton. After all the windows were broken I joined him in looting the cars for all the worthless items we could find. About the most valuable item I could discover was a pair of black Nike jogging sweat pants that were too small for me and tailored for a woman. A small white truck came cruising by. My boy leaped into the car taking cover in the back seat leaving a trail of blood in his tracks and staining my upholstery. I guess he sliced himself in several different places while breaking windows. I raced to the driver's side throwing the car in drive and hauled ass out of there. The small truck gave chase. I thought at first it was mall security because they patrolled the parking lots in small white trucks. When the truck followed us out of the parking lot onto Highway 285 heading north, I reconsidered my assumption. I must've been too plastered to realize it but my passenger behind me yelled at me to put the gun away. He claims I almost shot him. I asked him what the fuck he was talking about. He said he heard a gunshot and repeated again for me to put the gun away. I told him I didn't have the gun the gun was under the seat. "Oh really," he responded. "Then how come your rear window is missing?" "What?" I looked over my shoulder and saw that he was right. My rear window was in shambles. I swore to him that it wasn't me and proved it to him by showing him the gun that was cold and still had a full chamber of bullets. Whoever was chasing us shot at us.

I finally lost them turning off the highway getting lost in the spiraling rural dirt roads near Buckman Road. We pulled over and finished off the bottle of whiskey, whatever beer was left, and smoked the rest of the joint that was now a roach. Everything happened so fast that night. While we were meditating in the early morning under the quilt of stars above us and the bashful rustle of trees, I couldn't remember what had taken place all through the previous hours. My friend narrated everything that happened but I didn't believe him. The only thing I remember from our exploits that night was waking up the next morning in Barrio La Canada around seven thirty sicker than a rodent freezing my ass off because the rear window to my 1979 Ford LTD was missing.

The Flamenco Dancer

The house lights were turned off. The show was beginning. We apprehended our seats near the front. The atmosphere is redolent with awe and ignorance. Darkness embraces us all. Red hazy lights cast a dense illumination over the greasy shiny black hair of the fat singer sitting directly opposite the audience center stage against the backdrop. He soliloquizes a metaphysically challenged haunt from his mouth. The solitary voice crescendos and decrescendos and flutters throughout the building, building terse anticipation for those that have never been here before. The song he is wailing permeates the eardrums of the listeners and every kind of quiet conversation comes to an expected pause. Immediately you recognize you're imprisoned inside the myth of the gypsy. Everything stereotypical and commercial you've learned about gypsies seems present. The isolation, the desperate shrill voice, the abandoned alley hidden somewhere in an urban tundra, the earrings and loose, raggedy clothing of the musicians, the paying members of the audience sitting in their Earth tone summer clothes. The fat singer's high-pitched yell sounds like an Indian yelp but with more of an Arabic morning prayer. The lights are fading to purple and blue and then darker purple and then a darker blue. He carries on his narcotic descant for some time calling forth the spirits of those that wander aimlessly through this meaningless world. Another light, light white, flashes on a younger culprit hitting a makeshift drum that looks like a square aluminum can covered in scale made of bone. The sound is stentorian. The rhythm is something similar to a Caribbean Latin flavor with improvised African jaunts included in the pattern out of step, vigilantly tapping the language known to those that are dead and don't know it. Both performers steady a syncopated vibration developing a timorous mood to welcome the dancers onto the stage. More lights explode from the somewhat elevated mini-stage front center. The dancers pirouette their European ass in front of a bunch of Amerikan tourists. There are three guys and three girls, somewhere between the ages of eighteen and forty-two. The women are breathtaking. The gentlemen look gay. There are two short guys and a tall dude that doesn't look like he should be dancing flamenco. There are two shorter somewhat corpulent chicks and one younger skinny taller one dancing opposite the tall dude that looked like he had no business dancing flamenco. They were overbearing. The men were dressed in black slacks with gleaming black shoes and a black button-up long sleeve shirt covered by a colored vest with their hair slicked back. The women wore off-shoulder long white flowery skirts that provided a cool wind every time they turned around. The patterns on the dress matched the color of the male counterpart's vest. If you looked momentarily you could see the plump breast cleavage of the maidens vibrate as they stomped their heartbroken feet volcanically on the wooden floor of the stage to the beat of the makeshift drum. The men would stomp and then the women would stomp and then the men and then together they stomped and together they sweated and they would clap their copas hard and send a million smacks to your presence as you wish they would stop because the reverberation was too loud. Sitting near the front had its drawbacks. Every time the male dancers twirled a shower of sweat would sashay in your direction landing on the napkin underneath your cheap overpriced drink resting on the tabletop slowly creeping toward you drop by drop. Once and a while the sweat would swat one of your cheeks or cascade down your forehead before you could realize it wasn't your own.

A guitar joins the session and it sounds like the guitar player is strumming a twelve-string instrument instead of the six. A string could pop anytime. Their faces are so intense it looks like they're forced to hold their shit throughout the performance to add that Latin mercurial fever. After the first dance the entire crowd except for us stands up and cheers and claps and shouts out "Oles" to the dancers. The dancers are smiling like schoolchildren who just received a condescending pat on the top of the head from an elder. I admit that when you first experience the flamenco dance by a troupe that can hold its own you're taken with the act as much as anybody else. The rapidity of the foot tapping, the accuracy of the two to three to four to five to six pirouettes, the jumping, the knee drops, the shouting commands from the musicians, the precise improvised steps that looked like it took years of rehearsal to master but felt like anybody could do it. The intensity. There is no intensity like the intensity of a flamenco dancer's concentration. But after a while the routine becomes monotonous and you grow weary of the sweat soaking you; the pomposity of the countenance of the dancers taking themselves too seriously, especially the Spanish ones; the same pattern of moves over and over again; the thunderous clapping of hands and stomping of feet; and the stupid gringo tourists in the audience shouting out distilled "Oles" at every unwarranted occasion. It got to the point where a drunk gringo tourist couple was clapping copas out of rhythm and the dancers on stage had to stop the performance. The leader of the troupe told them to not do that. An ensuing argument occurred where the gringo couple tried arguing with the leader of the troupe about how other dance troupes allow the audience to participate and that the dancers should be professional enough to dance through anything. The couple agreed to stop when threatened with security removal.

The show took nearly three hours with a brief intermission. The second half of the show was pretty much the same thing as the first half only in the second half the leader of the troupe, this much older flamenco dancer wearing too much vibrant make-up and looked like the best of her dancing days were behind her, trots onto the stage for a showcase dance and the audience automatically gives her a standing ovation and numerous "Oles" for reasons I will never comprehend.

After the show some of the audience members venture upstairs to the social bar where a bunch of degenerates are singing karaoke. My brother and his date are drunk. Some of the flamenco dancers finally made it upstairs and start smoking and singing like spoiled European pigs. Hours pass and everybody's drunk. A few people start dancing on a small open space in front of the karaoke machine. I like to dance and I was drunk so I started dancing with no one in particular trying to show-off my turns and twists acting like one of the flamenco dancers. There were two other couples swaying next to me looking at me and laughing. All of a sudden I was swept off my feet by strong stringy muscular arms. It was one of the shorter flamenco dancers. He twirled me round and round the floor making me dizzy. I went along with the show. I figured we were just having a good time providing entertainment for the onlookers who seemed quite amused. He was pretty strong. He placed me down like a ceramic vase. We acted like a couple conducting a frail tango taking turns leading one another and turning one another until at one point we both fell to our knees and he stared into my eyes with a mischievous smile full of excitement and I stared back feigning engrossment when I feel these fingers cup their grip around my balls.

Right away I stiff armed him, lifted my index finger on my right hand and waved it from side to side letting him know that that was no way to go. He seemed to have understood and backed off. I went over to my brother and told him what had just happened, feeling violated. He laughed at me and told me to go dance with him some more. I told him let's go. On our way out the flamenco dancer came over to apologize. I accepted his apology and informed him that I'm not interested in men I'm heterosexual. The bastard hardly spoke any English but understood what I was attempting to relate. He apologized again and offered to cook me dinner if I went back with him to his place he was staying at. As he was asking me what was my favorite kind of fish I told him to forget about it and had to yank my wrist from his hand on the way out the door.

It happened to me again a few years later. I was at Bar B on a Thanksgiving evening drinking by myself at the bar because I have no friends I can truly call friends. There weren't many people around. The bar seats were empty. I chose one at the end of the bar in a corner where I wouldn't be disturbed. I was sipping on Chivas Regal with two ice cubes in it when some flaming joto comes stumbling through the front doors talking loud like an obnoxious bitch swaggering his way to the seat next to me. I didn't look in his direction but knew he was swallowing me with his eyes. I finally turned his way and saw a skinny middle-aged crew cut albino looking blonde thing winking at me. He asked me my name. I gave him a false one. He told me I looked sexy with my tattoos and attire. I said nothing. He kept asking me if I had a boyfriend and if I didn't would I like him to be my boyfriend. I told him in the most serious, respectful manner I could summon that I was not interested in men, I like women I don't prefer to stick my dick in some dry shit stained hole when I can place it into a soft, warm, moist filet. He giggled telling me how cute I was and placed his hand on my arm. I gently removed his hand and asked him not to do that again. I said that I have no problem with gay people for all I was concerned I didn't think that sexual preference should be such an antagonistic political issue. The only sexual political issue worth discussing was patriarchy and male dominance and female repression and whether or not you want to suck dick was more of a personal issue than a political one and shouldn't be placed at the forefront of any political agenda because growing-up in Santa Fe during the '80s and '90s I've encountered and interacted with many kinds of gay and lesbian people. I always got along with many of them as people except for the ones that wouldn't talk to me because I wasn't one of them. I'm well aware that many gay people have been persecuted for years and that coming out is a lot healthier than suppressing it and confusing yourself to the point where depression and possible suicide becomes viable and friendly. I have questioned my own sexuality and have reached a solid conclusion that I don't have sexual fantasies about men. I have them about women. I told him I had done a theatrical play in Santa Fe about gay issues with an almost entirely gay cast and how some of the men excluded me or shunned me and looked at me in a weird way because they knew that I knew I wasn't gay. I realized then that many gay men are uncomfortable around a virile masculine man who walks straight and they may even feel somewhat threatened, like women do around women that are prettier, depending on the type of individual. Also, I had witnessed firsthand the bestowment of political power to a gay constituent that became the first openly gay official in the city that's not so different and how I discovered that gay people are not that different or inferior or unequal from the rest of us because this gay official has become one of the worst egomaniacal little tyrants allowing the so-called power to go to her head and now other important political issues occupy less consideration in her view unless it is a high priority gay issue. Gay issues or any other special interest issue should not come before some of the more important pressing issues such as equal civil rights for all, food for all, affordable housing, and sustainable communities. He didn't seem too interested in my rhetoric. "You're cute," he told me again and I turned away after I told him not to speak to me any more. The bartender asked me if I was all right. He said this dude comes in the joint all the time harassing customers and to let him know if he bothers me any more. I thanked him and said that that probably wouldn't be necessary because I let the bitch know that I'm not gay and not interested.

The faggot wouldn't lay off. After about a few minutes he slid over next to me closer and whispered into my ear that he wanted to "suck my dick." I shook my head and warned him not to do anything stupid I didn't want to have to physically fuck him up. He smiled and shoved his hand between my thighs reaching for my crotch. I jumped out of the seat and pushed him off his seat. He landed hard on his back on the floor but got back up easily because he was a fuckin' worthless drunk. He was laughing the whole time. Two bouncers grabbed him by the arms and threw him out of the establishment. The rest of the night the Chivas was on the house.

Sangre de Gallo

There are all kinds of cults in Santa Fe. New age, Eastern, Western, Christian, Catholic, Jewish, etc. All these uninvited newcomers and transplants, especially the ones with no culture, the ones we dare not name by their best known name, develop less than intellectually invigorating small religious circles consisting of their closest newly formed friendships where at least five to ten reprobates worship some overweight ramshackle hustler posing as a guru, or god, or dog, or something. They feel they are drawn to this place by some unknown power. It's called greed. The first time I came to this revelation I was holding my mother's sacred hand sucking on my middle extended finger wondering who all these people were roaming around the desert with diapers on their heads protected by armed guards brandishing AK47s. It was supposed to be a day of prayer and like any prudent brainwashed Catholic inimmaculate virgin, I was there to pray.

The people appeared dismal, dead, and controlled. My mother's ass was being kissed by two female servants offering their services asserting that they have been assigned to her for the day because I keep forgetting that my mother was supposed to sort of be someone that's supposedly supposed to be important. I think the proper term is dignitary. There were plenty of dignitaries getting their asses greased in preparation to kiss some other ass. We were escorted to the exalted leader; the universal one; the spiritual equivalent; the yogi bear of the forest; the sideshow sandman calling the shots. I always wondered why people are so willing to submit to a power that's supposedly supposed to be higher. Why do some people sacrifice their will to participate in another human's depraved version of spiritual abundance? How can anyone willingly take orders from anyone else? Nobody has the answers and if you ask me all religious so-called leaders are charlatans perpetuating eternal sham.

When we walked into the leader's room I understood why people follow. A big fat greasy ugly looking pig motherfucker lay on his divan with his beer belly protruding from his cotton slacks and his shirt unbuttoned exposing a thicket of hairy chest dripping juices from fruit being fed to him by two pale starving looking bitches and two others massaging his feet and one other I swear to your God one other slave fanning him with a peacock's hind feathers. I swear to your God I'm not joking. This is what I witnessed from one of the most powerful cults operating in the Santa Fe area. All the invited dignitaries bent down and kissed his ring to receive blessing or anointment or some shit. It was disgusting. People called him divine. He had this off-kilter permanent hackneyed grin stuck to his face and he never looked you directly in the eye. Obviously he was materialistically rich like termites in wood. They said he had a direct connection to the Supreme One. I thought he looked like this homeless guy I always saw around town whom I used to take a piss on when he was sleeping on the sidewalk. The way he exploited women he was obviously a grotesque chauvinistic maggot. There's nothing holy about wearing ten extravagantly high-priced rings with rubies, sapphires, emeralds, and diamonds. That's like Phil Jackson claiming to be Buddhist and signing million dollar contracts while saying it. He disgusted me and his little army of cult followers disgusted me. When it was my mother's turn to see him he rose from his lazy position and embraced my mother like a Middle Easterner. I think he was supposed to be one of the real things from India or around those parts. He sure looked human to me and therefore not worthy of any sort of adoration or admiration. He kissed my mother's ass and had her sit down next to him and provided her with his sincerest attention and affection provoking the other self-important political dignitaries to take offense. He acknowledged my mother's presence. He did this for no one else.

She was said to have the power. I think I inherited it from her. For a long time now personalities pop up in my life who try to steal my soul. I was just a baby the first time. My mother found this ex-Montessori educator in the phone book. My mother needed day care and she and my father decided to try something unorthodox. On the way over to the location my mother felt something wasn't right. Upon arrival she knew what it was. The lady who ran the place took to me instantly. There were about seven other kids around but she insisted she loved me the most. I was so precious. I probably wasn't older than four years old. Before I could let go of my mother's hand she scooped me into her arms and greeted me with a dishonest overzealous inspiration. I noticed her teeth were exceptionally yellow with severe bleeding gums and breath that reeked of Echinacea and oleander. She had dark placid eyes, one crossed. I thought I heard her say something to me without moving her lips like Danny in *The Shining*. Her hair was hazel brown, tangled, and very, very long, like her fingernails. She covered her skin with a single piece full length gown made out of gunny sack material and sported a huge turquoise upside down triangular stone swinging from her neck by several strands of midnight purple yarn. Her prickly forearms were bulwarked in silver bracelets. She told my mother that she would have nothing to worry about, that I was one of the special ones. She wouldn't let go of me. She kept hugging and pressing me between her wilting breasts. As she was staring at me with a serious reference for many seconds my mother grabbed me by the arm, pulled me away from her and hurried me out of the classroom. Looking back over my mother's shoulder I could see the strange woman blowing me a kiss and smiling with a sad sadistic hesitance wishing me good look and saying we'll meet again without moving her lips.

It must be the mountains. The Sangre de Cristo Mountains surrounding Santa harbor voluminous amounts of unsavory spirits. And not just the super rich assholes who developed all over the foothills and lower small valleys. My father used to say it was God's country. The name itself means "holy faith". The "city of holy faith." The type of fuckin' weirdoes who end up here proves that this place is much more than enchantment. There's so many holier than thou con artists circulating throughout Santa they should provide a directory to contact them. They're always drawn to me and I don't know why.

He thought he was a hip-hop entity. He claimed he was from outer space and he was returning there after he completed his apprenticeship. I asked him what his apprenticeship was and he'd remain silent for a few seconds and then tell me he couldn't say, I wouldn't understand. This is how a lot of our conversations concluded. I never really thought much of him. At least not as much as he thought of himself. He was three years younger than I and would try to dominate everything all the time. I'm not an aggressive person by nature or choice. Most of the time I'd remain silent and wish I was somewhere else than with him wherever we were going and whatever we were doing. Hip-hop was the only thing we had in common. He had a provisional studio with up-to-date software for formulating your own instrumentals. Later on we would add the vocals by huffing into a bargain-basement microphone. He possessed the setup, I exploited. There is a price to pay for everything.

We had been working late. Guru this, guru that. He couldn't stop talking in adoration of some dirtbag he once referred to as a guru. He'd quote his guru's sayings and try telling me something I didn't know already. Consciousness this, consciousness that. Never had I traveled to his domain before because he lived in a quaint compound with sixteen other people. His guru owned the place and all the occupants shared everything. He was the youngest and consequently the least respected and mostly taken advantage of. The studio was located in the yurt. The place had a bad vibe. The kind of vibe you get when you examine a homicide scene. We recorded some music for several hours and then took a break. The night was still and the moon bombastic. Outside I could hear drumming noise at a circumspect distance.

"What's that?" I asked.

"The Drummers."

"Drummers, what kind of drummers?"

"Drummers to begin the ceremony," he intoned.

"What kind of ceremony?" Why I was curious I would never know. I should've known better.

"You want to see?"

The only reason I went is because I knew he lived with some women. Upon entering the door to a circular interior I witnessed a packed room of roughly thirty plus dirtheads stripped naked banging on multitudes of various handmade drums creating a deafening, ghastly noise almost as lurid as Sun Ra's orchestra.

"They're calling the spirits."

"What spirits?" I inquired with a dumbfounded emphasis.

"The spirits from outer space. Space is the universe, the ultimate dimension that we'll be returning to. This life is an illusion. An illusion of love filled with humans incapable of communicating their true inner feelings. Once I complete my apprenticeship I'll be able to travel through time without hesitation. The only reason we think we can't do it now is because we hesitate." He went on for hours illustrating the different virtues of his guru and how his guru tells him what he's looking for is on Earth and how his guru buys him gifts and takes him on business trips from Las Vegas to Los Angeles to Chicago and lends him his new luxury car and supports his mother and other things I wasn't really supposed to be aware of. To this guy his guru was the end end of all ends to end. He told me I should meet his guru and showed me a four-pronged plant his guru bequeathed to him.

"You have to cut the leaves a certain way and take it at a certain time of year and you will have the greatest experience you'll ever know. In order to take it though, you have to be willing to become an apprentice and obey the teachings without questioning."

"What's in the plant?" I asked.

"Nothing you'd know. You wouldn't be able to understand." I always hated his arrogance. He was so arrogant he made William F. Buckley Jr. look like a practicing Taoist. He knew it all. Everything there was to know about everything. The wisdom imparted to him he kept repeating all the time sounded more shallow than Christian sermons, but just as urbane.

The noise was killing me. Every one of these dirthead hippies tried acting like jungle natives slamming the skin over the drum a bit too bellicose. Overgrown thickets of pubic hair symmetry captured my attention. I almost gagged due to the extreme foul odor that occupied the room. Phalluses were jangling everywhere and titties flopped by. You could tell everybody was fucked-up on something. There was nothing spiritual about this fiasco. I turned to leave.

Before I could exit the doorway I encountered him. He was small in stature, fatter than a penguin, wearing an Armani suit accessorized by sunglasses beneath a crumpled Panamanian hat. Two ugly women with long narrow noses and jet-black hair flanked his sides and two oversized Arian Vanguard looking motherfuckers had his back. He smiled a smile that seemed never to leave his face except probably when he was upset with one of his disciples.

The noise ceased. Everybody went silent and stared at us.

"Hello," he charmingly declared as he removed his sunglasses and hat. He placed his hands under my jawbone and squinted into my eyes. His hands were colder than concrete in winter. I started to feel weak. My thoughts inside my head rambled on in a broken language I could not calculate. I peered one last time into his eyes and saw blankness. When I pushed his hands away and threw him to the ground I could hear many footsteps clambering behind me on the dirt road. I sprinted my way out of the vicinity. Finally I came upon the Old Las Vegas Highway and was able to find my way back into town. I was somewhere near Eldorado. It took me over an hour to reach downtown and call a taxi. I never heard from my hip-hop friend again.

Another weirdo tried taking me to Ecuador. He said I could stay with the shamans in the rainforest for over a month. Sitting in the booth he passed me a small bottle and told me to drink it. It was ayahuasca. The ayahuasca would let me know if it was in my destiny to go. I stalled. I didn't want to drink it. Taking something like that requires proper preparation. It was a sacred plant and not anything to toy with. I respected it, he didn't. I had to make the decision sober.

The only reason I considered his proposal was because I wanted to take the ayahuasca. I wanted to cleanse my soul.

I had the money and was ready to go. I knew him from a long time ago. He was connected through distant relatives so I felt I could relatively trust him, somewhat. He was always trying to get me down there. He told me how beautiful it was. How you can enter the forest and play with monkeys and eat them. The native people were an endangered species and it was important to visit them now. Enticing as he made it all sound my only reservation was traveling to the tropics. The year before I had visited my brother in the Virgin Islands, somewhere around twenty degrees latitude, and returned home carrying a virus that almost killed me. The first day back home I started throwing up and didn't stop until I lost ten pounds in two days. It took me more than a month to fully recover. The tropics were unkind to me and I wasn't in any kind of shape to accept his invitation. I vacillated on a final answer. He and his business partner kept pressuring me to buy my ticket right away and kept trying to shame me into participating. It was a group travel. I'd be the only one from Santa Fe going but I wouldn't be alone. He promised me women, a good time like I've never known before, women, and time to meditate and plenty of young women, virgin if I brought enough money in cash in small denominations.

At first I had no real doubts. The tropics weren't enough to scare me off. I figured I survived the previous trip so at least I had an idea of what to sort of expect. But being at zero degrees latitude was a giant step from twenty. I didn't care. I felt I needed to go. I needed to confront whatever was waiting for me over there. He gave me a weekend to make up my mind. Before we parted ways he presented me with a black and white necklace made of porcupine quills holding a circle of dyed black and white dried berries with a hollow center. He warned me that the shamans would feel closer to me now and probably visit me in my dreams. He placed it over my head and around my neck. For four days, from Thursday to Sunday, I pondered and questioned my own existence and attempted to rationalize any kind of justification I could conjure to convince myself that it was the right thing to do. Locked in my room, pacing back and forth in geometric circles, obsessed with the contours of the floor, listening to System of a Down's first album, I became confident that I could handle the trip. A few weeks were left before departure so there was enough time to receive the specified inoculations and get into some decent shape and perhaps even improve my Spanish to a communicative level. Talking and talking to myself repeatedly turned into a juvenile game with only one loser. I lay for hours on my bed and my reading couch speaking silently to the other world seeking advice from phantasms unheard and unseen. The decision was mine to make. I had to psyche myself out ferociously. The amulet started to burn my chest through the shirt I was wearing. I took it off and placed it on the most powerful shrine I have at home. I knew I had to go. I wanted to go. I wanted to take the ayahuasca. There was nothing that was going to stop me. Something was calling me. I was preparing myself to die.

The hours were agonizing. The weekend took forever. I had to come up with an answer by Monday. Whatever would happen in Ecuador would change me forever. There was even a good chance I wouldn't return to Santa Fe any time soon. All of my plans for the summer would have to be put on hold. Everything in my life would've required such a demand. I was sacrificing everything for this, maybe even myself. At the time I didn't know the difference between a good shaman and a bad shaman. I was aware that there are many fakes out there posing as shamans to make money, but I figured this might be the real thing since it was in Ecuador and the guy who was taking me was a resident there part-time out of the year. He and his business partner showed me pictures and video and their website and ran down a whole program of what a joyful experience I would have.

I didn't doubt that I would. Only two things bothered me: (1) I never trust anybody, period; and (2) they showed me a picture of a real old man and a very young girl and narrated to me how this seventy some year old man was wedding a thirteen year old girl. They tried to assure me that this was a custom of theirs for the shaman to pass on his magical powers to a seed and he needed fertile ground to do so. To say the mere idea of it disturbed me would be lacking. I became too suspect and skeptical to be overwhelmed with what seemed like quite an adventurous undertaking. Some things aren't worth selling your soul over.

I figured by Monday or Tuesday or early in the week sometime I would come to a conclusion. Something would happen that would let me know which course to take. Sunday brought about a mighty thunder and dazzling lightening storm unlike any I'd ever seen in Santa Fe. It was too early to be monsoon season. Lately the weather had been warming up since spring had just opened her doors for a glimpse. The storm was freezing. The rain was heavy and vicious. It would come and go at incalculable intervals. Between downpours the thick gray clouds overhead seemed close to the ground and kept moving in and out of one another like they were lungs expanding and detracting. The sky was breathing. I couldn't stop staring and touching the amulet that swung from a santo of Saint Francis de Assisi my father had given me. My father has the magic as well. He's the one who saved me from that tropical virus by giving me a smudge all over my body. He managed to exorcise the wicked spirit that followed me home. It was a very crucial decision I was making. Severe contemplation was required. I couldn't peel my eyes away from it. I adulated over it like a hungry window shopper wanting something she can't afford. I was falling in love with it. How beautiful it looked in the dusky downcast given off by the filtered sunlight beneath the clouds. I could feel the power and the voice of the storm calling for me. After a few hours passed I realized I was becoming infatuated with an object of unfamiliarity. I decided to take my dogs for a walk in the trails behind my house leading to the infamous dog park. When I ventured outside the rain disappeared. The air was cold and sent a shock through my body waking it up. I hadn't exited the house in three days. The thoughts in my head became excruciating. I was obsessed with the whole idea of going. It was starting to make me feel ill. Along one of the main trails on the way back my dogs closed in on something that was there and kept sniffing relentlessly and groping whatever it was with their paws. When I got closer to where they were I shooed them away and uncovered a dead carcass of a rat. Not just a rat like a pet rat, but a fat, plump, swollen dirty gray and brown furry rat the size of a football. It was turned on its back with its little legs jutting stiff into the air and its mouth flayed open enough to see its razor like teeth. The eyes were squeezed shut. The tail was almost as long as a ruler. I had never seen a rat like this before. It resembled one of those sewer rats you're supposed to see in New York or from the movie *Ben*. There were no rats around here nor have there ever been. It was monstrous. My dogs kept trying to find out what it was. I had to scare them away from it. I was scurrying out of that location when something inside me told me to bury the rat. I couldn't just leave it there. I went through that path almost every day. Other people traversed that trail as well and it wouldn't do well for their dogs or themselves to be exposed to it either. I picked-up the nearest stick I could locate and dug a superficial hole as fast as I could. The rat lay still. I maneuvered the body with two sticks into the hole and covered it with dirt and rocks. The rain appeared once again in torrents. The thunder exploded above me. I watched the electric display in the mountains to the outlying east and removed south. Wind intrusive etched a heavy presence in my mind as I ran home.

The atmosphere reminded me of when I buried a rottweiler I once had. I found him one cold winter morning frozen dead in the doghouse. I should've known it was coming. The day before I took him out on a short walk. When it was time to leave he didn't want to go back home with me. He kept pulling and tugging in the opposite direction and whimpering telling me it was time to depart from the family. His eyes were the epitome of sadness manifested inside a tragedian mask. Eventually I dragged him home and the next morning I found him dead. My father and I had to scrape him off the ground. He was real heavy. I dug about a four feet grave through the frozen dirt. When we rolled him over into the grave every neighborhood dog released a mournful shriek howling en masse and didn't desist until the blade of the shovel patted the mound firmly.

When I came across the rat I knew that was the sign for me to decide otherwise. Many times you have to see the signs when embarking on a major decision that will affect your life interminably. The heat in the tropics at zero degrees latitude would have killed me for sure if the mosquitoes didn't finish me off first. In the Virgin Islands I stopped counting after forty of them had eaten me in only three days. I wasn't about to go through that again. But there was another reason for my not going. Something was awaiting me there. It might've been death. Either physical or spiritual. Something or someone wanted my soul. I wasn't willing to find out. On Monday I phoned the guy and told him I would be unable to attend this year. He wasn't too gleeful about my decision, but he had no choice but to accept it. My father wanted to keep the amulet. At first I agreed. It was a well-crafted specimen and artifact from a place that would soon be wiped off the map due to oil exploration and logging. The amulet had an influence over me that was unnerving.

Several days after my final answer was given, I couldn't help but feel melancholy and loathsome. I wouldn't speak to anybody. I remained silent for forty-eight hours straight. I wasn't sure I had made the right decision. In my room the amulet called me forth and I carried conversations with it apologizing to the spirits for letting them down. What was wrong with me? It got to the point where I was getting nauseous every time I entered my room. I knew it was the amulet but I didn't believe it. I looked at it one more time and involuntarily determined it was representative of some unknowable dark force. My father wanted it but I knew I had to get rid of it. Without procrastination I lifted the necklace off the santo, jumped into my car and drove miles out of town into the mountains to leave it hanging on a tree limb hoping it would return to its desired source.

One month later the guy returned from Ecuador and informed my father and I that one of the shamans had died in a canoe that tipped over.

The Great White Liberator

As I awoke one morning from uneasy dreams I found myself transformed in my bed into the dumbest leader of the free world the world had ever known. The first sensation of the day was the damp coolness I could sense further down the road heading to my toes. It took me several minutes to move my right hand into a position to find out what the coolness was. When I felt the moisture it was cold and sticky. I panicked and leaped out of bed throwing the sheets off revealing a small circle of dampness that was in the process of drying. I couldn't tell if it was urine or not, or my urine for that matter, until I leaned forward far enough to sniff the contents of the wet surface. I poked it with my index finger and tasted it. It definitely was my urine. Looks like I peed in bed again.

I didn't realize who I was until I peered into the mirror and vociferated a shrill shriek more terrifying than poverty. I had shrunk in stature overnight, my hair was mostly gray and white interspersed with burnt splotches of a bad dye job. My uncircumcised penis was now two inches instead of two and a quarter. I was overweight with a fat ass. The reflection of a withered corpse's face showed that I couldn't stop smirking. I was an ugly motherfucker.

This can't be happening to me. Before I could adjust properly my brain started experiencing pain every time I would attempt to formulate a thought. The English language made no sense. The world around me was turning dull. I couldn't remember the answer to the mathematical equation 2 + 2. Flashbacks of my old self kept trying to appear steady. My old self would not give in so easily. A battle was taking place between who I thought I once was and this new personality. It was disturbing, some of the things I underwent to become this certain nobody that the world was unfamiliar with. All of a sudden I found myself hating faggots and niggers. I had an insatiable yearning to kill something. I hated anything that had to do with learning or thinking too much. Money, booze, cocaine and sodomizing Jesus were the only things on my preoccupation. The only thing I knew for certain was that I was not supposed to do anything until The Architect came to get me.

I had to get dressed. When I opened the closet doors there was only a pair of blue jeans and a black t-shirt. My custom fit blue suits with the white shirt and the red tie and the little flag button were missing. Many shined shoes were gone. There was only a pair of combat boots and raggedy outdated Nike Air sneakers. Everything seemed out of place. The room I was in was certainly not located in The White House. None of my house nigger servants came by to arouse me, bathe me and shave me. For the first time in my life it appeared I would have to do everything by myself for myself.

Before I could try to think about doing anything the phone rang and startled me enough to provoke a girlish squeak. I thought it might be The Architect. I picked up the phone. On the other end of the line was some unfamiliar voice of a man asking me if I wanted to participate in a Fiesta float for the big parade tomorrow. I responded that I usually attended church on Sunday. I don't really. I like to tell people that. Sundays are usually the days Big Dick comes out of his bunker and plays with me after his customary appearance on *Face The Nation*. Intellectually I'm worse than an immature child. "Parade" was all my brain registered. The idea sounded intriguing. I asked this voice what a Fiesta float is and what the parade was for. He told me that being a lifelong resident of Santa Fe I certainly was aware of what Fiestas was. I felt confused. My long silence must've prompted him to explain. It seems that Fiestas is some sort of annual moral debauchery where tourists get to witness a huge crowd of rowdy drunk locals gather at some location called Fort Marcy to burn some Old Man Gloom that was actually introduced into the ceremonies by some white guy in the twenties. Fiestas itself is the celebration of the Spaniard's double attempt at conquest of this part of the New World. By murdering enough indigenous natives the Spaniards were able to claim Santa Fe as theirs exclusively. Anything that has to do with genocide excites me. I asked the voice on the other end to go on. He told me that I would be participating in a float with two others. He would be the one to drive the vehicle that carries the wagon end of the float. The other two guys with me would walk along the float disguised as Lady Liberty, Uncle Sam, and The President of the United States. A patriotic float! Anybody who knows me is well aware of how much I love to talk about patriotism. A parade that celebrates genocide is the perfect place to show off your patriotism. My co-conspirators had already claimed Lady Liberty and Uncle Sam so there was nothing left for me to do but act like The President of The United States. He could count me in I told him. Great he answered. We made plans to rendezvous at the DeVargas Mall on Guadalupe Street during registration.

The only thing that troubled me was what he said about being a lifelong resident of Santa Fe. I didn't know there was such a thing. I didn't know Santa Fe existed until I visited here about a year ago with my wife. She attended some dance show while I played golf and drank cheap scotch with a buddy of mine in a wonderful place called Las Campanas. It was like paradise. A place where only the super rich thrived and no second-class citizens were allowed. Everybody had fat wallets and full coverage health plans. To think that a place like this existed in a region I still thought was part of Mexico. That's what I get for failing geography. The rest of Santa Fe was to be ignored. I heard it was a strange place with lots of fudgepackers and lick-her licenses. The Architect informed me that it was one of the last bastions for liberal nostalgia and that I wouldn't be welcome. But he has yet to experience the gross amount of wealth concentrated in the hands of the few the way I did. I came to discover that The City Different was pretty much the same as the rest of the country: a few rich white men who ran everything, a mass of mixed middle class citizens that didn't matter and kept dwindling in numbers, and an obscene amount of wretched folk hibernating in the inner city or at the ends of town where they couldn't be seen nor heard. It was fantastic. I still couldn't figure out what I was doing here, but I knew there was a reason. God always has a reason. God Bless Santa Fe.

The next morning I got up early. There was nothing to wear but the blue jeans, t-shirt and sneakers. I was not about to wear combat boots. Looking in the mirror to examine how I dressed I was horrified to discover that the t-shirt I had on was a black t-shirt with a red, black and white Nazi flag of the swastika on the front. Above and below the flag in white lettering were the words "Vote Republican." I removed myself from the presence of the mirror immediately. Every time I see that insignia I get scared and start to reminisce about those spooky tales my father used to tell us as children about our ancestry and bloodline. I tried taking and tearing the shirt off my body a million times but it seemed permanently attached to my being. I was caught in quite the predicament. I was scheduled to meet my new acquaintance in less than an hour. There was no way I could walk in public wearing that shirt. I absolutely would not betray my faith in such a disrespectful manner. What was I supposed to do? I really wanted to be part of the parade.

The Architect warned me that something like this might happen to me one day. He said that if I stayed too long in Santa Fe I might get infected with all that liberal nonsense about equal rights and a world without war. Santa Fe was a place of black magic and Santeria curses. Karma was known to have a strong presence here. I tried praying to Jesus to get rid of this garment from my nakedness but nothing happened. I called out for help amongst my many Secret Service caretakers but nobody arrived. Time was running out. Nothing can ever get in the way of pretentious presidential frivolity. I can't stay in this room all day. I have to grow up and act like a mature adult who is capable of making decisions on his own. It seems I can't do a goddamn thing about the fate Providence has assigned me. Everybody is always telling me what to do. I'm tired of being a puppet. I never wanted to be President in the first place. I was told to do it in order to distract the populace from what is really happening. What is really happening out there in that wide world? Hell, I don't know. All I know is that I have a rare opportunity to participate in a parade and a shirt with a swastika on it. Perhaps if I brave the public they won't notice. Maybe because this is Santa Fe people will think this is some sort of Indian symbol. No, that will never work. Most of the population in this country is about as stupid as I am. You know, it really doesn't look that bad. Jews might take offence but I don't care about those people. It looks rather befitting if you ask me. After all, we are the party that loves war. We make war every opportunity we get to wield power. We hate Jews, niggers, gooks, Arabs, and spics. We take care of the rich at the expense of the poor. We are into White Supremacy and exploit Christianity for our own earthly ambitions. We will conquer this world once and for all and nobody is going to stop us. Yes, I think I can wear this t-shirt and represent my country and birthright appropriately. After all, Los Alamos is only minutes away. I look remarkable if you ask me. This should be the new flag of The United States. Death to all those that think they can create a better world than the one we're living in. My daddy is right. I am The President and it's high time I start acting like it.

I had to do the Robert DeNiro *Taxi Driver* scene in front of the mirror one last time before I departed. Outside the sky is very clear. Vast endlessness camouflage the atmosphere pockmarked sporadically with a lost puff of cloud here and over there. They will evaporate by noon. It is hot. Hot like the underworld. The light here is vibrant and clear. No wonder artsy fartsy fairy people re-locate here. The immediate future looks preposterous. Lots of people out today. Churchgoers were about to be released. The parking lot and street would soon be filled to its limit. A long trail of cars filled Guadalupe Street for almost a mile. He told me he might be somewhere in the middle closer to the front of the line. Like everything that's great about this country, registration was based on a first come first serve basis. I think I might've heard once that the Fiesta parade can get political as far as politics can be addressed in such an offbeat tiny town. Most of these brutes resemble a fabric of barbarity similar to extended relatives I have back in the fatherland. A lot of them look Hispanic. Maybe I might be able to pick-up some votes today. Seems like plenty of political whores bare their colors on such a fine day for a fine cause. There's floats of all sorts and themes and gallant pageantry: second rate musical floats, good causes floats, uh…traditional floats, high school bands, little cute cheerleaders on sports cars sitting with their logs crossed so their little skirts won't fly up in the air, floats with uh…princesses on them uh…knights and stuff, you know throwing candy at kids cheering on the curbside collecting as much candy as they can like spoiled greedy little bastards, horses shitting and things, people acting like Don Quixote and Sancho Panza doing all kinds of neat things enjoying their way of life in the city that is holy faith. Hundreds of floats enter the parade every year. It is a moment when the local collateral nobodies and religious freaks can come out of the closet and feel important for once in their lives.

I covered the line twice searching for him amongst the busy bodies. I found out the Fiesta Council that puts on the spectacle hands out prizes for three main categories: best traditional float, best political float, and best beautiful boat or superficial looking float. Because we entered what was probably the most patriotic float in the charade, I was gonna make sure our float would win best political one. There was good competition though. I noticed our wonderful and heroic police officers had at least five or six entries. People running for office were present because it was election time. There were several Vote Republican Party entries, a rarity in Santa Fe. There were plenty of makeshift concoctions slandering my pathetic opponent in the election. Every Christian church in town had a float in the parade. Many were handing out literature to the onlookers and preaching the Lord's good word. The best float I saw that could give us competition was the Christian Life Organization. They had a huge picture of a dead fetus wrapped in an Amerikan flag hoisted to the truck that pulled it. I saw that the Christians were definitely out today and not afraid to express their feelings. I felt like I didn't belong in Santa Fe any more.

I finally found my co-conspirators. To my tarnished astonishment I beheld a dark comical representation of yours truly portrayed as a Nazi Cowboy. I was roughly six foot tall, had on black pants, a black shirt with the essential red and white armband on an outstretched hailing right arm holding a mechanical hand with a black leather glove on the end, a black beach crunched cowboy hat, and an erection jutting out the black crotch. I was placed in the center of the cage sticking up above the lid. My face had on dark shades and a square stumpy mustache drawn on with permanent marker. On the back of the float were posted photographs of notorious Nazi War criminals. Inside the float was not only unpardonable, but should be illegal in this Christian Nation of ours. Decapitated heads of heads of state in my cabinet swung lax from the lid of the cage like captured trophies of hunted animals. There was the black chick that doesn't talk black; the black dude that doesn't look black; Rommel, Big Dick, and my daddy. The guy doing Uncle Sam was crazy and acted like a psycho mad dog of an Uncle Sam. Lady Liberty was stoned, looked like a homeless bum covered by a dirty toga that could pass for John Belushi in *Animal House*. Our leader was a gentleman in a wheelchair who reminded me of some subversive hippie type with nothing better to do with his time than devise smart-ass marionettes of my good name. I asked him what the hell this was supposed to be about. He was a puppeteer and artist who worked with sculptures made from many found materials. I have to admit his work was well crafted. I had a stroke of verisimilitude. He had been working on me for some years now and has used it in his Friday demonstrations at the intersection of Cerrillos and St. Francis. The Architect told me something about those so-called protests. I guess they've been going on since before the war began. The Architect told me he had sent some operatives down here to spy on these troublemakers. The only intelligence we received out of the operation we called Operation Sanitize All Mobilizing Assemblies was that there was nothing intelligent about the whole affair. Our operatives returned home with emphysema. They spent one day a week for months on end outside at one of the busiest and congested intersections in the state inhaling severely toxic fumes. They were almost run over twice. The cars come sidling up to the curb very close nicking clothes to cause a ruffle. Not to mention purposely getting run over by some right-wing nutbag targeting the most vulnerable geriatric subjects risking their lives to express their discontent. Plenty of scumbags are paid to fly by the demonstrators fast and reckless. We do everything we can to disrupt social mobilization. There is comforting irony in watching losers protest a war of oil while sucking fumes from the exhaust pipe. The guy that called me on the phone the night before had been attending the Friday protests regularly. He said the theme of the float was True Amerikan Patriots Escorting Terrorists And War Criminals To The International Criminal Court In The Hague. I didn't understand. He told me not to worry about it. All I was required to do was walk alongside the float throughout the parade. The route was about two miles. The sun ascended and heated. He handed me a mask of myself I could wear if I so chose. I agreed to wear the mask because I wanted no one to recognize me.

Our float didn't seem to complement the parade. People kept coming by examining the float in detail and commenting on it. Some reactions were affirmative. The majority of them were negative. One guy argued with the creator of the representation for nearly an hour before the show started. He said that this was uncalled for. He said that we didn't have respect and all we were doing was spreading hate on a day that celebrates love. I listened and observed. Something I don't do very often. He had a convincing argument. I really wanted to walk the parade, but quietly I was apprehensive. Santa Fe was supposed to be liberal and I didn't think I would fit in in any form. I was about to tell the guy in the wheelchair that as much as I wanted to be part of the festivities I couldn't go through with it. I overheard him telling the other guy he was arguing with a story about something that happened to him that changed my view of life forever.

The guy in the wheelchair was out at the intersection the Friday before doing his normal protest thing. He stationed himself in a middle island with his life-like image of me as the centerpiece. Minutes into the routine he was joined by a tall fat redneck holding a Pro-Republican sign. The standing Republican man started arguing with my partner in the wheelchair for no reason. A struggle ensued in which the Republican man tried grabbing the sign out of the hands of my partner. My partner held on to the sign. The outstanding Republican got angry and hit my friend in the wheelchair with the sign pushing him off his wheelchair into the middle of oncoming traffic. My friend was almost killed. Police officers interfered along with other on-looking protesters. Nobody was arrested and when it came time to testify as to what happened the other Leftist protesters distanced themselves from the guy in the wheelchair denouncing him as an unstable loon. The following day the local newspapers carried a front page story about the incident criticizing the guy in the wheelchair and the other protesters for creating a potentially dangerous environment. The cops and city council threatened to shut the demonstrations down. Upon hearing this I decided to alter my life right then and there. This is Amerika, where ordinary people are supposed to have the right to say any goddamn thing they feel like saying. That way the secret intelligence agencies can track you down easily and smoke you out! Express yourself and have your name put on a list. I should know. It's starting to come back to me.

As my former self I used to attend anti-war rallies and make vitriolic speeches denouncing this administration. When election time came around, many of my political street signs were vandalized and destroyed. I found out inadvertently from a distant cop cousin of mine that I was the number one suspect. What bullshit we tolerate and adore. Something wasn't right about what that Republican asshole did. Something wasn't right about the way the world is being run and I think I might know what it might be. It comes as no surprise that a Republican would behave that way. Only a Republican could knock a paraplegic off his wheelchair. Injustices such as these had to be remedied. The right wing is out of control. Activism construed as dissent that achieves nothing but incrimination is the solitary answer.

Meanwhile, the guy continued arguing with my new friend. He shamed all of us and commented that the presentation of our artistic float was obscene. Two young yuppie looking type fucks dressed as hippies were standing nearby. One of them jumped in the conversation and told the arguing dickhead that if he wanted to see obscene he should see the float in front of their hippie tye-dyed van. When he narrated to us what it was I couldn't believe it. I did not believe what he told me. Things like that do not happen in Amerika. That kind of shit only takes place in those backward Arab regions of the world breeding hate and terrorists. Amerika is pure and innocent. Unsullied by the mollycoddle critics that are incapable of misunderstanding that military might is the only way to go. We walked together to the mystery float in question. The portrait in front of my blinded eyes perturbed me enigmatically. I saw a float sponsored by the state police in conjunction with the county sheriff's office. How does one describe it? Little tottlers saturated in full military and police force regalia popping caps from plastic toy automatic Kaloshnikovs and M 16s at pedestrians sauntering by to have an admiration. They looked adorable. One little fella was wearing fatigues brandishing a Rambo knife saying he was going to kill the next person to walk by. Others were decked out in menacing black uniforms and mirrored sunglasses practicing their handcuffing techniques on one another. The parents were busy adjusting the collar or the ammunition belt making sure their precious jito carried the essential cartridges to load his .45 magnum as the rest of the Hispanic family posed for pictures using the children soldiers as backdrop. Brainwashing begins very early in this country. Everybody thought it was cute. The guy arguing with my new friend commended the innovators of this wholesome thematic role-play. I was horrified. I stood there frozen for ten minutes disbelieving that fascism like this takes root in Amerikan soil. When I heard there were four more like it in the parade I experienced my first attack of the undefeatable, the indomitable, the almighty powerful ignoble con-of-science. I sneaked a photograph of the scene to remind me of what kind of place I was living in.

The parade was beginning to move. Horses to the front and rear and everybody else in between. Horns blaring, music blasting on bad loudspeakers, candy starting to drift even though it is illegal, and a caravan of good hard-working US citizens taking the day off having a good time even if there's a war on. Twenty seconds into the mask and I couldn't breathe. I started sweating extravagantly. My body temperature rose. It felt appropriate but I wore it too convincingly. I did not possess the option of taking it off even if I wanted to. Certain sacrifices would have to be made if I was to accomplish what I intentionally set out to do. We agreed that our goal for the day was to undermine the Fiesta charade. Lady Liberty was smoking a cigarette. Uncle Sam was on the wagon. Already into our dilatory march onlookers were booing and making violent, threatening catcalls. I can't add the times I was threatened with death by people that love their country. The righteous patriotic fanatics threw middle fingers at me, yelled at me to go home, and one fervent patriot spat in my face that was actually a mask. I couldn't understand why someone would do something like that to a person he doesn't know. Nothing made sense anymore. I became frightened by the prospect of completing the parade route on foot. Some loathsome force kept throttling my legs forward. The route was the same route that it always was: cruise up Paseo de Peralta looping right onto Palace Avenue following the flock into The Plaza showboating in front of the grandstand getting judged constantly moving forward to West Alameda right again on Guadalupe completing a full circle around the historic plaza down to where you began your journey. Life is always like that: you end up where you started. Jesus said that. Jesus is my favorite philosopher. I'm not too high on him as a practitioner. Maybe I should be more like him instead of trying to talk like he did. I'm starting to see how what I've done has affected the world. Throughout the parade I experienced more hate than I've ever wanted to see in my existential mode.

What that big fat Republican did to my newly acquainted comrade confined to a wheelchair was not only wrong it was discomfiting, mean, and unforgivable. I may be a bit fucked up but I'm not that fucked up. Most of the people I encountered through the course of the parade hated what we were doing, turned the other cheek, didn't understand, or threw trash at us from the roadside. Some people were enthusiastic by giving the thumbs-up and laughing and joking about our submission. Some, but very few.

Despite the ridiculous discrepancies in political opinion here, two things were for certain: Santa Fe was not a Liberal hotbed and everybody paid attention when they paid no mind. I wish I could grab people's attention like that when I make my dreary speeches. Maybe I should become a radical Leftist saboteur. I should really support the poor instead of patronizing them. I should leave women alone and render myself available for those that might seek consolation. I should put a ban on guns. I decided to practice some of what I preach. To traverse the length of this parade in hostile environment was a suicide mission, but it would set me free. I pretended I was one of those faceless terrorists I'm always telling you about lurking in the bushes. I would complete my mission unaffected. War is a game played by power stockbrokers, mad scientists, and brave young men with heavy balls and light heads. I've never been to war nor never want to see one. However, I am entitled to my imagination and today I imagined that I really did live in a free nation because any truly free nation would be guarded by free thinking people who would listen to its malcontents regardless of how obnoxious they are. To exercise your right to freedom of speech is not the same as exercising your right to speak freely.

The more people direct their hate to me the more I love them. I was transforming before the eyes of the world without anyone noticing. I found myself alone despite being flanked by three other individuals just as concerned about the true state of the world as I am. I lost myself conquering the fears that corrode a dream. Three quarters of the way finished I unearthed the truth about myself. I am a piece of shit. I am Amerikan. I am a gringo. I've been responsible for the murders of more people than I can fathom. I am responsible for all those people starving to death in Africa because I am a selfish prick. Do not believe what others might say about me; I am a kind compassionate man. It is my bosses that are to blame. Nobody has ever seen them, not even I. What has been presented to you is farcical at best. The personalities you respond to are not real. They are computer-generated reproductions of subconscious pubescent fantasies. The truth of the matter is that no one really knows why September 11th had to happen. Could any reasonable person out there not see it coming? Do people actually believe this country earned its wealthiest nation in the world title by being polite and deferring to others? The most I can come up with is that the consequential War on Terror is nothing more than a duel between two bored over-privileged sons of billionaires. You don't actually believe in all that crap about freedom and democracy do you? Those are just words. Words have no meaning. They are tools that can be manipulated in a variety of ways by the advantageous. I'm not as foolish as everybody thinks. I could tell you the answers to the question why. Why did my son have to die? Why did we go into Iraq in the first place? I'll tell you why.

The reason we are trapped in Iraq is because nobody in Amerika gives a shit about Iraq. Parents don't really care about their children dying for my personal profit. If they did they would defy the government and do everything possible to discourage their kids from signing up or leaving and have the support of the citizenry to back them. You live in fear. There is not enough of you organized in any way to even attempt to slow us down. You can't stop us. We're everywhere. We're better than God. We bombard your children before they hit puberty. We got files on every child in public school and keep track of their development and select the best of the worst sadists to conform in line when the army recruiter comes calling their freshman year of high school. We put tons of pressure on the indigent to join the armed forces. Poor people will do anything for money. They will kill, torture, suck dick and die all in the name of abstract concepts that have nothing to do with anything. You idiots supporting the war and the troops can't possibly visualize how things come to pass. The only thing Amerikans care about is watching TV, fast food, convenience stores, who won on *Amerikan Idol*, trying to look like what they've been taught is supposed to be beautiful, indulging in vanity, going to the movies, buying records, attending parties, dressing up for the holidays, going out to the bar, getting laid, making money, buying cars, going on vacation, visiting the therapist, and mellifluous forms of recreation that have no relation to reality. You're getting overweight because you're supposed to. Oprah is about as invigorating as sticking your tongue into an exposed outlet. The thing that makes me laugh the most is I bet a lot of you assholes thought the price of gas would go down after we stole the oil in Iraq. What a bunch of maroons! Basic economics tells us the opposite is more likely to happen. But you wouldn't know that because you don't understand how Capitalism works. Nobody does. You will keep paying. Paying and praying, that's what I always say. I lied to the world a million times and nobody could do anything about it. Democracy is for shit and luxury is non-negotiable. You are comfortable. Confined to comfort. You are misinformed. What can I tell you that you are not already aware of? Where are your freedom fighters? You and I are in the same boat. We are all guilty. We are guilty for contributing to this war constantly, every two weeks for most of you. The taxes we extract never come back but are utilized to attack sandnigger villages and metropolises. Jesus is a bitch of a burden for those who choose to believe. Consume some more. You are all whores for one price or another. Those that reveal are concealed. Those that teach are beseeched to cut that shit out. We will persecute any that defy the law of the land that is designed by the hour by those taming power. Funny how persecute and prosecute mean the same thing but when you change a few letters around prosecute becomes acceptable while persecute becomes suspect. I am sorry, I honestly am. I'm sorry for all those Arab civilian casualties we killed in the first few days of Operation Iraqi Freedom. We would've kept better count of them but only Amerikan lives have any real market value so our controlled media monopolies suppress harmful information such as how many Iraqis are killed daily by our soldiers for no goddamn reason. We show you only the Amerikan loss of life so we can continue to fuel the spew of hatred that permeates your pure red Amerikan blood. Most of those suicide car bombings we show you are orchestrated by us. Peace to the war machine that controls everything. But I don't rest any kind of blame on my compatriots. Guilt yes, blame no. The blame stays with the Liberals. They're a bunch of pussies and that's about all I have left to say about them. I could never become a dedicated Leftist. I don't give a fuck about people lamenting the pain and suffering that never seems to abate. Who really cares about starving people? Military contracts must be fulfilled. The right wing is the only way. Travel first class and the cargo will be lighter. The world is fucked up because average people make it that way. The elite were born to rule. It's genetic. Prayer in school should be a requirement. If a woman thinks she can have an abortion let her dig into her closet for a hanger. Education should be unaffordable. Health care is not for everyone. Iran is next and yes we will use low-level nukes like we do in Iraq so nobody will complain much less have a clue of what is going on. We'll whore Israel out for the job of starting it. The Earth is obsolete. The Earth is the past. We must look to the future of biospheres and underground facilities. The colonization of outer space still has potential if we could only figure out what we're doing. Everything will be itemized and you will be compartmentalized like animals for sale in a pet shop. You no longer have the illusion of having control over your life. You are Amerikan. I am Amerikan. Get to work on time and shut the fuck up. You are a member of the deadliest cult in the solar system. You may be able to break the bonds of filial loyalty but you will never overcome the chains of political ideology. Submit and serve. That is the quote of the day. Everything you ever thought you knew about life has now been rearranged. Violence is a virtue of the strong, a vice for the meek. Right now you are being filmed. Yesterday you were filmed. Tomorrow you will be put on display. Smile and wish us a very nice day. Only the few can be rich. The many will be forced to wait in line. As for God, duty, and honor, who really gives a shit? You died because it was time for you to go. Soldiers are returning crippled and psychologically maimed because they weren't careful like we told them to be. It's too late for a knee jerk reaction. The world is more complicated than you originally thought it was.

For a moment there I thought this float was having a deleterious influence on me. I imagined briefly that I could have feelings like a normal human being. I had an urge to break free of my personal bondage but have eternally accepted the fact of my fate: I am Nazi. Resenting authority is for the depraved. I wanted to atone for my wrongdoings and repent like a Penitente torturing myself in a parade of self-flagellation feeling the physical pain of the blazing sun underneath my skin, the coldness of the hard concrete ruining my kneecaps and limbs, the apostasy of my people as I witnessed the destruction of all human understanding and compassion. I'm Amerikan like the rest of you, therefore a slave. I am in the wrong by being part of the right but the left has no refuge left. From here on out I dedicate my soul to defending the prerogative of the select. Let the dumbfucks die and allow the devil to divvy them up. It is not worth putting your privacy on the line for a bunch of selfish spoiled jerks that have no interest in saving life from those that would destroy it. You are all hypocrites. I am a hypocrite. It all depends on the type of hypocrisy you practice. A con-of-science is not fit to endure a lapse of forgiveness. There is no way to con science. Science is the ultimate con. I am a murderer, a liar, a thief, and an excellent criminal. I am the gringo. The Great White Liberator. I represent the people of Amerika. I could never relinquish my demiurgic heritage. I must claw and kill in order to be placed ahead of you when it's time for promotion. It's easier when you relax at the top. Cash rules everything around me and I yearn to be like everybody else that's getting away with it. There is only one life to live, live it well, even if it means living in hell.

The weekend before I had achieved something magical. Notwithstanding the litany of murderous deeds beneath my belt, I had saved the life of a helpless creature. Exiting the house in the morning on my way to work, I came across a baby bird that fell from a nest stashed inside the base of the porch lamp. My black cat wanted to snatch it away. An army of ants began to tug and bite at the flesh of the crying bird prostrated on it's back. The bird made screeching sounds, heaving it's frail chest viciously like an oxygen pump. Without thinking I picked the newborn up, plucked the ants that were stuck to the surface below the feathers, and returned the baby to the nest. In less than a month the baby matured and sang boisterous ballads serenading me every morning. Shortly after the bird left the nest. I don't know why I tell you this other than the notion I have that I am aware that there is an undercurrent and oppositional force to the madness we witness every day. The world is not as fucked up as many would have us believe. If everything all the time was really that shitty and dangerous, the human race would have destroyed all of it a long time ago. The fable of the bird discloses the truth that there is still hope for any and all of us. It requires a small amount of effort to create something great. Healing takes time. Love is forever.

I never had so much fun in my life. I really felt free for the first and subsequently last time. My favorite moment during the charade was when we were approaching the grandstand where they were judging the floats. So-called dignitaries and respectable people in suits hang around the grandstand area. Chains of cops locked and loaded protected the crowd from themselves. Every time I would pass a cop I unintentionally started doing a high-boot goose step to prove to them my affinity with their ways. I tried stopping but nothing worked. The shirt and mask held me prisoner to what was going on around me. I recognized who I was, what I had become, and where I was headed. In front of the grandstand the emcee was introducing our float to the hundreds of spectators present. Lady Liberty and I worked out an improvisation of guerilla street theatre to perform. I used one of the toy machine guns I lifted off one of the children soldiers when no one was looking and chased Lady Liberty around the street trying to assassinate her. I knocked her flat on her back, adjusted the make-believe barrel to her dome and pulled the trigger a dozen times. The judges of the contest rushed us out of the vicinity as quickly as possible before we could enact the fucking Liberty in the ass routine. Toward the end of the parade the company in the float separated from Lady Liberty and me. We had to sprint almost half a mile to catch up with our party. At the end of the march we sat on the trailer pulling the dummy cooling down and catching our breath. The audience began to drift. Driving slowly to the finish there was still time for one more snide remark. Some dirty indigent local spic reared his foul face and shouted at us what a goddamn shame, we were a bunch of communists that should go back to Red China. I was too tired to respond. I didn't want to bother with an idiot. One idiot is better than one and a half. Yet, we had traveled too far and struggled too long to let this fucker off the hook without a rebuttal. I desired to impart to him a summary rejoinder of what this moment meant to me. Much had changed inside of me but the heart remained the same. In lieu of my past and present I remembered the little bird that almost died for nothing and decided to commit myself to something meaningless yet feasible. What I think and what I do are disparate entities. The life ahead of me cannot be the one I lived. The parade experience taught me what I could be with a little effort. Before our crew could escape his whereabouts, I turned around towards the heckler and proclaimed loud enough for him to hear that I was not a communist, he was wrong. I am an anarchist.

Printed in the United States
77902LV00002B/91-93

9 780865 345348